P9-CLV-170

09/2014

BELIEVE

"Entertaining and emotionally satisfying . . . McCarthy's signature clean writing style and an easy-to-follow story line makes it incredibly easy to become involved in this book . . . A sweet new adult love story that takes us on a journey of friendship, self discovery, forgiveness, and love." —*Smexy Books*

"I was completely caught up in this story." —*The Book Pushers*

"A great love story filled with steamy romance and drama." —*Dark Faerie Tales*

SWEET

"[A] riveting addition to the rising new adult category." —*Library Journal*

"A sexy, romantic, emotional coming-of-age new adult that uses a different approach to defining the romance than the usual NA offerings. Crisp writing, indulgent humor, and a smooth flowing story line makes it incredibly easy to become fully invested in this book . . . A wonderful love story that takes us on a journey filled with love, laughter, growth, and angst." —*Smexy Books*

"Full of steamy romance and entertaining banter . . . [McCarthy's] writing is very captivating." —*Dark Faerie Tales*

"A wonderful second book to the True Believers series. I love the characters that McCarthy has created." —*The Book Pushers*

"Sweet and   ith creating real stories."   *:ket to Anywhere*

TRUE

"McCarthy's entry in the burgeoning new adult subgenre is a page-turning, gut-wrenching success . . . Their troubles are real, their love True, and readers will root them on past the very last page."

—*RT Book Reviews*

"A sweet, romantic, dynamic coming-of-age new adult that takes a much-needed detour from the usual emotionally draining, overly dramatic offerings . . . Crisp writing and a smooth story line makes it incredibly easy to become fully invested in this book."

—*Smexy Books*

"By turns sweet, steamy, gritty, and heartbreaking, *True* is an outstanding read."
—*On a Book Bender*

"One of those books that you just can't and won't put down . . . Extremely realistic and relatable . . . [A] dramatic and beautiful story."
—*Harlequin Junkie*

"Ms. McCarthy did a wonderful job with this story."
—*Under the Covers Book Blog*

PRAISE FOR NOVELS OF ERIN McCARTHY

"Sizzling hot, jam-packed with snappy dialogue, emotional intensity, and racing fun."
—Carly Phillips, *New York Times* bestselling author

"A steamy romance . . . Fast-paced and red-hot." —*Publishers Weekly*

"Characters you will care about, a story that will make you laugh and cry, and a book you won't soon forget." —*The Romance Reader*

"Priceless!" —*RT Book Reviews*

continued . . .

Titles by Erin McCarthy

A DATE WITH THE OTHER SIDE
HEIRESS FOR HIRE
SEEING IS BELIEVING

The Fast Track Series
FLAT-OUT SEXY
HARD AND FAST
HOT FINISH
THE CHASE
SLOW RIDE
JACKED UP
FULL THROTTLE

The Vegas Vampires Series
HIGH STAKES
BIT THE JACKPOT
BLED DRY
SUCKER BET

The Deadly Sins Series
MY IMMORTAL
FALLEN
THE TAKING

The True Believers Series
TRUE
SWEET
BELIEVE
SHATTER

Anthologies

THE NAKED TRUTH
(with Donna Kauffman, Beverly Brandt, and Alesia Holliday)

AN ENCHANTED SEASON
(with Maggie Shayne, Nalini Singh, and Jean Johnson)

THE POWER OF LOVE
(with Lori Foster, Toni Blake, Dianne Castell, Karen Kelley,
Rosemary Laurey, Janice Maynard, LuAnn McLane, Lucy Monroe,
Patricia Sargeant, Kay Stockham, and J. C. Wilder)

FIRST BLOOD
(with Susan Sizemore, Chris Marie Green, and Meljean Brook)

ERIN McCARTHY

SHATTER

BERKLEY BOOKS, NEW YORK

THE BERKLEY PUBLISHING GROUP
Published by the Penguin Group
Penguin Group (USA) LLC
375 Hudson Street, New York, New York 10014

USA • Canada • UK • Ireland • Australia • New Zealand • India • South Africa • China

penguin.com

A Penguin Random House Company

This book is an original publication of The Berkley Publishing Group.

Copyright © 2014 by Erin McCarthy.

Penguin supports copyright. Copyright fuels creativity, encourages diverse voices, promotes free speech, and creates a vibrant culture. Thank you for buying an authorized edition of this book and for complying with copyright laws by not reproducing, scanning, or distributing any part of it in any form without permission. You are supporting writers and allowing Penguin to continue to publish books for every reader.

BERKLEY® is a registered trademark of Penguin Group (USA).
The "B" design is a trademark of Penguin Group (USA).

Library of Congress Cataloging-in-Publication Data

McCarthy, Erin, 1971— Author
Shatter / Erin McCarthy
pages cm.—(True believers ; 4)
ISBN 978-0-425-27510-8 (paperback)
I. Title
PS3613.C34575S53 2014
813'.6—dc23
2014017916

PUBLISHING HISTORY
Berkley trade paperback edition / September 2014

PRINTED IN THE UNITED STATES OF AMERICA

10 9 8 7 6 5 4 3 2 1

Cover design by Rita Frangie.
Couple © Solominviktor; *Tattoos*: formulas © Ojka; periodic table
© Zern Liew; algebra © AnastasiaSonne/all Shutterstock.
Interior text design by Kristin del Rosario.

CHAPTER ONE

I HATED LIVING ALONE. I WAS NEVER MEANT TO LIVE ALONE. And I don't mean that in the pathetic way where I couldn't be happy with myself unless someone was validating me with their company or whatever. I mean that I was just super social. I liked having people around me all the time. Conversation. Laughter. Growing up with three younger siblings, the house was loud all the time, and to me that was comfortable, homey, happiness. Some people, like my friend Rory, need alone time, and they can get lost in their private thoughts, a whole universe going on in there that no one else has a view to.

Not me. My thoughts for the most part came out through my mouth in a steady stream of talking and I loved that constant interaction with my friends.

But I had to move out of our roomie's apartment because of what I had started calling RAN (Robin and Nathan and their drunken hookup), and into a crappy little studio that was dark and way too quiet. Maybe if I'd at least had a boyfriend to cozy up on my daybed with me, I could deal with flying solo in the housing situation. No boyfriend, though, because my ex Nathan had decided to be both mean and stupid and have sex with my friend Robin while we were still dating. Yeah. He so did that. She so did that. Even though she was seriously drunk and didn't remember a thing, it had still been really hard for me to forgive her and impossible for me to forgive Nathan.

It was hard to be single in a world filled with perfect pairs. Salt and pepper. PB&J. Chili and hot dogs. Not to mention couples like Rory and Tyler. Jessica and Riley. Even Robin—who, drunk or not, had still ruined my relationship—even Robin had Phoenix. How unfair was that? She *lived* with her boyfriend, totally happy, while I was alone and for the first time ever in my entire life, miserable.

I didn't do sad. Grumpy wasn't me. I was usually optimistic, high-energy. Basically a cheerleader for life, always having a good time, always believing the best in people. So I wasn't the most super-intelligent, highest-IQ chick in the room. I knew that. It didn't matter, because I always liked everyone and I tried really hard to be nice. It took basically something awful like murder for me to hate your face. Or something like cheating on me with one of my best friends. But even then, I didn't hate Nathan. I was hurt. Hurt in a way that was weird to me because it wasn't going away. It wasn't like a cry at the end of a sad movie or the pang in your heart when you read a story about someone being bullied online.

This was different. It was a hurt that came over me in gigantic cold waves and settled inside my chest. It just lingered on and on, every day, making me feel like I was someone else, someone I didn't recognize, someone who had nasty thoughts and who cried unexpectedly. It made me forget to do homework and forget my phone in my room and forget where I was going.

It was a new feeling and I didn't know how to get rid of it, how to make the sadness stop popping up like some jerk-off Jack-in-the-box.

Shoving my hands in my pockets I trudged across the street to the coffee shop to meet my new tutor for chemistry, the cold wind instantly whipping my hair across my face and into my lip gloss, where it stuck. Sigh. I was flunking chemistry because I couldn't seem to focus. The formulas danced in front of my eyes when I looked at the online study sheet for our final exam next week. It was like temperature and molarity were twerking with each other. Rory, who was pre-Med, had tried to help me study, but I had ended up crying and she had ended up horrified.

I wasn't sure that I wouldn't wind up leaky-eyed on my tutor, too, but I was willing to risk it. I couldn't stay in that apartment alone in the dark for one more minute. The lighting sucked and with it getting dark so early every day, it felt like every corner of the room was a black hole filled with happiness thieves. Like there were little men hovering in there, snagging my confidence and hope while I watched TV and slept. It was a weird thought to have, but I was having a lot of weird thoughts, and they were foreign to me. It was like suddenly discovering your thoughts are in Hindi and you don't know why and you don't speak that language.

Pushing the door open, the warmth of the room washed over me and I gave a residual shiver. My hair was still stuck to my lip and instead of pulling it away, I decided to chew on it a little. It felt good, like I was six years old again and had the right to nibble my hair. I looked around for a nerd. I had never met the tutor, who was a grad student. My professor had given me his e-mail and said he was the best for helping undergrad students understand concepts. His name was Darwin, according to Professor Kadisch and the e-mail address. That couldn't be his real name. Or maybe it was. But anyone who went by that name, nickname or not, had to be a nerd. Which was perfect, because only a nerd could save me from failing this course and having to retake it next semester.

It wasn't very crowded in the coffee shop but as I moved inside, I didn't see any obvious candidates for a Darwin. There were three girls studying together, and two couples. See, couples were *everywhere.* You couldn't exist without stumbling over like a hundred perfect pairs of people who believed they were in love every single day. Some of them probably even were in love, though I had my doubts about Couple Number One. They looked bored. Couple Number Two? Love. And say hello to jealousy, Kylie, your new best friend.

I pushed those thoughts to the back of my mind where there was a box labeled Things That Suck and went back to searching for my genius tutor. And why weren't those thoughts in Hindi? Geez, so not fair.

There were two guys sitting by themselves. One was wearing hipster glasses and had a tattoo sleeve, his head bobbing to the music fed through his iPhone. Nope. The other one looked a little young to be a grad student, but he had acne and curly hair that went to his shoulders. He was staring intently at his computer screen, papers spread out all around him. This was clearly my man. He was going to have to be a superhero to save me from repeating this class, and, frankly, he looked up for the job. I also felt that I was perfectly safe from bursting into tears in his presence. Nothing about him seemed compassionate or friendly.

Approaching him, I smiled. "Are you Darwin? I'm Kylie. Thanks for helping me study."

But he just glanced up at me blankly. "What?"

"I'm Kylie. Professor Kadisch gave me your e-mail . . . we arranged to meet here." Then as his expression never changed, I realized I was barking up the wrong nerd tree. "Are you Darwin?"

"No, I'm Christian."

"Oh." I gave him a smile of apology, readjusting my backpack on my shoulders. "Sorry to bother you."

"No problem." His Adam's apple moved as he swallowed, his upper lip curling up to indicate it was in fact a huge problem. He was annoyed at the interruption.

Feeling stupid, I turned on my heel and went for an empty table. Darwin must be running a few minutes late. I would check my e-mail on my phone and see if he had canceled or something.

"Kylie?"

I stopped short, and turned. The other guy had pulled out his earbuds and he was giving me a smile.

"Yes."

"I'm Darwin." He stood up and came toward me, sticking his hand out. "Nice to meet you."

This was Darwin? For real? Huh. I shouldn't have been so quick to judge. I hated when people assumed I was just another dumb blonde. But seriously, this guy was cute. He had eyes that crinkled when he smiled in greeting, a patch of beard on his chin, and eyelashes behind his glasses that made me bitter on behalf of wispy-eyelashed blond women everywhere. He was about five eleven, lanky but not skinny, and despite the jeans and T-shirt, looked every inch a man, not a kid.

"Nice to meet you, too." I took his hand and shook it carefully. His grip was appropriately solid, but not grabby or lingering. His palm wasn't damp. "Thanks for helping me out. I've been . . . struggling." That was an understatement.

"Sit down and we'll see where you're at." He pulled out a chair for me and sat in the one he'd been occupying before, his tablet propped on his bag so he could see the screen.

I sat down, feeling disarmed by his friendly smile. I wasn't sure, but I thought I would have preferred a stern and studious tutor. I wasn't sure I could handle kindness without comparing it to the cruelty Nathan had shown me. That's what I kept doing. Every time someone was even remotely and casually nice to me, I immediately wondered why Nathan could have so intentionally and viciously hurt me. Which then made me feel terrible. Like maybe there was something wrong with me. That the more he had gotten to know me, the more he thought I wasn't entitled to his respect. I didn't want to think about that, but I couldn't help it. It charged in without warning.

As I pulled out my laptop and found my study guide, I studied Darwin.

His hair wasn't military short, but not long either, just enough length to look appropriately effortless with a hint of hair product. I knew hair product. You could not fool me. He was definitely using it, but it was most likely just a molding mud he ran through his hair post-shower in a pea-sized dose. A man who cared enough to control frizz was a notch up in my estimation. But if they spent more time on their blowout than I did, we had a problem. There was a fine line for acceptable male grooming practices. In that middle territory between high maintenance and caveman was where I found men to be attractive.

Not that I found him attractive. I didn't find anyone attractive. I had been in love. You don't just suddenly start finding other guys attractive when your heart has been hand-fed to jackals.

"So what do you think is the main issue?" he asked me, shifting a little closer to me so he could take a look at what was on my screen.

"I'm failing chemistry."

He laughed. "Well, I know that. But when did you start having problems?"

"When the class started."

His lips pressed together and he pushed up his glasses. "Okay, let's just start going through the study guide together and we'll see if we can figure out what's tripping you up."

"Okay," I said doubtfully. The coffee shop was warm and I shrugged out of my jacket.

His hand came out and helped me drag my left sleeve all the way off. "Thanks."

"Sure." He draped the freed sleeve over my chair. "So why can't isolated atoms be measured?"

Um. I thought about it. But I seriously had no idea. None whatsoever. I didn't even remember discussing atoms at all, but since this was a chem class, we must have at some time. "Because they're alone and there's no one to hold the measuring tape?"

He gave me a grin. "No. It's because we can't determine the location of the electrons around the atom's nucleus."

"Right." Oh my God, I was already lost. Wait. I had never been found.

"But we can estimate the size of an atom by assuming that the radius of an atom is half the distance between adjacent atoms in a solid. This is best for elements that are metals, because they form solids composed of extended planes of atoms of that element. The results of the measurements are called metallic radii."

I tried not to panic. "So . . . do I just have to memorize the definition? Is the exam just going to ask me to define 'metallic radii'?"

"Yes, and there may be an example where you have to estimate the size of the atom." He ripped a piece of paper and started drawing a formula. He was left-handed and his pen moved efficiently and confidently. "See? Like this."

Yeah. No. I figured if I at least got the definition and bombed the formulas, I would maybe get a D and that was all I needed to pass. "Uh-huh," I said, noncommittedly.

"The metallic radius becomes *larger* as we go down a column of the periodic table because the valence electrons are placed in larger orbitals."

I could feel my lip starting to tremble and I blinked hard, afraid I might embarrass the hell out of myself and start crying. He might as well be speaking Klingon for all I understood what he was saying. Actually, I might understand Klingon better. I went through a *Star Trek* phase in middle school.

When I didn't say anything, he glanced over at me and his face became alarmed. "What's wrong?"

"I think a whole semester of chemistry is a lot to cram into one night," I said in a small voice.

"Good thing you have the best tutor." He winked at me. "They don't call me Darwin for nothing."

"Is that your real name?"

"No. It's Jonathon."

"That's a nice name."

"Thanks. I got saddled with the Darwin nickname when I won the state physics competition in high school. It stuck."

For some reason, that made me feel better. "I played volleyball in high school. My nickname was Bump."

He laughed. "Really? And how did you feel about that?"

"I hated it. Who wants to be called Bump? It made me feel like my butt is big."

Darwin, or Jonathon, gave me a puzzled look. "Isn't a bump a . . ." He used his wrists to demonstrate hitting the ball.

"In volleyball, yes. But it doesn't have that meaning off the court." It was a teasing slur that could be interpreted in a thousand ways depending on the circumstances, but I wasn't going to spell it out for him.

He glanced down behind my chair. "I think your butt is fine."

That's what I got for bringing up my butt in the first place. My tutor giving me a lame compliment to shut me up so we could get back to atoms and whatnot. "Thanks. Am I supposed to call you Darwin or Jonathon?"

"Whichever one you like. I answer to both."

"I'll test them both out and make a decision," I said to him, standing up. "I'm going to grab a latte, Darwin, can I get you anything?"

He smiled, his mouth turning up like he was fighting the urge to laugh. "Sure. I'll take coffee. Black. Costa Rican blend. Thanks, Kylie."

I dug in my backpack for my wallet and he tried me to hand me five dollars but I shook my head. "It's on me. For helping me. It's the least I can do." Especially considering I was a totally hopeless case.

He nodded. "Thanks. And hey, we'll just divide the material into the major components and break it down one section at a time. You'll be fine. You'll ace this."

Sigh. I used to be optimistic like that. When the earth was younger, and I hadn't been cheated on by the guy I'd given my heart and the key to my back door to.

CHAPTER TWO

TWO HOURS LATER MY HEAD WAS SPINNING, BUT I AT LEAST had a game plan for further studying. Darwin/Jonathon had shown me that the class was divided into elements, mixtures, compounds, gases, and measurements. He subdivided each of those for me into additional categories and talked me through every definition and gave example formulas, which I almost maybe understood if I squinted and thought really hard.

I had three days before my exam so if I spent every waking moment between now and then reading the notes over and over and over again, I might pass. Maybe.

But I was getting a little loopy. While he was in the bathroom I was going through some online study sites and I found a bunch of chemistry jokes. I couldn't help it. I copied one and e-mailed it to him.

He was looking at his phone as he came out. "Did you just e-mail me while I was in the restroom?"

He really was cute. It just wasn't right. His jeans fit the way they were supposed to and I found it interesting that he only needed a T-shirt in November. His tattoo was a complex sleeve of numbers and diagrams.

I nodded. "Yes, I did. Jonathon." I was still testing his dual-personality names.

He gave a low, husky laugh as he settled back into his chair while reading his screen. "Really, Kylie?"

My head was propped with my palm and I smiled, feeling comfortable with him. He smelled good. Like coffee and clean.

"What did one ion say to the other?" he read back to me, even though I knew what it said since I'd sent it. "I've got my ion you."

I laughed. I couldn't help it. It was stupid, and even I understood it.

To his credit, he laughed with me. "See? Chemistry is *fun*."

"Oh yeah. It's a laugh riot. Hey, what do you do with a dead chemist?" I asked him, glad to rest my brain for a minute. I was a little afraid it was smoking from overheating.

"You barium."

No way. He'd heard this one before. "Damn it! How did you know the answer?"

He tapped his temple. "Me use my head."

"Well, *Darwin*." I let the nickname roll off my tongue. I still wasn't sure which one suited him better. "I guess I should let you get back to your regularly scheduled life. Thanks for all your help."

"You're welcome." He efficiently packed up all his stuff. "You'll do fine on this exam as long as you don't panic."

Easy for him to say. "So what all is in your tattoo?" I asked, reaching out and running my finger along his arm, over the maze of numbers.

He looked startled that I had touched him and I realized that probably wasn't appropriate. But I came from a touchy-feely family and I had always been someone who reached out and made contact without any thought about it. I hugged my friends, I put my hands on arms when I spoke to people, I squeezed knees. If I liked you—and it was rare I met someone I truly didn't like—I touched. The me before the RAN incident wouldn't have even thought twice about it, but now I suddenly felt like I needed to apologize or something. Like he would think I was hitting on him.

But he just started pointing out parts of his sleeve. "The periodic table of the elements. Avogrado's number. The molecular graphic for propane."

After that, I couldn't follow any more. "But won't professors think you're cheating? If you have stuff on your arm?"

The smile he gave me was patronizing. I don't think he meant it to be, but his answer told me how clearly stupid my question was. "When you're studying reactions kinetics and advanced nucleic biochemistry you don't need to cheat on basic chem."

"Oh." I felt heat in my cheeks. Most of the time, I was perfectly happy with who I was. But then there were other times, like then, where I just didn't want to be the dumb blonde. Just once, I wanted to be taken seriously, instead of having everyone think I was cute, but ten IQ points off from needing the short bus. "Duh."

"In between are dates representing people and events that are important to me. My birthday. My mom's birthday. The first time I—" He looked up and gave me a grin. "Well, you get the idea."

So genius or not, he was still like any other guy. Needing to brag. "Are you seriously telling me you inked the date you lost your virginity on your arm?"

"I never said that."

But he did wink at me, and I thought he was actually growing even cuter the longer I sat with him. "Honestly, it should look like a total mess, but the artist did a really good job. It's very cool."

"Thank you." He pushed his chair back. "You ready to head out?"

"Sure." I stood up and pulled my coat off the chair.

"Do you have any tattoos?" he asked.

"No. I do have a piercing, though."

"Belly button?"

"No." Let him interpret that however he wanted to.

His eyebrows shot up. "Are you telling *me* you have your love button pierced?"

I laughed. "Love button? And I never said that." I winked back at him after echoing his words.

"Oh my God," he said, standing up and picking up his messenger bag. "You're dangerous."

I wished. "To be dangerous you have to be evil or super-smart and I'm not either."

"Those aren't the only ways to pose a threat."

Suddenly I was afraid to hear what he might say. So to distract myself, I looked at my phone, and was immediately sorry I had. I had a text from Nathan.

I love you.

My smile evaporated and I shoved my phone in my pocket. I didn't want to see that. He kept coming at me like that, trying to apologize, begging me to take him back. But how do you trust someone who not only hooked up with your friend, he spent the next two months trying to repeat it?

He didn't love me. You didn't treat someone you loved like he had me.

Resolutely, I put a smile on my face and looked at Darwin/Jonathon. "Thanks again, Jonathon. Have a good night." I started to walk away, wanting a private moment to myself.

"I'll walk out with you," he said easily, falling into step beside me. Damn it.

"Are you okay?" he asked, as he held the door open for me.

Cold air hit me the face. I winced. "Fine. I'm stressed, but I'll do the best I can on the exam. If I fail, well, at least I tried."

"I'm not talking about the exam."

Puzzled, I glanced over at him, hovering on the sidewalk, not sure which way he was going. "What do you mean?"

"Whatever was on your phone upset you."

That it was that obvious made tears instantly rise to my eyes. "No, it's fine." I gestured to the left. "I'm this way. Have a good night."

"You're walking?" He frowned.

"It's just a block."

"It's dark. I'll walk with you."

"No, no, it's fine." I started walking, anxious to get away from him. He was being too nice and I felt vulnerable, like a loser. I couldn't keep a boyfriend or understand basic chem. What he considered chemistry for dummies.

But he continued to walk with me. "You're a junior, right?" he asked casually, like I wasn't struggling not to cry.

I nodded.

"What is your major?"

"Education. I want to be a kindergarten teacher." I gave him a wan smile. "I don't need to know chemistry to teach that."

"I bet you'd be good with kids."

"I love kids."

There was silence between us as we walked, the heels of my boots sounding extra loud in the dark, the street, which was normally filled with students, mostly empty. It was a bit of a creepy walk at this time of night and I'd known a girl who had been mugged. I would pee my pants if I were mugged and if I wasn't feeling so bummed, I would be more grateful for him walking with me. But mostly I just wanted to get home.

Then I realized what I was going home to—a dark, silent room.

And the tears I'd been holding back fell along with a sob that burst out unbidden.

We were in front of my building and I just about ran to the door, digging in my bag for my key.

"Kylie." Darwin/Jonathon touched my arm. "Hey. Look at me."

I shook my head.

"Do you want to talk about it?"

I shook my head harder.

But then, because I'm not someone who stuffs my feelings down, and because all my thoughts come out like a toddler commentating from their car seat on every car, cow, and house they see out the window, I blurted out, "My boyfriend cheated on me with my best friend."

"*What*?" He sounded horrified. "Are you fucking kidding me?"

It gave me a sense of relief that his reaction was so strong. "That's what I thought. I mean, it's like the worst thing ever."

"I hope he is your *ex*-boyfriend."

"He is. Because the thing is, okay, so it was a drunken hookup which is really bad, but I don't know, maybe I could have forgiven him for that. But I found the texts he sent her for months afterward, creeping for a repeat. He said it was the best blow job he'd ever had and that she had a . . ." I shook my head. "Never mind. It just was obvious he wasn't even remotely sorry."

"Wow. That's rough. He sounds like a complete asshole. I'm sorry."

My shoulders fell as my breath expelled. I ran out of words for a second. It was the right thing for him to say, but every time I heard someone offer sympathy, I just felt worse. Because while they were all genuinely sorry for me, they were also a little bit glad it hadn't happened to them. "Thanks." I finally found my key and I noticed my hand was shaking a little as I tried to unlock the exterior door to my building.

Darwin/Jonathon put his hand over mine to steady it. For a second, I just stood there, drawing in a breath to calm down. He waited then helped me turn the key to the right.

He was close behind me when I looked up at him, my hip shoving the door open. "Thanks," I whispered.

"He's an asshole," he repeated, his voice serious, eyes earnest.

"Do you want to come in?" I asked, because I really, really didn't want to be alone. My thoughts were too scattered, my anxiety high. Failing chemistry, moving out of my old apartment, hating my jealousy over my friends' relationships . . . it was hitting me hard. I didn't want silence.

His eyes shuttered for a minute and I felt silly. He was like twenty-five years old, a grad student with labs and research and probably a brainiac girlfriend who did physics for fun. Why would he want to spend the rest of his night with an undergrad who didn't know biochemistry from her butthole and kept threatening to cry? "Sorry, I don't know why I said that. I'm sure you have better things to do. Things that don't involve me boring you with my pathetic love life." Shame wasn't an emotion I'd felt a lot in my life, but the last three months it had become a familiar feeling. One I hated.

I stepped into the vestibule, intending to close the door behind me, letting Darwin off the hook. But he came with me. "I'd love to."

Oh, God, he totally felt sorry for me. The shame increased, but at the same time, I still didn't want to be alone, so I didn't hold firm and send him home like I should have. I trudged up the stairs to the second floor and he reached out and put his hand on the small of my back when I stumbled a little on the third step.

Darwin was clearly a nice guy. Whatever he was getting paid by the university to tutor wasn't enough. How many hours a week did he spend coaching crying undergrads? Probably half the freshman class was failing chemistry. Yet here he was, being pretty damn sweet when it was obvious he could be doing about a million more interesting things.

"Do you have a roommate?" he asked.

"No, it's just a studio. I moved here in September after classes started, so I had to take what I could get and this was it. But I couldn't live in an apartment with Robin after what happened, so this was the best solution." I unlocked the door and shoved it open. Flicking on the light, I felt depressed all over again looking at the glum. "It has terrible lighting."

He wandered in to the small room and bent over to inspect my two lamps. "You only have twenty-five watts in here. You could get brighter bulbs."

"Oh." Of course I could. But that had never once occurred to me. I was too busy feeling sorry for myself to be logical. "Yeah, I guess I could do that."

He dropped down onto my bed, which also acted as my couch, because I had no furniture and no space. "It takes a while to settle into a new place."

"I never wanted to be here. So it's hard to care." Setting my backpack on the floor, I sat next to him, crossing my legs and tucking my feet under them. "Do you have a roommate?"

"Yeah. My friend Devon. I'd rather live alone, honestly, but I can't afford it."

"And I would rather live with people. I'm social." My phone buzzed in my pocket.

I wasn't going to look at it. I didn't want to look at it. It could be nothing. It could be Jessica or Rory or my mother. But compulsion drove me to pull it out and check. I was sorry I did. A pit formed in my stomach as I read the text from Nathan.

This wouldn't have happened if you had stayed here this summer like I asked you to. We would still be together and happy.

My lip curled. So it was my fault that he had fucked my friend? Because I wasn't around for a few weeks?

"Why don't you block him?" Darwin asked.

"I don't know. Maybe because I keep wanting and waiting for a better apology."

"I don't think there's a better apology for what he did. I don't think he can ever really give you a good enough reason for why he had sex with your best friend."

I nodded. "You're right." I knew it. "I also know it's not my fault, but I can't help but feel like if only I'd done something different . . ."

He held his hand up, palm out. "Stop right there. There is no way that you could have done anything different so that it would have prevented this. If a guy is willing to cross that line, you could be perfect and it still wouldn't matter. Don't put yourself through that."

The tears started again. I nodded, my lips trembling.

"It's not your fault he's selfish, stupid, immoral, and an asshole."

"Well, I don't know if he's stupid." I could concede the rest, but for some ridiculous reason I felt the need to defend Nathan, even just a little.

"He got caught, didn't he? That makes him stupid. Besides, any guy who would waste his time hooking up with a chick when he has *you* is an idiot."

I smiled. "Thanks. Even if you are just saying that."

But he shook his head as he peeled off his jacket. "I'm not just saying that. You're beautiful, Kylie, and more than that, you're sweet."

I did like to think that I was nice. "I try to be a decent person. But it seems like that's worked against me."

"Don't let one guy's dickheadedness change who you are. Don't let him ruin you. You're attractive just the way you are."

Confused, I wasn't sure what to say. I knew he was just being nice, and I hated that it even mattered to me what anyone's opinion was, but I felt needy. It had me seeking validation in a way I hadn't since probably middle school. "You think I'm attractive?"

It was an embarrassing thing to ask. I wanted to choke myself for letting it slip out.

Darwin nodded, though. "I find you very attractive. So attractive that I have to admit to being distracted the whole time I was tutoring you."

A shiver inched up my spine. "You were not." He hadn't looked at all like he'd been undressing me with his eyes. But then again, maybe nerds were smart enough to hide it, unlike the douche bags I usually hung out with.

"Oh yes, I was." He was leaning against the wall, hands resting on his knees, and his expression was hooded. "I can tell you that you wear two necklaces—one is a cross, one is a heart with a ruby in the center. You have on a braided bracelet and if I had to guess, you are a 34C bra size. You have a tiny mole on your neck, you're really fond of lip gloss, you always twirl your hair with your left hand, never your right, and you are a natural blonde."

Oh, my. A blush covered my face and it was partly from embarrassment and partly from a sudden arousal that caught me completely off guard. "How do you know I'm a natural blonde?"

"You don't have any exposed roots and your eyebrows are the same tone as your hair."

Were all intelligent people this observant? Rory was the same way. Though Rory had never nailed my bra size. I wasn't sure what to say.

"Is that creepy?" he asked. "I only told you to illustrate my point that I find you attractive."

"It's not creepy. It's flattering." It was. And he was very sweet to massage my damaged ego.

"Good. I want you to remember that, whenever you start to doubt that you had anything to do with Dickhead cheating on you. It was his problem, not yours."

I felt like I should I give him a fee for the therapy. "Thanks, Darwin. I find you attractive, too."

He gave me a smile, the corner of his lip turning up in a way that made me focus on his mouth, made me wonder what it would feel like to have it on mine. I kind of really wanted him to kiss me, just to see.

"Now you're just flattering me."

"No." I shook my head, feeling myself leaning closer toward him, without even intending to. "The first thing I noticed when I sat down next to you was how good you smell."

His nostrils flared a little. "How I smell?"

"Yes. You smell masculine."

"That's evolution," he told me. "A female instinctively responds to the scent of a male and she is subconsciously drawn to the specimen she thinks will ensure her progeny's survival."

Whatever. "I think it was more that you don't smell like sweat or cologne."

"It's still the chemistry of attraction."

He had shifted closer, too, and I could see that he had an erection. It hadn't been there before, and now it was. Bam. The sight of it so clearly outlined beneath his jeans had me tingling in places I had thought no longer existed. I hadn't had a single sexual urge at all since RAN and now a warm sensation was pooling between my thighs and spreading out to all my limbs. My nipples felt constrained in my bra. My 34C bra.

"Can you just show me instead of explaining it to me?" I asked, and I was shocked to hear the flirt, which I thought had taken a permanent vacation, return to my voice for the first time in four months. "I learn better hands-on."

"With visual aids?"

I nodded, biting my bottom lip.

"Come here," he urged, holding his hand out to me.

I did, crawling up between his legs, breathing in his scent, taking in his narrow lips, his eyes, so dark behind the lenses of his glasses. He reached out with his thumb and wiped the tears that were still lingering on my face in itchy, wet streaks.

Then he kissed me.

CHAPTER THREE

IT WAS A DELICIOUS KISS, THE KIND THAT STARTED SLOW and tentative then grew deeper and deeper until I needed to pull back and snag a breath. For a heartbeat, I stared at him, my mouth hovering over his, the light reflecting off his glasses so I couldn't read what was in his eyes, but he didn't give me enough time to speak or think any further. He put his hand on the back of my head and erased the space between us, and for some reason it mattered to me that he didn't pull me to him, he came to me. It wasn't a lazy kiss, a hey, baby, give daddy some sugar, kind of lame, puckered-lip sloppiness.

This was like when you went tubing on the river and you drifted along, eyes closed, face turned up toward the sun, relaxed, warm and cold at the same time, aware of every sensation, fingers trailing behind in the murky water. Like each moment mattered, time caught in a mental camera roll, captured in sparkling perfection, time slow and easy, yet disappearing faster than you could have ever imagined. Jonathon kissed like that, his tongue teasing the inside of my mouth, his fingers massaging the back of my head, his legs and arms forming a warm circle around me. It was like he had nowhere to be and nothing to do except this, and he didn't grind or grab or push my hand onto his junk.

It was like he could kiss me indefinitely, and I could hear my breathing grow ragged, could feel my body growing hot, heavy, eager. When he briefly pulled back to study me, smiling a little, I saw that I had fogged up his glasses. I gave a soft laugh.

"What?"

"Your glasses are steamed up."

I expected him to smile or laugh with me, but his expression was serious, intense.

"It's because you're damn hot," he said, his voice low, before he pulled my bottom lip into his mouth and sucked on it.

"Oh," I murmured, leaning on him sideways, my hands around his neck. My response wasn't meant to be an agreement, it was just an involuntary reaction to the sensation of him sucking on my flesh, the tugging echoing at all the warm spots of my body. I squirmed a little as he dipped down and nuzzled along my neck, amazed at how turned on I was from so little contact. My fingertips dug into his shoulders and he eased me back onto my bed.

"Can I take your sweater off?"

That he asked me instead of just tearing at my clothes stunned me and I just nodded. Something about him made me speechless, and it felt bizarre and confusing, yet arousing. I didn't need to chatter away to keep his interest, and I didn't feel like he wanted the porn star partner Nathan had always craved. This was slow and easy, and as Darwin stripped my sweater off carefully, making sure he didn't accidentally pull my hair, I didn't feel the need to pose or pout. Instead, I reached up with one finger and pushed his glasses up since they had slipped, and it felt natural to do that.

"Thanks," he murmured.

He kissed me again, a deep, sexy kiss that had me rubbing my leg over the back of his calf, straining to meet my hips to his.

His hand rested on my hipbone, heavy and large, as his tongue slid across my lower lip and down my neck. I shivered. "Oh, God." His fingers jerked a little on my hip.

My bra strap had fallen off my shoulder and he shifted his hand to pull it all the way down my arm. I finished the job, lifting my hand to remove the strap entirely. He repeated it on the other side and while his hands explored my breasts over my bra, his mouth continued to float over my flesh, sometimes on my neck, sometimes my cleavage, sometimes my lips, so that I never quite knew where he was going. It went on and on, minute after agonizing minute, and I moaned, my hips grinding more desperately against him. I hadn't had sex since August and I hadn't devoted this much time to making out since tenth grade.

He paused long enough to strip off his own T-shirt, revealing a chest that had more definition than I could have ever expected for a guy who spent all his time with beakers or whatever they had in chem labs. I ran my fingers over it, wanting to feel him. His skin was warm and wherever I touched, goose bumps appeared, and for some reason that pleased me. When I reached the button on his jeans, I popped it, and he drew back to look at me.

"I was wondering if we were going there," he said. "Is that a yes?"

For a second, I felt a little confused. He really hadn't seen sex as a definite conclusion? That seemed hard to believe. But it cemented my decision. I had already decided to without going through any actual decision-making process, and this forced me to stop and think and be one hundred percent certain. Did I want to have sex with Darwin? Oh, hell, yes. My body was on fire and he seemed like a guy who wanted to do everything to the best of his ability. For every tool who had told me I wouldn't be disappointed, the majority of the time I had been, but the amount of effort Jonathon had given to making out made me certain in this case I wouldn't be.

I nodded, biting my lip. "It's a yes."

He didn't speak, he just popped the back of my bra and lifted it off of me. He studied the tag.

"What are you doing?"

"34C. Damn, I'm good."

I laughed. "Or a pervert."

"Not usually. But you bring out the pervert in me. I told you that you were dangerous."

"I'm not taking responsibility for you staring at my breasts."

His mouth descended onto my nipple.

"Or doing that." Oh, God, that felt good. He took his time, sucking slowly, his hand cupping the weight of my breast. I could feel his erection thick against my leg, the heat from my body feeling trapped inside my jeans. I wanted to be naked. I wanted him to be naked. I jerked his zipper down and slid my hand inside his pants.

He paused to give his own moan when I made contact with his business, squeezing down the length of him.

But he still didn't hurry. He didn't shuck his pants to his knees and pump into me for five minutes, slapping the side of my ass at random intervals.

Not even close. He moved his mouth over me, trading breasts, licking down my middle, tongue dipping into my belly button. His hands trailed behind everywhere his tongue touched, and the feathery brushing over top of the wet path he'd created had me sucking in air on desperate gasps, my grip tightening on his cock.

"Darwin," I murmured, still needing to test both names on him. I couldn't figure out which one suited him better. Normally nicknames feel more personal, but that didn't seem quite accurate with him.

"Yes?"

"I don't know," I told him, free hand digging into the back of his hair, urging his mouth back to my nipple. "I have no idea why I just said that." I didn't. I couldn't think.

"Maybe you wanted to ask me something?" he suggested, glancing up at me with a wicked smile.

It should be illegal for a guy to be both that intelligent and that goddamn hot. He held all the cards. "You're right. I wanted to ask you to take my pants off."

His nostrils flared. "I'd be happy to." Moving down my stomach, he undid my button and took down the zipper. He gave a tug but the jeans didn't do much. "I'll be really happy when these fucking skinny jeans go out of style."

That struck me as super funny for some reason and I giggled.

"What?" he said, smiling at me. "It's true. These are a pain in the ass."

I had no response for that. And I wasn't sure why I was laughing, exactly. Maybe because for the first time in forever I felt . . . sexy. Wanted. Even if it was for right now, and right now only.

Instead of answering him, I just gripped the waistband of my jeans and shoved them, along with my panties, straight down my thighs. "There. You can take it the rest of the way."

The way his eyes darkened and he muttered, "Holy fuck," as he stared down at my body was very satisfying. "You weren't lying about the piercing."

"No." It wasn't something I would have sought out. I'd done it at Nathan's urging, who had seen too much sex on the Internet. He'd insisted it would be super hot for him and super sensitive for me during foreplay. Except there never was foreplay. About all he had ever done with it was flick the hoop with his finger and occasionally tug it when he wanted my attention. I had actually been meaning to take it out, but just never quite got around to it. I was used to it, though, and when I was getting turned on, it did give it an extra tingle.

For a second his hand hovered over me, before lightly cupping me. His eyes shifted up to meet mine. "You shave."

Since it wasn't a question I didn't answer. I'd been shaving since freshman year in high school because of bikinis and volleyball and later because of boys. I liked a clean surface to set the table.

He shook his head slightly and I frowned, wondering what it meant, but he kissed me before I could ask, while his finger slipped inside me. Words disappeared. What he found was that I was already wet. What I found was that Jonathon had long fingers that knew just where to stroke. This was no twenty-year-old jamming his fingers into me like he was scraping a peanut butter jar. His touch was gentle, exploratory, and when he got a positive reaction from me, he settled in with a steady rhythm that probably could only be topped by my own touch, and I'd had years of practice. He had only been doing it for five minutes. While his finger stroked, his thumb teasingly brushed over my clitoris, flipping the ring back and forth, creating extra friction and stimulation.

I turned my head, too many sensations pouring over me. I needed air, I needed a break. But that only freed him up to drop his tongue over my nipple again, flicking it in a steady rhythm that matched what he was doing to my clitoris. Back and forth, back and forth, tongue and thumb until I was squirming on the bed, my grip on his arms desperate. I scissored my feet trying to get my pants all the way off so I could fully spread my legs.

He knew what I was trying to do and without breaking rhythm inside me, he shifted off my breast and leaned down to jerk hard on my jeans, freeing my legs.

"Thank you," I breathed, letting my hips drop apart.

"I'm the one who should be giving thanks." He rubbed his jaw and swept his eyes over me from head to toe. "You are honestly the hottest thing I've ever seen. I want to lick every single inch of you."

I wasn't going to say no to that. He was already halfway to

accomplishing that goal anyway. My hand was trembling, like it had been when I had tried to open my apartment door, as I took his wrist and pulled his touch away from me. I was too close to having an orgasm and he didn't even have his jeans off yet.

"No finger?" he asked.

I shook my head, wondering again where my voice had disappeared to. I never stop talking. Ever. But I had nothing to say. I just wanted to feel.

"Tongue?" he asked.

It would probably kill me but the very thought of what he could do with his touch there had me nodding eagerly.

The corner of his mouth turned up. "First let me take my pants off. I feel a little overdressed."

"Like an Eskimo in the Everglades," I said.

He laughed. "Kylie, you are a funny girl." Then he sat up and stripped his jeans and boxer briefs off, his erection springing up at the freedom.

My mouth felt hot, my saliva thick. My necklaces were stuck to my damp skin and the tickling of his hair on my stomach as he descended over me had me shivering. Then I felt the first touch of the tip of his tongue on me, just below the navel. He cut a line straight down, playing with the ring before bypassing it and going to the last stop on the bus line before coming up and starting all over again. This time he lingered longer, toying with my piercing, taking it between his teeth and tugging gently so that I had damp palms and hitched breathing, and heavy eyelids.

His thumbs massaged either side as his tongue moved from

playing with my clit to deep into the core of my body, then back again.

"I like your love button and its bling," he murmured.

"I like you liking it." Even if he insisted on calling it such a stupid name. For a scientist I would have expected something more anatomically correct.

None of which mattered when he did what he was doing, for longer than I could keep track of, for so long that I almost forgot how to breathe and definitely forgot how to think. "Oh, God," I cried out, biting my bottom lip and trying to hold back an orgasm.

But he gripped my thighs and worked me deeper. "Come for me, Kylie."

I couldn't have stopped it if there had been a million dollars riding on it. It was big, a swollen wave of pleasure that crashed over me, knocking great gusts of satisfied sound from my mouth. It was epic, lasting long enough to have my eyes fully rolling back.

Then it was over and before I even had time to think or blink or swallow he was between my thighs, arms resting on either side of my shoulders.

"Birth control?" he asked.

"Yes," I said, my voice hoarse from moaning.

But then I felt the tip of him just inside me and I shoved his chest. "No, I meant, yes, we need birth control, not that I'm on it."

"Oh, sorry." He jerked backward. "Sorry."

Rolling onto my side I wiggled out from under him and stretched for my purse. I dumped it completely on to my nightstand, desperate to not delay the action too long. Three condoms fell out last, having sunk to the very bottom of my bag, neglected for months. I threw them at Darwin. "Here."

As I fell back onto the bed and shifted my legs apart again he quickly covered himself with a condom and moved back into position. His glasses had slipped down his nose again but he didn't seem to notice. For a second he just paused, hovering there, staring down at me. I fought the urge to lift my hips and instead just waited for him.

His jaw worked. "You're very beautiful." He bent over me and drew in a breath, deep in my neck, his lips tickling me as he spoke. "I like the way you smell, too."

Then he gave me a kiss and pushed inside me. It was more than I expected, both physically and otherwise. All his careful prep work had left me super sensitive and very wet and there was none of the usual feeling of tugging, that rough invasion. It just . . . fit. Like he belonged deep there, inside of me, and after five minutes of him stroking in and out easily, I was already halfway to another orgasm.

"That's it," he urged me. "You got it."

For a second I was confused, but then I realized he wanted me to come again. My excitement was exciting him. The comforter was twisted in his grip and his thrusts were coming harder, faster. There was a sheen of sweat on his forehead and he was pulsing inside me the way a guy does just before he comes. I squeezed my muscles around him and enjoyed the groan of appreciation he gave.

It hit me hard, the second one, like a speeding car hitting a wall. I breathed his name. "Jonathon."

And I knew after that moment I'd never be able to call him Darwin again.

He was Jonathon.

Jonathon gave one final thrust then came, his teeth gritted.

For at least a minute, we were frozen just like that, our heavy breathing the only sound in the dim room. Then he gripped my hips and rolled me over, on top of him, as he collapsed back onto the bed with a sigh. With him still inside me, I rested my head on his chest and swallowed hard.

"You're a really good tutor," I said.

He gave a startled laugh and choked on it. His hand slid over my ass. "God. Professor Kadisch would kill me. After he fired me."

"Well, I'm sure in the hell not going to tell him." Jonathon had helped demystify chemistry for me and made me come twice. I had no complaints. I scratched my fingers across his chest and yawned.

He patted his hand around the bed until he found his jeans, which were wadded against the wall. He dug into the pocket and retrieved his phone. "I should probably go. It's after midnight."

Holy crap. We'd left the coffeehouse at 9:45. I couldn't remember the last time I'd had sex for two hours. Okay, like maybe never. No wonder it had been so good. "Wow. I didn't realize it was so late."

I shifted off of him and we both gave a little sigh. As he tugged off the condom, he asked, "Do you have a bathroom in here?"

Pointing to the door across from the bed, I nodded.

When he stood up to ditch the condom in the trash can, I

watched him walk across the room naked. He had a nice butt. I yawned again and rolled onto my side to face toward the room, making praying hands to prop my head up. I should probably pull my clothes on, but it seemed like too much work. I was comfortable naked and with my body.

After he flushed, he came back and gave me an appreciative glance. "Damn it, I wish we weren't about to start finals. I'd like to start that all over again instead of studying."

For a second I thought about suggesting we do it again after finals, then dismissed it. I wasn't going to throw that out there. Not when I was feeling so yummy delicious satisfied. Jonathon gave me a kiss as he leaned over my body to grab his jeans. Better to just leave it alone.

A minute later he was dressed and reaching for his bag. "Let me know if you need any more help studying."

"Okay. Thanks."

He pushed up his glasses and for a second I thought he was going to say something else but he just gave me a soft smile and turned and left, holding the door so it closed carefully instead of with a slam.

Rolling onto my back, I sighed, shoving my jeans off the bed with my foot. My vagina was pleasantly sore and I felt more relaxed than I had since, well, The Incident. My phone had fallen onto the nightstand when I had dumped my purse and it buzzed, indicating a text. I wasn't even tempted to check it. I didn't want to ruin this feeling, this perfect contentment.

After I slipped under the comforter I drifted off to sleep.

That night I slept better than I had in four months.

CHAPTER FOUR

I LEFT KYLIE'S APARTMENT AND FOR A SECOND, JUST STOOD in the hallway, shaking my head. What the fuck? Sex with a student I was tutoring? That was a first. And a last. Jesus.

Jogging down the one flight I hit the front door hard, welcoming the cool air on my body. I was still hot from the sex, from the exertion, the arousal, the view of her gorgeous, smooth, naked body, lounging on her bed, looking built for sin. Her expression had just been sweetly satisfied, her smile knowing yet innocent somehow. She was a complete dichotomy.

Fuck. Fuck. Fuck.

I was twenty-five, goddamn it. I had control over my body. Usually.

Walking fast, I backtracked to the coffee shop and unlocked my car in the parking lot. Tossing my bag on the passenger seat,

I adjusted myself and got in. My balls were sticking. For a second, I sat there immobile, brain dead from the memory of seeing her clean-shaven and pierced pussy for the first time. A fucking crowbar couldn't have pried me away from her at that point.

Yet it wasn't just her body. It was her. She was nothing but mixed signals. She dressed in tight jeans and showed cleavage, sporting a tan that couldn't be natural in November, and she was clearly comfortable being naked. Yet she cried over her stupid boyfriend instead of being angry, and she looked at me with shy, worried eyes, her teeth digging into her bottom lip when I had been walking her through ionic compounds. There was nothing ballsy or brazen about her. It made me intensely curious.

None of which could totally explain how I'd found myself buried inside her instead of going home to study for my own finals.

Fortunately, it was a short drive to my apartment.

Unfortunately, Devon was still up, sitting at the kitchen table, books spread in front of him. "Are you insane?" he said as a greeting as I slunk in, knowing I probably smelled like sex.

I could taste Kylie on my tongue and I wanted to let it linger awhile, but not there in the kitchen with Devon. His words made me feel guilty. "What?" I asked defensively.

"Why are you going out when your first exam is on Monday? Spectroscopy, if my photographic memory recalls."

I just grunted.

He finally glanced up, looking annoyed. "And why the hell didn't you text me to meet you out? Just because I'm Indian doesn't mean I want to spend all my time studying. I resent that."

Ignoring that bit of ridiculousness, I sighed and decided to tell the truth. "I wasn't out having a beer. I was with the new girl I'm tutoring in chem."

"Until midnight? Is she a total moron?"

For a second I wondered how far off from the truth that was, then I felt like a complete asshole for even thinking it. Kylie wasn't stupid. She just didn't have a brain for science. I wasn't sure she was going to actually pass her exam, despite our cram session. The concepts just seemed to float around her head, but never actually penetrate it. Maybe it was that she was distracted by her personal drama, but I didn't think that was all of it. It just wasn't her thing.

"We weren't studying the whole time."

"What is that supposed to mean?"

"I had sex with her." I went into the fridge, because suddenly I needed a drink of water. My tongue felt too thick for my mouth. I spotted a twelve-pack of beer and decided that sounded even better. I snagged one.

"You *what*? I repeat, are you fucking insane?"

"Probably." I held the cold can to my forehead. The image of Kylie writhing beneath me had popped up in my head again and I had a renewed boner. I hung around in the fridge for a minute before closing the door and facing my best friend.

He was making an expression that was so ludicrous I almost laughed. Almost.

"Was she hot?"

"Of course she was hot! I'm not going to bang a chick three hours after meeting her if she looks like my uncle Mike."

"Valid point. I concede the stupidity of my question. But how exactly does that happen? Hey, here's molarity, oh, and my dick inside you."

Now I did laugh. "Shut up."

Devon pulled his earbuds down and tossed them on the table. "No, I am dead serious. I want an answer. This shit never happens to me. I want to know what I'm doing wrong."

"Well." How did I explain what had happened? "She's struggling with chem."

"Established." He waved his hand. "Jump ahead."

"I'm trying to explain, asshole." I popped the beer tab and took a sip. The cool liquid felt good on my dry mouth. "She was trying really hard, though, and she was sweet and funny. She looked up these incredibly idiotic chemistry jokes and it was . . . cute." The women I dated were usually serious, like me. Kylie had amused me, made me smile.

"Then?" Devon looked thoroughly impatient with my storytelling.

"Then she started crying about her ex-boyfriend so I walked her home. And that's it."

"That's it? That is not the fuck it. How do you go from a chick crying to coming? It does not work like that."

"She was upset because her ex cheated on her. She felt unattractive and I was comforting her." As I said it, I realized how ludicrous that sounded. It hadn't seemed that creepy at the time.

His eyebrows shot up. "Oh, I'm so sorry your boyfriend

fucked someone else. If you suck on my dick you'll feel so much better." He picked up a balled-up piece of notebook paper and threw it at me. "God, I hate you. That would never work for me. I would end up with a black eye and a testicular torque."

The paper missed me. "I didn't say it like that, douche."

"Word for word what did you say?"

"I don't know. I don't remember." Which was a lie. I remembered every word, every kiss, every touch. But some things were none of Devon's business. Like that piercing. I took another huge sip of my beer.

"Are you going to see her again?"

I paused. But then I said, "No."

Kylie had made no move to give me her number, and she hadn't said anything about seeing each other again. She'd even been noncommittal when I had offered to help her study a little more. Not that she needed my particular brand of, uh, studying, before her exams. Suddenly I felt like a jerk. I should have never gone into her apartment.

But then I wouldn't have had that amazing sex.

My grip tightened on my can.

"Why the hell not? We can think of ways to make her cry so you can comfort her again."

I bent over and picked the paper up and threw it back at him. Hard.

He caught it and grinned. "Was it at least good?"

"Yes," I said shortly. "I'm going to go take a shower."

"Thank God. I can smell you from over here, you dirty whore.

Darwin's theory of fuckability. Can't wait to see the formula for that one."

Yeah. Someday it would really be damn nice to live alone.

I CURLED UP ON JESSICA'S COUCH, HAPPY TO NOT BE ALONE. Rory, Jess, and I were sprawled out studying. Robin, who didn't have traditional exams because she was taking all art classes, was out with her boyfriend, Phoenix. I was glad she wasn't there, and that made me feel guilty. I wanted to just sprinkle pixie dust and make all my shitty feelings toward her go away, but it was hard. I knew she was drunk and didn't even remember sleeping with Nathan, but she had still done it. I'd been shitfaced plenty of times and I'd never fucked anyone's boyfriend.

So it felt more comfortable not to have her there. Like old times. When it was just Rory, Jess, and me in a triple in our old dorm. Both Tyler and Riley and their younger brothers were out catching a movie. Cuddling under a blanket, I bit the bottom of my pen and went over the chemistry notes Jonathon had made for me again. Rory was lying on the floor, chin propped up by her fists. She had a giant to-go cup of coffee sitting next to her.

I knew she was studying and I shouldn't interrupt her, but I also knew she was always around the chemistry lab. "Hey, Rory, do you know some guy who is a chemistry grad student named Darwin?"

She glanced over at me before going straight back to reading. "Sure," she murmured. "He's a kinetics genius."

Whatever. "Isn't he totally cute?"

Now she swung her head completely and stared at me. "I guess. Yes. He's attractive. How do you know Darwin?"

I waved my notes at her. "He is the tutor I met Thursday night. He helped me study."

"How do you get a cute tutor?" Jessica asked, sprawled across the easy chair on the other side of the coffee table. She was wearing yoga pants and lying on her back. "When I was still at UC, the one time I tried to get calculus help I got a girl with a mustache. I mean, hello, there are at-home wax strips. Try them."

"Not everyone has your aesthetic," Rory told her. "Besides, maybe there are religious reasons she can't alter her body."

Jessica waved her hand. "Fine." She had enrolled in cosmetology school in October and while we were studying for our college exams, she was studying for her own first round of exams. Apparently even stylists need to know the muscles in the head and I was looking forward to when she would need to practice shampoo and massage techniques.

"But my point is, I did not get a hot tutor while Kylie apparently did." Jessica studied me. "You are so crushing on him."

"No, I'm not!" I protested, because I wasn't. Not really. I honestly didn't expect to ever see him again. But he had been exactly what I had needed right then, whether he knew it or not. "I totally had sex with him, but I do not have a crush on him."

Jessica shrieked. Rory's head fell off her hand.

I grinned. Well, it was fun to drop that little bomb.

Rory looked totally scandalized. "You had sex with Darwin Kadisch? Are you *serious*?"

Wait a minute. "His last name is Kadisch? But that's my teacher's last name."

"He's Professor Kadisch's son."

"He is?" Oops. "I did not know that. At all." That seemed bad. "Is that bad?"

"It's only bad if one of you tells the professor," Jessica said. "Which I seriously doubt he is going to do unless he and his father have a TMI relationship with each other. And you're not going to tell."

"No. Definitely not." I chewed my lip. "He said he wasn't going to say anything. He actually said Professor Kadisch would kill him. He didn't say anything about him being his dad. That's weird."

"His father is head of the undergrad chemistry program," Rory said. "He must've been trying to stay professional."

Jessica snorted. "Sure, he was. That's why he and Kylie were playing naked Twister. Because he's totally professional."

Rory made a face. "Good point. I guess the real question here is . . . was it good?"

"Rory asks an excellent question. Was it good?"

They both stared at me expectantly. I let them sweat it for a second.

"Oh yeah." Then I couldn't help it. I threw myself back on the cushion and rolled around, kicking my feet. "Holy shit, it was soooo good. I feel hot just thinking about it." I did. My cheeks were burning and so was my vajayjay. It had been three days and I was trying to set the experience aside and study very seriously, but he popped into my head when I was least expecting it.

Jessica laughed. "Well, that's good. Was he huge or something?"

"No. I mean, maybe slightly above average. It was more that he took his time. It was two hours and mostly, it was about me." I cuddled the blanket and sighed. "I really needed that."

"I haven't seen you this excited since Voldemort fucked you over," Jessica commented. "This is awesome."

I had forbidden my friend's to use Nathan's name in my presence so he became he-who-shall-not-be-named and then Voldemort. It worked for me. "Don't spoil my post-sex happiness by mentioning Sir Dickhead," I told her.

"Sorry. I'm just really glad to see you having fun."

"Was it kinky sex?" Rory asked, looking very curious.

"Rory!" Sometimes she said things that seemed totally out of character. "What do you mean by 'kinky'? And, actually, no. However you could possibly define 'kinky,' it wasn't."

She shrugged, her auburn braid falling over her shoulder. "I don't know. I guess I just envisioned him trying to defy the laws of gravity."

I had been taking a sip of my orange soft drink and at her words, I choked and sprayed it out of both my mouth and my nose. "OMG!" I was laughing and coughing at the same time as my friends both lost it, too. There was orange pop all over my notes and the coffee table. It dribbled down the front of my hoodie. "You kill me." I wiped my nose.

Rory sat up, still laughing. "God, this floor is so hard. I think I've dented my elbows."

"It's better than that stinky-ass carpet that was here before Riley and I ripped it up."

"True."

I let them go off on a carpet thing for a minute, happy to day-dream about Jonathon. Who would have thought nerd sex would be so hot?

When I rolled onto my side and reached idly for my drink again, I realized they were both grinning at me, no longer speaking. "What?"

"You look downright dreamy." Jessica grinned. "So when are you seeing him again?"

"Oh, I'm not."

"What? You let him leave without getting his number? Girl, you're slipping."

"I have his e-mail. I could get in touch with him. And I could have said something to him before he left, but I don't know. I didn't want to ruin it." I ran my finger over the formulas he'd written in my notebook. "I don't want to find out he really is some huge asshat. It was fun, and it made me feel sexy for the first time in a long time, and I just want to leave it at that."

Rory nodded, but Jessica looked sketch about the whole thing. "But if it was good, don't you want to do it again? It's not like every guy is willing to be going down on you for two hours. Trust me on this one. I've done some research."

I tried to explain. "But what if it was just A Moment? One of those like rare combinations of the right time, the right place, the right level of hormones or whatever. What if we did it again and it sucked? Not only would it suck, it would lessen the good factor of the first time. You know what I mean?"

"Yeah. I guess so."

"I just want to lock it in a box labeled 'Awesome Sex with a Nice Guy' and keep it safe there. Right now he's the only one in that box so he has plenty of room to move around."

Rory laughed. "I can understand that."

"Was he circumcised?" Jessica asked. "I've always wanted to know what dealing with an uncircumcised guy is like."

She made it sound like you had to be animal tamer to handle an uncircumcised penis. Circle it carefully, hands out, so you didn't spook it.

"Of course he is," Rory told her. "He's Jewish."

"He's Jewish?" I asked blankly. I had to admit I had not given one single thought to his ethnic or religious background. Not a single one.

"Well, presumably. Professor Kadisch is and their last name is German-Jewish."

"You scare me," Jessica told Rory. "How do you know shit like that?"

"What? It's common knowledge."

"Not in my world." Then she glanced back at me. "So he was circumcised?"

I nodded. "Definitely." I hadn't gotten that up close and personal with it, well, not with my eyes, but I had stroked him with my hand and that soldier had been wearing a helmet.

The front door opened and Jessica whispered, "Shh!" urgently like we were twelve and someone's mom was coming in to the room.

Which was why we all looked totally guilty when Riley, Tyler, Jayden, and Easton came into the living room, a gust of cold air following them. They were talking when they first stepped in, but Riley paused in the middle of kicking off his boots.

"What? Why do you all look so guilty?"

Rory bit her lip and shook her head. Jessica pretended to be studiously looking at her book. "What are you talking about, honey? How was the movie?"

He raised his eyebrows. "Fine." Then he turned to his brother. "Ty, are you with me on this one? Don't they look like they're either talking about something that is going to embarrass the shit out of us, or they are planning something that involves me doing manual labor?"

Tyler had kicked his boots off, too, and he padded into the room on his socks, dropping to the floor beside Rory. "I agree with you." He kissed his girlfriend and starting massaging her shoulders, clearly trying to butter her up. "Come on, Rory, be honest. Were you guys talking about us?"

"No," she told him and it rang with sincerity because it was true. "Ah, keep doing that. It feels good. I'm all in knots from studying."

He made a face but he kept doing it.

Jayden, Riley and Tyler's younger brother who had Down syndrome and was basically a laugh-riot all the time, hung his coat on the hooks Jessica had installed by the front door. "Man, I'm glad I don't have to study."

"Me, too," Riley said, going over and kneeling over Jessica on the chair to give her a kiss.

"Ow, get off of me," she said. "Your knee is crushing my shin."

Riley completely sprawled across her just to annoy her, kissing her neck with obnoxious sounds.

"Stop it," she said, laughing, trying to shove at his chest even as her head bent to give him better access.

Two weeks ago, watching both my friends with their boyfriends would have sent me from the room, unable to deal. But now I really didn't mind. I just pulled my feet up when Easton, who was only eleven, decided to flop onto the couch with me, worming under the blanket. In a minute, he was parallel with me, moving into the crook of my arm. I know his brothers thought it was weird that Easton really dug both Rory and me. I didn't. Rory volunteered at an animal shelter and I loved kids, having spent every summer in high school as a camp counselor. It seemed natural to me that a kid who had a negligent mother before she died, and none now, would want some affection. Tyler and Riley tried really hard to fill that void, but their way of showing love tended to involve a lot of fist-bumping and hair-rubbing.

Easton said, "Can I have a sip of your pop?"

"Sure."

But Tyler had eagle ears when it came to Easton. His head popped up from the other side of the coffee table. "No, it's too—"

"Too what?" Easton asked, already reaching for the can.

"What the hell are you two doing under a blanket together?" Tyler asked. "No. Uh-oh. *Hell* no."

Riley looked up from Jessica's boobs and sighed. "Oh my God."

I got totally offended. "What? He's just sitting next to me. He misses his mother."

"Our mother never hugged him and you are not a forty-year-old woman."

"So what?" I asked, exasperated. "He thinks of me like a babysitter. Don't you, Easton?"

Easton nodded.

"A babysitter he'd like to bang if he knew how," Riley said with a snort.

"Oh!" I gasped. "You're disgusting!" I actually covered Easton's ears with my hands. "You shouldn't say things like that in front of him. He's just an innocent child."

Tyler's eyebrows just about disappeared. "As much as I wish that were the case, he's seen and heard a lot worse than what Riley just said. Is he innocent in terms of girls? Of course he is, technically. You're right, he's only eleven. But in terms of life? Sorry to say he isn't even close to innocent, Kylie. He has a bit of a breast obsession right now and I think he is playing you, taking advantage of your sympathy."

"He does," Jessica confirmed.

"Oh." She should know, she lived there, even if I had a hard time thinking of an eleven-year-old as anything other than a child still. "Sorry, I didn't realize." I released Easton's ears and thumped the blanket down between us so our bodies weren't touching. "Better?"

Tyler just laughed. "Uh. Maybe not quite, but thanks." He kissed the top of Rory's head. "You ready to go home?"

"Yes. It's going to be an all-nighter, though."

"I'll make you coffee before I go to bed," he told her. "Kylie, you want a ride home?"

"Yes. Thanks." Though the idea of returning to my poop apartment didn't make me happy. I sighed, wishing things had worked out differently. Tyler had moved in with Rory and Phoenix had moved into Robin's room, so now it was couple city over there instead of the four of us girls the way I had pictured it, the way we had planned it last year. Jessica lived with Riley in the house he'd inherited from his mother. Or been saddled with, as he liked to put it.

On the ride back, me in the backseat, I checked my phone as Rory and Tyler discussed needing to go to the grocery store. Boring.

I had an e-mail from Jonathon. I clicked on it and it said simply, "Good luck tomorrow. You can do it. ~ D"

Now, that gave me a bit of a tingle in my vajingle.

I typed back, "Thanks. ☺"

There really wasn't much else to say.

Then I realized I had a text from Nathan. I deleted it without even reading it.

And took Jonathon's advice and finally blocked him.

That felt almost as good as sex with Jonathon.

I remembered the feel of his tongue over me.

Nah. Sex was *way* better.

CHAPTER FIVE

I GOT A C- ON MY EXAM. OKAY, SO I WASN'T MARIE CURIE, BUT it was a passing grade. It made my semester grade a D+ and that was passing. Good enough.

After I saw the score on the following Thursday as I was cramming the last of my stuff into my suitcase for winter break, I e-mailed Jonathon. "C-!" I wrote. Then after I signed my name, I wrote, "And that's good, in case you were wondering. ☺"

An hour later he responded with, "Awesome job! You deserve it."

Even though Jessica had grown up in the same hometown as me, she wasn't going back for break because her mother wasn't speaking to her. Some stupid BS about not liking Jessica having sex. Particularly sex with Riley, who she deemed a thug. Which was hilarious because Riley was a totally hard worker and he *adored* Jess. But I had known her mother long enough to not be shocked. Her mom was a nutter who cared more about present-ing the right image than her kids.

I was lucky because my own mom was nothing like that. She was awesome and we were super close. I was actually looking forward to getting to hang out with her over break and see my younger sister and two little brothers. The eats were always good at home, too. I wanted to eat my weight in Christmas cookies and green bean casserole.

Except when Christmas finally arrived I had been feeling off for a few weeks and my nose wrinkled at all the smells colliding in the house. The rooms all felt overheated and at one point I stuck my head out the back door to get some fresh air.

"What are you doing?" my brother Matt asked. He had grown since summer and he towered over me now even though he was only fifteen.

"It's hotter than a crotch in here," I said, taking quick, short breaths. "I feel sick."

"If you're like getting the flu or whatever stay away from me. This is the first year Mom and Dad are letting me go out on New Year's Eve and I am so not missing it."

"I don't have the flu." I was starting to worry about what I had and it wasn't a virus.

When we sat down to dinner my grandmother's green bean casserole looked like worms crawling across a patch of wet grass. Bile lurched up my throat. I concentrated on breathing through my nose and taking tiny sips of water. The only thing I ate was mashed potatoes. Fortunately, no one seemed to notice because they were making plans for a big family vacation, a three-generation kind of thing, the following summer.

I counted on my fingers under the table. Seven months from Christmas was when they were talking about the trip. My grandfather offered me wine now that I was only a few weeks from my twenty-first birthday, but I waved it off. I could smell it from three feet away and it seemed sour to me. When had I had sex with Jonathon? The last week in November. Four weeks earlier. I tried to remember when the last time I had my period was. Definitely not since then.

It was before that, before Thanksgiving, because I remembered being at zumba with Robin, and I had just started in the restroom right before class. I hadn't had any tampons so she had given me one of hers, which were natural and chemical free. Part of her whole sober living thing was going all organic, and while I got it in theory and supported the concept, I found using her hippie tampons annoying because there was no applicator. Then it had leaked during zumba, because salsa dancing meets aerobics isn't for a halfhearted tampon.

When had that been, though?

At least a week before Thanksgiving because we went to Rory's dad's house for Thanksgiving dinner and I was relieved not to have to deal with it. It's always super awkward ditching used tampons in someone else's bathroom. Pulling my phone into my lap under the table, I scrolled through the calendar. That had been more than five weeks ago. Cruising toward six. Definitely late and then some, which wasn't usually the case. In fact, it was never the case. Then I counted forward from the approximate date I would have started and ended on the last Thursday before exams when I had been with Jonathon. Fourteen days.

Holy hell.

I was going to throw up. I shoved my chair back, my phone spilling onto the floor. I ignored it and everyone's exclamations of surprise and ran to the bathroom, spewing mashed potatoes into the toilet. Oh, God. Disaster. This was a total disaster.

My mother knocked, then came in as I was flushing, reaching for the toilet paper with trembling fingers, my eyes watery and a string of saliva hanging from my mouth. She took over, wiping my mouth and cheeks. "Are you okay?"

I shook my head, starting to panic. "No! Mom, I think I'm pregnant." I shared almost everything with my mother, and if anyone would know what to do, it was her. I was actually glad I was at home instead of school.

She didn't even blink. "I was starting to think the same thing, actually."

"Really? Why?" I asked, stunned. I hadn't had a clue until about two days earlier.

"You've been complaining about PMS for three weeks now. No one has PMS for three weeks, but half the signs of pregnancy are the same as having PMS. Sore breasts, cramps, fatigue. Then the nausea clearly started."

I sat back against the wall, my hands on my knees. "This is bad."

"It's not the best," she agreed, but she reached out and stroked my hair. "But let's make sure before we do our freaking out, okay?"

"Too late. I'm already freaking out."

"Okay, I'm going to run to the store right now and get a test."

"It's Christmas Day," I protested. "Nothing is open."

"That convenience store is always still open. It's probably their best business day of the year."

I chewed my lip. I wanted to know for sure, but at the same time I wanted to avoid the truth as long as possible. "What are you going to tell everyone? They're all eating dinner."

"That we called the doctor and got you that antiviral flu prescription so you don't get laid up for three weeks."

"Oh." I hugged my knees to my chest. "Maybe I'm wrong. Maybe I really do have the flu."

"There's only one way to find out. Now why don't you lie down in your room while I'm gone? And don't pee."

What I really wanted to do was shit myself.

Instead I stared at the ceiling of my bedroom and pictured having this conversation with Jonathon. Hey, remember that night we were studying and one thing led to another? Well . . . it led to a baby, too. Isn't that just wild?

Yeah. Crazy.

Over and over I kept remembering the moment when his penis had pressed against me condom-free before I had shoved him away. Seriously, that could not be enough contact to cause pregnancy. Could it? I mean, I knew technically a guy didn't need to ejaculate, that sperm hung around in that clear stuff that leaks out when they're turned on, but still. What were the odds?

Probably pretty damn high.

My stomach lurched again and I concentrated on breathing through my nose.

Twenty minutes later my mother was back with a brown bag that she handed to me. I made her come into the bathroom with me, pushing the button to lock the door behind me. "Tell me what I'm supposed to do," I said, pulling the box out and handing it to her. "I can't read the directions. I'm freaking out too much."

She pulled her reading glasses out of her cardigan pocket. My mom was beautiful, her figure still toned and athletic. She had a few wrinkles, but she was aging gracefully, her hair dyed blond now but still thick and lustrous, still long. I appreciated her more right then than possibly I ever had before. Her lips moved as she read then she looked up and pulled the glasses back off.

"All you have to do is hold this end with the blue tip under your urine stream. After you pull the tip off, obviously. Then you wait two minutes."

I took the stick from her and did it as quickly as possible.

"Set it down flat after you put the tip back on. Here, put it on the paper. Now step away from it while I time it."

I did, sitting on the edge of the bathtub. I closed my eyes and sang a Britney Spears song to myself to keep myself calm and pass the time.

"It's time. Do you want me to look or do you want to do it?"

"I'll do it." I couldn't be a total wimp about it. I held my breath as I leaned over to glance at the stick, keeping my distance. Oh, shit. "It's a plus sign. Does that mean what I think it means?"

"Yes. You're pregnant."

Fuckity fuck.

For some reason my chemistry professor's face popped into

my head. Nothing like having to tell your chem prof that you're pregnant with his grandchild. How random was that? Somehow I doubted that would improve my grade.

I gave a hysterical laugh that dissolved into tears. My mother pulled me into her arms and I sobbed on her sweater, tears and snot smearing all over her.

"It's okay, it's okay," she murmured, her hand smoothing over my back, up and down in steady strokes. "Nobody died."

"I'll be dead when Dad finds out. He's going to kill me." Or maybe I just wanted him to kill me and put me out of my misery.

She laughed. "No, he won't. You're not sixteen, for heaven's sake. You'll be twenty-one in three weeks. I think your father is well aware that you're a woman."

I didn't feel like a woman. I felt like an idiot. A terrified idiot. I peeled myself off her chest and wiped my nose with my sleeve. "What am I going to do?"

"That's up to you, baby. What do you think Nathan will say about this?"

My lip curled and I felt my stomach cramp again. "Nathan is not the father, thank God. I haven't been with him since August. There is no way."

"Oh, I just assumed you had gotten back together. I know how much you were in love with him."

"Mom, he had sex with Robin. No. We are *not* together." I reached over and ripped a tissue out of the box on the back of the toilet, my sobbing fit seeming to be over.

"Well, who is the father, then?"

"My chemistry tutor." I blew my nose. Hard. "He's basically

a genius. Or at least on paper he is. This is actually his fault and he of all people, Mr. Science, should have known better."

Her eyebrows rose.

"But at least your first grandchild won't be a moron. It will probably be born wearing glasses, though." If I sounded irrational and bitter it was because I was.

"Kylie, that's a bit ridiculous. You can't possibly be berating his intelligence."

What I was doing was freaking out, plain and simple. "He does wear glasses. And this is his fault." Which was completely unfair of me. What, like I wasn't there, too? Like I had been totally clear about the situation before getting naked? No, I was just as much to blame and that pissed me off. I knew better. This wasn't my first rodeo. I had safe sex. Except for two seconds with my chemistry tutor and I got caught. Busted. Knocked up.

"What do you think you'll do, then? Are you two dating?"

"No." I sighed, my nose swollen, face itchy. "I guess what I'm doing is having a baby. I love kids too much not to, and you're right. I'm almost twenty-one. I'm not a teenager." Then I added completely pointlessly, "Why couldn't this happen a year from now? Then I would at least graduate while I was pregnant."

"Because it happened this year," my mother said with a smile. But she took my hand and squeezed it. "I'm proud of you. You'll be a wonderful mother, Kylie Ann. I've known that since you were three. And Daddy and I will be here to help you however we can."

I nodded, my throat suddenly tight. If I was half as good of a mother as she was, I'd be just fine.

"I was only a few years older than you when I had you."

I didn't bother pointing out that she might have only been twenty-three but she'd been married to my father and out of college already.

She turned on the water. "Wash your hands and let's go in and tell the family."

Yay.

My mother wasted no time. Everyone looked up from where they were sitting in the family room, my brother Jake wrestling with the dog on the floor, my sister Ainsley banging away at the piano.

"Everything okay?" my father asked, busy laying logs in the fireplace to set them ablaze. The man loved to burn stuff.

My mother glanced at me for permission and I nodded. I couldn't speak if my life depended on it.

"We have some Christmas news," she said cheerfully. "Kylie's having a baby!"

I had to give her props. She was spinning it. Making it sound like this was something we had all been hoping for. Like tickets to Florida for the entire month of January.

Shock on my entire family's faces gave way to horror, which gave way to acceptance. Then false conviction that I would be able to handle it and everything would be fine.

Basically what I had just emotionally experienced myself.

That night I couldn't sleep. I stared up at the ceiling, wide-awake, trying to imagine myself with a baby in my stupid studio apartment. Trying to imagine getting huge. Pushing a human being out of my vagina.

I had always wanted kids. Four, like my mother had. But later. Like after the age of twenty-six, when I had logged a good five years teaching and I was starting to get the baby bug. My foxy husband would have a good job and we would be living in a suburb of Cincinnati, somewhere like Mason, where the houses were brick colonials in tidy subdivisions, and the schools were good. We would join a nondenominational Christian church, the PTA, a golf course. We would vacation in the Maya Riviera with our precious and beautiful blond children and I would jog to keep up my body. I would do a marathon by thirty, to prove I could do it all, raise the kids, craft and cook and decorate, and make my health a priority.

The husband figure in this scenario was hazy but I had certainly never envisioned a glasses-wearing nerd with a tattoo sleeve and a magic tongue. Nor had I ever pictured that while I was living out this life of perfection with my generic and faceless husband, that the father of my first child would be pulling in the driveway every other weekend to pick her up, her Dora the Explorer suitcase packed and ready to go for Daddy time. Or worse, her daddy wanting nothing to do with her.

I rubbed my hand over my flat belly in the dark and felt a surge of protectiveness. That was Jonathon's choice, to be involved or not, and I couldn't blame him if what he did do was walk away. Parenthood was likely not in Jonathon's plans. Certainly not with his one-night-stand chem student who pulled a D in the course.

Reaching for my phone I scrolled through all my Christmas texts and social media messages. For some stupid reason I wondered if I would hear from him. Why, when I hadn't heard a peep from him in four weeks and when he was Jewish and maybe didn't even celebrate Christmas, I had no idea.

Because I was an idiot was the only logical explanation.

I tossed my phone aside with a sigh and counted how many days until I went back to school. Six. Six days to figure out what to say to Jonathon besides *WTF, you knocked me up, genius.*

That probably wouldn't start things off on the right foot.

Then because I couldn't resist, I grabbed my phone again and sent him an e-mail before I totally chickened out.

Hey, can I meet with you when I get back to campus? I really need help with something.

That was the truth, and then some.

WHEN I GOT THE E-MAIL FROM KYLIE SAYING SHE WANTED TO see me, I admit it, I was pleased. Granted, I knew that she was most likely seeking a tutor for the entire second semester, assuming she had continued on to advanced chemistry to fulfill her science requirement. I personally didn't think that she would be able to pass, considering how she didn't have a full grasp of the material from the first course, nor did I want to be her tutor, because there was no way in hell I could see her once a week and not want to repeat what we had done.

I hadn't seen her in a month and I *still* wanted to repeat what we had done. It hit me at the weirdest moments. Like I'd be hauling boxes for the moving company I worked for every Saturday and suddenly I would have an image of her beneath me, eyes limpid, fingers digging into my arms, her amazing body arched and open to me. Then I would have a hard-on while trying to lift a couch with a coworker and, seriously, it made me feel fourteen. Or I would be in the lab and I'd see a blond head pass by and I'd wonder if it was her and then I would be distracted as hell. I had actually fucked up several experiments that way and my father had given me The Look, the one that I hated. The one that showed he was just waiting for me for fail, and that he was wondering how I could be his kid.

Being distracted by Kylie and her sweet smile and warm body was not an option.

Nor was dating her, though I didn't think for a minute she wanted to date *me*. She probably dated athletes and frat guys, not someone who got excited by reactions kinetics. To her, I was probably boring, and I could understand that. It wasn't like we could possibly have a single thing in common.

Other than great sex.

Which was the thing I just couldn't quite seem to get past.

And I did want to see her.

I locked my car and headed across the parking lot to the coffee shop. Kylie had actually asked me to come to her apartment, but I had been really uncomfortable with that and had made an excuse about only having an hour and I would really love to grab something to eat. If we went to her place, there was no way I wasn't going to be tempted to have a repeat. Which I couldn't do, I reminded myself yet again.

I had gone out twice with a physics PhD student, and while she didn't exactly set my pants on fire, she seemed nice enough, and highly intelligent. We had things to talk about. She was attractive in a distracted sort of way, though I could have done without the denim overalls/Converse combination. It made me feel like she was the world's smartest toddler and it wasn't a turn-on.

Kylie was already in the coffee shop, sitting at the table we had been at the first time we met. She was sipping hot tea, the steam rising in front of her, the string for the bag dangling over the side of the cup. I wouldn't have pictured her as a tea drinker, but what the hell did I know? I didn't actually know her at all. She was wearing a pink fuzzy scarf over a gray tank top and a gray hoodie. Her hair was up on top of her head in a twisted bun, and she wasn't wearing any makeup. Just lip gloss. It didn't look like seduction was in her plans.

And why was I disappointed about that?

Fucking idiot.

I went over to the table and I smiled in greeting. I felt like I should touch her. Like I should hug her or kiss her forehead or something. I mean, we'd had sex. Amazing sex. I had touched every single inch of her, and the last time I had seen her she was bare-ass naked sprawled out on her bed yawning in satisfaction. But now she was sitting and there was the teacup and it all just felt weird, so I settled for squeezing her shoulder as I rounded the table for the other side and dumped my bag.

"Hey," I said to her. "How was your break?"

"Okay. How about you?"

"Busy. I worked a lot." I pulled my wallet out of my bag. "I'm going to grab some food. Can I get you anything?"

She shook her head. "No, I'm fine, thanks."

I frowned as I went up and quickly ordered a sandwich and a coffee. Kylie looked pale, like she'd had the flu or something. And she hadn't exactly looked me the eye. She had been studying her tea intently, brow furrowed.

When I sat back down, food in hand, she was still in the exact same position. "Is everything okay?" I asked her, popping a sweet potato fry in my mouth.

Finally she took a deep breath and lifted her head. When her eyes locked with mine, I paused in reaching for another fry. Something about that look . . . it was ominous.

"Jonathon, I'm pregnant."

I had heard the expression regarding veins turning to ice and had always thought it was a ludicrous description of a physical improbability. Now I understood exactly what they meant. It was like I immediately froze, crystallizing from the inside out, jaw clenched, muscles locked, brain synapses snapped in two.

"You're pregnant?" I repeated stupidly.

She nodded. "Five weeks."

Oh, Jesus Christ, she really was telling me what I thought she was telling me. Holy shit. Holy fucking shit. My heart started to race and my palms grew damp and clammy. I put my index finger on my chest. "Me?" I asked, voice gravely and unsure.

Impatience crossed her face. "Of course it's you or I wouldn't be sitting here having this conversation with you. Before that night I hadn't been with a guy since August, so there's no question about it. None."

For a second I thought I was actually going to pass out. Like all the blood rushed out of my head and my vision blurred and I thought I was going to take a facer into my tuna melt. I tried to breathe and gripped the edge of the table. "Holy shit," I muttered.

She nodded in agreement. "That's kind of how I felt about it."

The black spots receded and I took a sip of coffee to clear the bile from my throat, scalding the roof of my mouth. "What are you going to do?" I asked, because I knew ultimately I had no say in what she did. It was her choice and maybe she was only telling me because she needed money. I wasn't even sure how I felt about that so I just waited to hear her answer.

"I'm keeping it." She set her cup down and the look she gave me was vaguely defiant. "I love kids. I'm an adult. It's just not the right choice for me emotionally to have an abortion or to give it up. You can be involved or not involved, that's up to you, but I thought you should know."

I nodded. "Thank you." Part of me was relieved. I didn't think I would really like the idea of a total stranger adopting and raising my kid. Which was fucking ridiculous because Kylie was pretty much a total stranger to me. My kid. "Oh my God, how did this happen?" I shoved my glasses up my nose and ran my fingers through my hair, shifting uneasily on my chair.

It was a rhetorical question, but she seemed to think it required an answer.

"It has to be because you started to before we had a condom."

Well, of course, that's what it had to be, but why did it sound like she was blaming me? Feeling defensive, I said, "I thought you were saying you were on the pill. It was a misunderstanding."

"But you were still willing to have sex without a condom? Haven't you heard of STDs?"

The look she gave me was so disdainful I felt shame rise, hot and thick in my mouth. She was right. Totally right. And here I considered myself the more intelligent of the two of us and she clearly had more common sense when it came to her sexual health than I did. Plus she was a good four or five years younger than me, which just really made me feel like an ass. I had no excuse other than that I had been basically struck stupid by her sheer sexiness.

Because I had no answer to that, I got childish. "Why weren't you on the pill anyway? Everyone is."

"Because it gives me acne."

Oh, that was just great. "So we're having a baby because you didn't want to get a pimple for Greek Week or whatever?"

I had gone too far and I knew it immediately. Her eyes snapped with anger and her nostrils flared. Even though she kept her voice down so no one would hear us, she leaned forward and hissed at me, "First of all, *we're* not having a baby. *I* am. I'm the one who will be carrying it for nine months. I'm the one who will get morning sickness and indigestion and stretch marks, and I'm the one who will be giving birth to this baby. And getting up at three a.m. to feed it. Second of all, birth control is the responsibility of both parties involved so I don't want to hear it. It's pointless for us to do this. It's done. I'm pregnant."

SHATTER

For a second I just stared at her, nodding like a chastened schoolboy. She was right, and holy hell, she'd put me in my place. This was a new side of her. "You're right. I'm sorry. I'm just . . . in shock."

Her expression smoothed. "Trust me, I understand. I've had six days to think about it and I'm still in shock."

Then her lip started to tremble and her eyes filled with tears.

Ah, shit. I shoved my chair back and came around to sit next to her. I put my arm around her and she turned into my chest, shoulders shaking as she started to cry in earnest. "It's okay," I told her. "Conception happens."

She gave a watery laugh in the middle of her crying. "That sounds stupid."

The whole thing was pretty stupid, but I didn't want to point that out. "How are you feeling? You seem a little pale. Are you having morning sickness?" I wasn't sure what else to say. What the fuck do you say to a woman you've knocked up? Sorry I have super sperm?

But it seemed to be the right tack to take because she sat up and wiped her eyes with a paper napkin. "I'm okay. I only threw up once when I first found out and then again a few days later. But that was mostly because the dog shit in the house and my brother left it for an hour before cleaning it up, so the smell just knocked me over when I walked in the front door. Other than that, mostly it's like you've swallowed a clam and it's sitting in your throat trying to crawl back up twenty-four/seven."

Horrified, my stomach clenched in sympathy. "That does not sound okay. Jesus. I'm sorry."

"It's not your fault," she said automatically, but then she looked at me and gave me a wobbly grin. "Well, maybe sort of."

How she could even smile was beyond me. I felt like I needed a shot of straight whiskey. "You seem to be handling this really well. Better than most girls. I'm impressed."

She shrugged. "I've always been a glass-half-full kind of person. How about you? Is the glass half full or half empty?"

"Technically the glass is completely full at all times. It's half liquid, half vapor."

Kylie gave me an incredulous look.

"What, it's true."

She burst out laughing. "I can't argue with that."

That made me smile. She really was pretty amazing. Here she'd just found out her whole life was changing and she was still smiling. I slid my hand across the table and took hers in mine, squeezing it, unable to speak.

She looked startled but then she gave me a look that made me feel thoughts that were totally inappropriate for the situation.

"I should go," she said. "Let you eat. And, Jonathon, take a few days to think about it, decide how you feel, what you want to do, and let me know. I'll understand either way. Honestly, I will. You shouldn't feel obligated."

I already felt obligated. How could I not? The weight of that was resting on my chest like a grand piano. How the hell was I going to financially support a baby?

"By the way, I didn't know Professor Kadisch was your father. I never would have guessed that."

Bringing up my father was the worst possible thing she could have done, though she obviously didn't know that. "We're not particularly close."

"Oh. I'm sorry." She looked sincerely compassionate.

Shit. Fuck. Damn. "I'll be involved, Kylie. I promise." My own father had turned his back on my mother and me for damn near two decades and I still hadn't totally forgiven him for that. I couldn't do the same thing and live with myself. "I'm going to try my best."

"Thank you. I appreciate that. That's all we can both do is just try our best." She stood up, and I saw she was wearing loose-fitting sweatpants and snow boots. She pulled her coat off the back of her chair and shrugged into it. "I'll e-mail you my number. It might be easier to keep in touch if we can text and call each other."

I nodded. A thought occurred to me. She didn't sound like she was suggesting there was anything between the two of us, but I definitely couldn't add trying to create some kind of relationship out of nothing on top of having a baby. "You know, right, that I want to be friends, but that's it? I don't think anything else between us is a good idea . . . and I've actually been dating some-one. I kind of really like her and want to see where this can go . . ."

My over-sharing and unnecessary explanation petered out when I saw she was practically baring her teeth in anger.

"You know what, Darwin? Go fuck yourself." She lifted her purse over her shoulder so it rested across her body hands-free. "I may not be as smart as you or whoever the hell you're dating, but I'm not stupid. I don't have any sort of dumbass fantasy going that you're the man of my dreams and that you'll marry me and we'll be happy. While you live in theories, I live in reality." Kylie whirled around and started toward the door.

"Kylie, wait." I stood up, contrite. Sometimes I really did sound like a total dick. I didn't mean to, but not wanting to be a dick doesn't excuse a dick move and that had been a dick move.

But she tossed over her shoulder, "Don't follow me! Seriously." As she stalked off, I thought maybe she called me an asshat under her breath.

I was an asshat. Sitting back down, I stared at my sandwich, vision blurring.

Why wasn't there a formula for life?

Numbers were easier to understand.

It looked like I had another important one to add to my sleeve. The conception date of my first child. I actually knew it, too. November 30. Thursday. 11:45 p.m.

Fuck.

CHAPTER SIX

THE COLD JANUARY AIR FELT AMAZING ON MY HOT FACE AS I left the coffee shop, already commanding my phone to call Jessica. I needed to vent. Why did guys always have to ruin a perfectly decent moment? Jonathon had handled my news pretty well, all things considered, though I didn't appreciate his hinting it was my fault for not being on the pill. But then he had been thoughtful, comforting, and while he looked like he had a fish bone caught in his throat, he hadn't hesitated to say he would be involved. That made me feel hugely relieved. I mean, either way, I was having a baby, and while it might be totally awkward at first to co-parent with a dude I barely knew, I still wanted my kid to have a father.

Then he had completely pissed me off by telling me he was dating someone and pointed out in that voice—the one you used when you thought someone was simple or slow—that he just wanted to be friends. So freaking insulting. Like, what, I'd gotten pregnant on purpose to snag my chem tutor? Yeah, because that was about the stupidest doomed-to-failure plan ever and pathetic to boot. I may have been a lot of things, but pathetic was not one of them.

"Hey, how did it go?" Jessica asked as a greeting.

"Remember when I said that I didn't want to go see Jonathon again because I didn't want to ruin the good memory by finding out he's an asshat?"

"Uh-huh."

"I found out he's an asshat."

"Oh, no. Did he freak out? Please don't tell me he insisted it can't be his. Because I will have to beat the shit out of him if he said that."

Walking quickly down the street, the initial relief of the cold on my overheated skin gave way to shivers. "No, he didn't say that." Yeah, he had pointed to himself in question, but I thought that was more shock than anything else. Once I had told him it was his and I hadn't been with anyone else, he hadn't questioned that. He hadn't insisted on a DNA test or anything like that. "He said he would be involved. That he would try his best."

"So then why is he an asshat?"

"Because he told me he's dating someone."

"When you had sex with him? What a dick."

"No. He started seeing her after."

There was a pause. The longer it went on, the stupider I realized what I had just said sounded.

"I guess that's a little awkward, but I'm not sure it makes him an asshat. I mean, he didn't *know* you were pregnant. And you're the one who didn't want to see him again."

Why did she have to make it sound like I was the unreasonable one? "You just had to be there. To hear his tone. It was . . . what's the word when someone is talking down to you?"

"Patronizing?"

"Yes. Patronizing. That's what he was being."

"I'm sorry, sweetie. Just give him some time to get over the shock before you judge him. And then if he proves he's truly a Grade-A asshat, we'll deal with it."

That made me smile as I approached my apartment building. "Are you going to take a hit out on him?"

"No. I'll just have Tyler and Riley work him over."

"You can't do that. It's illegal. But thanks for offering." I was not going to think too closely about why the idea of Tyler punching Jonathon in his very cute face made me super upset. His cute face that was going to merge with my genetics. "Hey, I just had a thought," I told her.

"Should I be scared?"

I laughed. "Shut up! No, I just had a really good thought. My baby is going to be super cute. I mean, how can she not be cute with two cute parents?" Just seeing Jonathon again had reminded me of how nerdy adorable sexy he was.

I admit it, I had my shallow moments. Hey, honestly, we all do. But that wasn't what I was saying, well, aside from no one wants to think they'll produce a goblin child. The point was more that suddenly, it felt real, and I felt . . . okay. Even looking forward to meeting my baby, who would be cute simply because she was *mine*. I had a human being growing inside of me and suddenly that felt very awe-inspiring. Glass half full. That was me.

"I'm sure she will be adorbs. It's genetically impossible for her not to be. And I will buy her many pretty dresses. Unless she is a he and then I probably shouldn't buy him dresses."

I was about to reply when I pulled open the exterior door and found myself face-to-face with Nathan. "Oh!" My heart started to race. "Shit. Jessica, let me call you back."

"Are you okay?"

It depended on what Nathan wanted. "Yeah. Fine. I just don't have enough hands right now. Give me twenty."

We hung up and I stared at Nathan, chewing on my bottom lip. What the hell was he doing there? Had he heard I was pregnant? How did he even know where I lived? I definitely had not told him.

Unless it was just a coincidence. Maybe he knew someone else in the building.

"Hi," he said, and gave me a nervous smile. "How are you?"

"Okay." Pregnant. "How are you?" I had no idea why I asked that. I guess I was being polite.

"Not so great. Can I come upstairs? I really, really want to talk to you, Kylie. Please. Just let me apologize face-to-face once and then I'll leave you alone forever."

My heart twisted. Tears formed in my eyes, damn him. "So I need to do this to give *you* closure? To make you feel better?" Somehow, the pure selfishness of that made me profoundly sad, not angry. I had loved him with all my heart, but did I even really know him? Obviously not.

"No, no, of course not. I'm trying to say I'm sorry. Can we at least go inside and sit down on the steps? We're blocking the door."

There was no one around and it didn't matter, but I was starting to feel light-headed. This whole creating-a-placenta thing was kicking my ass. I was exhausted all the time. Pushing around him, I unlocked the interior door to my building and sat down on the bottom step with a sigh. It suddenly felt like a long walk to the second floor.

Nathan sat down next to me, his hands on his knees, legs apart. I stared at him, at the familiar curve of his nose, his jaw, the mouth that had kissed me so many times with so much tenderness and I wondered what really was going on in his head. I wondered if I would ever know the truth and if I did, if I would even recognize it as honesty. He turned to speak and started a little when he realized I was watching him.

Then he surprised me by starting to cry. That was so not Nathan. He joked, he got angry, he grinned. He didn't cry.

"I'm sorry," he said, covering his eyes with his hand. "I'm so sorry, Kylie, baby, you have to believe me. I never meant to hurt you."

It got to me. I didn't want it to get to me, but it did. Throat tight, I tried to hold on to my anger. Tried to remember that moment when I had found the texts he had been sending to Robin. "If you had sex with Robin when you were both drunk and that was the end of it, I would believe you. But that wasn't the end of it. You weren't sorry at all. You're just sorry you got caught."

He wiped his eyes and sniffled. "I'm sorry I did it. I'm sorry I texted Robin. But I missed you, Ky, when you were back home, and this is going to sound stupid, but I missed you so much it scared me."

This wasn't helping. "That does sound stupid. The thing is, there is literally nothing you can say that will make it okay that you were texting my best friend telling her that her pussy tasted like chocolate."

He winced.

Good. I wanted him to squirm. "Does that make you uncomfortable to hear that?"

"Yeah." He shifted on the step.

"It was really uncomfortable to read it."

For a second, he just stared at the floor then he looked at me, his nose twitching. "I deserve that."

I sighed. "What do you want?"

"I just want you to know it was real, you and me. Everything I said, all those feelings. I loved you. I love you still."

It shouldn't have mattered. It shouldn't have had any impact on me whatsoever.

But it did. It made me cry. I had devoted a whole year of my life to loving him. It wasn't fair. It wasn't fair of him to cheat. It wasn't fair of him to continue to try to cheat. It wasn't fair of him not to just leave me the hell alone and let me heal.

"Baby, don't cry. Why are you crying?"

He reached for me and I jumped up. "I can't do this. Go home, Nathan. Leave me alone. Please." I ran up the stairs, feeling flushed and nauseous.

There was nothing he could say that could undo any of his

actions. What I didn't understand was why he still cared, why he wanted to continue to insist that he loved me. Because in my world, you couldn't love someone and do what he did. The two can't coexist.

I was afraid he was going to follow me so I unlocked my door as fast as I could and closed it behind me, locking the dead bolt. I was leaning against it, breathing hard, when my phone buzzed in my hand.

It was him. Of course. Because apparently it wasn't bad enough that he had to cheat on me and humiliate me. Now he was going to stalk me until I absolved him of his guilt. In a moment of weakness before Christmas I had taken the block off his number and now I was sorry I had.

Are you going to the going-away party?

He was talking about the party at Riley and Jessica's house for Robin and Phoenix. She had transferred to Tulane and they were moving to New Orleans in just a couple of days. Because she got a complete fresh start. Clean slate. Happiness.

While I got Nathan lingering like a headache I couldn't shake, and a growing uterus.

I was happy for her, I was. Despite everything, I loved Robin and she had shown me over and over how remorseful she was for what had happened. Unlike Nathan. But I wasn't quite ready to wave a handkerchief in good luck at her bon voyage party. Especially because she had found what seemed like the perfect guy for her. Phoenix looked at Robin like he couldn't breathe without her, and he'd tattooed her *face* on his rib cage. Who does that?

No.

We should go together. Show them they can't break us.

Was he for real? He had lost his fucking mind.

You broke us. Not anyone else.

And suddenly I knew I was going to throw up. I dropped my phone and my bag on the floor and ran for the bathroom.

"HELLO?"

"Hey, Mom." After Kylie left the coffee shop I stared at the table for a while, thoughts racing around in my head in concentric circles, and I needed someone to talk to. Devon wasn't going to be the best source for advice on this one given that he thought procreation was for suckers, so I figured my mother was a better bet.

Besides, I needed to get this conversation over with. If Kylie hadn't ripped my balls off, it was possible my mother still might, and I couldn't concentrate when I was dreading castration.

"How are you doing? What's new, sweetie?"

More than there usually was. "Oh, you know, classes start in a few days. I, um, have a new student I've been tutoring." And having sex with. God, this was really, really awkward. I wasn't the kind of guy who shared details about his personal life with his mother. I hid my masturbation results in middle school like I was covering up state secrets or the evidence of the existence of aliens. When I had lost my virginity my senior year in high school I played it cool, as cool as you can when you've suddenly been given the key to nirvana. I didn't even talk to my mother about girlfriends unless I was past the three-month dating mark with someone. So, yeah, this was fucking awkward.

"An undergraduate?"

"Yes." I rubbed the patch of hair on my chin I never got around to shaving. "She's really struggling with chemistry, and, um, she's pregnant."

"Oh, geez, that poor thing. It can't be easy for her to be in school and to be pregnant. Trust me, I know."

"I know. And you handled it amazingly well, Mom." She had. My mother had raised me by herself with my father nowhere to be found. The only proof of his existence was the child support the government garnished from his wages every month. A freshman in college when she got pregnant, Mom had managed to graduate by the time I started kindergarten and find a job in marketing. It wasn't until I was seventeen and won the physics competition that my father suddenly appeared to claim his part in producing me.

"Is the father around at least?" she asked.

Here it was. Moment of truth. *Man up, Kadisch*, I told myself. Get it out. "I'm going to try to be."

Dead silence. She made a sound, like a gasp, and I winced, dropping my head into my hand. I was ashamed of myself, and selfish for wanting Kylie so much that night that I had been a total idiot. I'd taken advantage of her. It didn't matter that she had wanted me, too. She had been hurting and instead of being a shoulder to cry on, I had gotten her pregnant. Winning.

"Jonathon . . . you got one of your tutoring students *pregnant*? Oh my God, how old is she?"

"She's a junior," I said, because I didn't actually know how old she was. Further proof of my asshat-ness. "It was an accident, Mom."

"I should hope so, for Chrissake."

I didn't know what else to say. Part of me felt like she couldn't condemn me, given that she had personally made the same mistake and I was the result of that mistake. But at the same time, I knew she would feel that history was repeating itself, that I had taken advantage of Kylie the same way my father had taken advantage of her.

"She's not crazy, is she? She's not going to keep this baby from you, right? Because we'll sue."

Crazy? That's where she went first? What, like a chick would have to be crazy to have sex with me? "No, she's not crazy, and no, she's being really reasonable." My mom's reaction surprised me. "I thought you'd be on the girl's side in this one, considering what you went through, not jumping on her."

"I'm on your side if she's crazy or a bitch. You're my son. But if she's normal, then I'm on both your sides."

That was some kind of complicated woman logic. "I don't even know what to say to that."

But she was already on to firing questions at me. "How far along is she? Do you know if it's a girl or a boy? Where is her family, are they close by? Has she been to the doctor?"

None of which I knew the answer to, other than how far along she was.

"She's six weeks."

And then the worst one of all. "Are you in love with her?"

"No," I said, because there was no point in letting her hope this was something different from what it really was. "I barely know her, Mom. I'm embarrassed to say that, but it's true. I'm actually dating someone else now." That might be a bit of a stretch to say Lydia and I were dating, but it seemed important to make sure my mother didn't get the wrong idea about Kylie.

"What's her name? Not the girl you're seeing, but the mother of my grandchild."

Did she have to say it like that? But it was true. And honestly, I had nothing bad to say about Kylie. "Kylie. She's blond, pretty, and she's very sweet."

"That's good. Are you sure you're not in love with her? You sound like you like her."

"Mom . . . don't." Of course I liked Kylie. But did I like her, like her? Who the hell knew? I didn't really know her. Sure, I knew that I liked her smile, and her funny laugh, and the way her bottom lip tasted, and without a doubt I liked her naked body locked with mine, but beyond that I couldn't say anything with any certainty.

Fortunately, she dropped it. Unfortunately, she brought up my dad.

"Does your father know?"

"No. I just found out an hour ago. And I don't think I'll tell him until the semester is over." I wanted to add that I didn't think he would be particularly interested, but that seemed a cruel truth my mother already had personal experience with. "Kylie is actually in his class. I don't want to cause problems for her. And I graduate in May and I don't feel like hearing his opinion on what's next." On how I was disappointing him by not going on to get my PhD, which was basically out of the question now. I had been debating whether I wanted to pursue it or not, but with needing to support a baby, I needed a job more than another degree.

Maybe that was revealing too much about my father to my mother, though. My relationships with them were separate entities.

It was amazing to me that suddenly, within the span of an hour, my whole future had changed. I picked at the congealed cheese on my sandwich and tried to stay rational, not succumb to emotion. I felt like I might actually have a heart attack. "Mom . . . do you think I can do this?"

I heard the doubt in my voice and she obviously did, too.

"Oh, Jonathon, of course you can, honey."

"Dad couldn't."

"At the risk of bad-mouthing your father, sweetheart, you were more of a man at fourteen years old than he is at fifty. You can do this. I know you can."

I took a deep breath, feeling more calm. "I don't know anything about babies or pregnancy."

"You're a scientist. Do your research."

She was right. So three hours and three cups of coffee later, I had made my way through a refresher course on conception, just out of curiosity, plus the first two trimesters of pregnancy, and the legal rights of non-custodial parents in the state of Ohio.

I had also spent a ridiculously large amount of time browsing through baby name sites. Never once in my entire life had I given a single thought to the name I would like to gift my future conceptualized infant, and it was a daunting task. I gave up by the time I got to C names. It was insanity. Just the As and Bs alone presented the basic options, the bewildering, the just plain bad, and the beautiful. I couldn't deal. Besides, I wasn't sure that I was actually entitled to an opinion. That may be something Kylie felt was well within her rights to decide solo.

Having kids was never something I'd given much thought to. It was a nebulous concept, something way off in the future in my mid-thirties or even later, after I had achieved certain career goals. After I had proved myself. I didn't think I had ever even actually held a baby. My mother only had one sibling and Uncle Mike had kids who were in their late teens. My father had two sisters that I had never even met. I had grown up in an apartment with my mother and she hadn't been particularly friendly with the neighbors, and basically there just hadn't ever been an occasion to hang with a tiny human.

It was a damn good thing gestation was a lengthy process because I needed every second of that nearly eight months to figure out what the hell I was doing.

My phone dinged with an e-mail alert. It was Kylie, giving me her phone number. Plus it said, "If you could not tell your father just yet I would appreciate it. And thanks for not running screaming. ☺"

I tapped a message back to her, giving her my number as well. "I won't tell my father. Trust me, I don't want to. I did tell my mother, though. I hope that is okay. Don't worry, my parents never talk to each other."

Seeing that about my parents written in front of me on the screen just before I hit SEND, like it was a positive thing to tell her, hit me hard. I didn't want that for myself. For her and I.

Ever. I would do whatever it took to maintain a friendly and reasonable relationship with Kylie so that my child didn't have to grow up the way I did, wondering where the hell my father was and why my mother was so angry.

History wasn't going to repeat itself. Any more than it already had, that is.

So I sent a second e-mail. "Hey, Kylie, why was the mole of oxygen molecules excited when he walked out of the singles bar? Because he got Avogadro's number."

CHAPTER SEVEN

I LAUGHED WHEN I READ JONATHON'S E-MAIL. I COULDN'T help it. I even actually knew what Avogrado's number was, sort of, so I could appreciate the silliness. But more importantly, I appreciated what he was trying to do. He was trying to make me feel comfortable, to lighten the tension between us. To remind me of the night we had met, our one and only private joke.

It was sweet.

As I lay on my bed in my stupid apartment, eyelids heavy, tummy churning again, music softly playing from my phone, I stared at my laptop next to me and wondered how to answer Jonathon. I felt a little bad over the way I had left him in the coffee shop. Yes, he'd been patronizing, but Jessica was right. I had totally caught him off guard.

I didn't want to do this alone. I would, if I had to, but I didn't want to. I didn't like to do anything alone. And while I'd been telling him the truth in my pissy rant before I stomped off, I was realistic and didn't expect him to fall in love with me and want to be with me forever and ever behind a white picket fence. I was still an optimist. A romantic. In a secret corner of my heart, I wanted to see if there could ever be anything between us, because I wanted to have a child with not just a partner, but a lover, a best friend.

It was stupid. I knew it was stupid.

But while I might not need someone to go to the doctor with me, or help me change diapers, I wanted a shoulder to lean on, a masculine body next to mine on the couch, in bed. I had missed the intimacy since RAN and now I missed it all over again. The only time I had felt it had been that night with Jonathon, and I wanted it again, but I knew I couldn't have it. Though it wasn't like I could get pregnant a second time. Why couldn't we at least have sex? It was amazing sex and we could do it all we wanted guilt-free, right?

Wrong. Because, duh, it was stupid. It would complicate things. Like seriously complicate things. Then I would want a relationship with him and he was with mystery woman. Shit. I'd forgotten about the mystery woman. Whoever she was, I hated her. Why did she get his heart when all I got was his sperm? With Nathan he'd given me his heart, but his penis to someone else. Was it so hard for one guy to give me both his heart and his hard-on?

Apparently it was.

My phone rang. Jessica. Shit, I'd forgotten to call her back.

"Um, you said you would call me back in twenty minutes and that was like three hours ago."

"Sorry. Nathan showed up."

"What? Why would he do that?"

"I don't know." I honestly had no idea what his goal was other than to hurt me.

"You didn't tell him about the baby, did you?"

"Of course not!" The thought made me shudder. "Ugh. He never needs to know as far as I'm concerned."

"Agreed. He's a dick. Now listen, I talked to Rory and the boys and we think you should move in with Rory and Tyler now that Robin and Phoenix are moving out."

The thought was instantly appealing. "But what am I supposed to do with this apartment?"

"Sublet it. Someone sublet it to you."

I sighed and looked at Jonathon's e-mail that was still on my screen. "Don't you think that apartment Rory is living in is cursed or something? Everyone has moved in and out like five times. Besides, do Rory and Tyler really want a preggers roommate?"

"You can take the room upstairs. They spend all their time downstairs. And then you won't be alone and they can help you if you need it. We don't want you alone."

I didn't want me alone, either. "I'll think about it. That's nice of them. I appreciate it."

What I wanted was what I couldn't have.

If you had asked me what that was six weeks ago I would have said it was for Nathan to never have cheated on me.

Now it wasn't that at all.

What I wanted was to unwind to the beginning with Jonathon and date him, because I liked him. He had a nice smile. He was thoughtful. He smelled good. When I had seen him in the coffee shop tonight for the first time since November, I had wanted him to kiss me. I was fighting nausea but I had still seen him and felt an ache deep down between my thighs and I had wanted his mouth on mine.

He had squeezed my shoulder instead.

I had to be realistic that all we could ever be was friendly co-parents.

Sigh. And sigh again.

It took me twenty minutes to figure out how to answer Jonathon.

Sounds like a positive reaction. ;-)

He LOL'd me right back.

Then it seemed trying to be brilliant and flirty was too taxing for me because I fell asleep before I could respond.

TWO WEEKS LATER I DIDN'T CARE IF I EVER HEARD FROM Jonathon or any human being ever again. I was pretty sure that I was, in fact, dying. There was no way a microscopic fetus should be causing me to feel like I had the flu paired with mono with an extra dose of hangover on top. Every time I turned my head my stomach protested and every time I ate or drank I promptly puked it back up. I had the shakes and the sweats, and I dozed in and out of sleep. I hadn't left my room in three days and there was dried vomit on my comforter from when I hadn't been able to muster enough energy to get to the bathroom before I threw up. My room reeked. I reeked. My hair was limp and greasy. My face felt like it could be tapped for crude oil, so much yuck was gushing from my pores.

I thought about calling my mom and begging her to come and get me and take me home to Troy, but it was over an hour away and going home would be like admitting I couldn't handle adulthood. If I couldn't handle adulthood, how could I be a mother? Not to mention if I skipped town, I definitely wouldn't be able to finish the semester. So I wasn't going to classes as it was. But at least I could hopefully recover and make it in a day or two. Hopefully. Maybe. I had already called off so often from my work-study job at the gym that my boss had told me I was permanently off the schedule, but I couldn't even bring myself to give a shit.

When Jessica and Rory texted, I lied and said I was fine, just tired. For some reason it seemed important to deal with this on my own. Like I made my barfy bed and now I had to lie in it.

Trying to find a more comfortable position, I groaned when the shift made me dry heave.

It wasn't helping that Jonathon was overwhelming me with texts asking me questions I didn't know the answers to. Like who my OB/GYN was. Or if I had health insurance. I thought I did, because I always had been on my parents', but maybe that changed because of the pregnancy. I had no idea and I didn't have the energy to figure it out. He also wanted to know if I was going to do genetics testing for disabilities. If I needed any money for medical expenses. If I had thought about where I was going to live.

All I could think about was breathing through my nose.

I wasn't answering him. It took too much energy to type and when I tried to hold my phone in front of me, my eyes crossed and I felt like puking. Mostly I slept, swallowed bile, and watched old TV sitcoms on Netflix on my laptop. When he finally expressed concern that I either wasn't okay or that I was upset with him, I did manage to answer that I wasn't feeling well.

When the buzzer went off letting me know I had a visitor at the front door, I ignored it. My first thought was it was Nathan. But then I got a text from Jonathon as the buzzer rang again.

Downstairs. Worried about you. Can I come up?

Oh, crap. Could I look any shittier? No. No, I couldn't.

I debated telling him to go away. But he texted again.

Brought you a smoothie. And anti-nausea medication that is safe for the baby.

Okay, I could get over the fact that I looked like ass if he could make even one one-hundredth of my symptoms go away.

Thx.

I struggled to a sitting position, then weaved to the DOOR button and hit it, holding it as long as I could before I felt dizzy, to make sure he was in. Then I unlocked my door and collapsed back onto my bed. This was worse than any hangover I'd ever had.

Jonathon knocked on the door a minute later and I tried to yell "come in," but nothing but a pathetic whimper came out. He opened the door anyway and stepped inside.

"Kylie? Oh my God, are you okay?"

I tried to turn my head and I saw spots in front of my eyes. Suddenly Jonathon was down on his knees next to the bed, brushing my hair back off my forehead. His face looked concerned, his touch cool and gentle. "That feels good," I murmured.

"What's going on here? How long have you been in bed?"

"Three days. I think."

"Have you eaten?"

Just the word made my stomach lurch and I heaved, slapping my hand over my mouth. "No."

"Are you drinking water or anything?"

"A little."

"How little?" He picked up the water bottle off the nightstand and shook it. "How often are you filling this up?"

"I don't think I have refilled it."

"When was the last time you went to the bathroom?"

I frowned. That was a little personal. "I'm not sure. Not today. I don't think. What time is it anyway?"

"It's seven."

"Oh." I closed my eyes again, fatigue overcoming me. It was like when I'd been given anesthesia for my wisdom teeth removal. You wanted your eyes to stay open, but they drifted closed anyway.

He shook me a little and I tried to swat at him but I had a hard time lifting my arm. It was like I was underwater.

"Take a sip."

A straw was shoved into my mouth. I took a sip and swallowed. It felt good in my mouth. Cold and sweet. It soothed my throat going down. But then it hit my stomach and it went horribly wrong. I jerked to move the straw and threw up a dribble of pink smoothie and foul-smelling bile right down the side of my mouth and onto the mattress where it puddled under my elbow. Sexy times. That was me.

"All right, we're going to the ER. This is not normal."

"I'm not normal?" I asked.

"You shouldn't be this sick. And you're either going to be dehydrated soon or you already are."

I watched him go into the bathroom then he reappeared with a wet cloth and wiped my mouth and face with it. Ah, that felt good. Then he rifled through my dresser until he found a big sweatshirt. Helping me into a sitting position, he pulled off my sweaty tank top and replaced it with the sweatshirt. He put my Uggs on my feet over my socks and then he lifted me up into his arms.

"Put your hands around my neck," he told me.

I did, leaning against his chest, too exhausted to protest that he didn't need to do this. That I didn't need the ER. "You smell good," I murmured, his scent the only thing that hadn't clogged my nostrils and made me want to hurl in the last week. "Clean."

He gave a soft laugh. "Even in the midst of morning sickness the chemistry of attraction applies. Because I was just thinking that you are absolutely beautiful."

"You're just saying that." I sighed. "I'm a mess."

"I don't say anything I don't mean. Where is your purse?"

"I don't know."

He bent over and I held on. He grabbed something off the kitchen counter and then we were out the door and down the stairs. The cold air outside felt good and even though I was shivering when he set me in the front seat of his car and clicked the seat belt over me, I actually felt a little better. More alert and less sick to my stomach. When we got to the ER two blocks away, he carried me into the lobby and answered all the questions as they checked me in. I leaned on his shoulder, and then I stretched across his lap as we waited. His thighs were warm and his knee made a perfect resting spot for my hand. Jonathon stroked my head, his fingers working through my dirty hair gently.

Relaxed, grateful that I didn't have to think, that he was thinking for me, I fell asleep.

IT WASN'T UNTIL THE NURSE HAD KYLIE HOOKED UP TO AN IV that the panic started to recede. The way she had looked when I had gone into her room, all clammy and waxy, her hair dull, her eyes dark, skin bruised, had scared the absolute shit out of me. For a minute, I had the horrible thought that she had miscarried and she was depressed, but then I could smell the sour odor on her clothes and see how disoriented and nauseous she was. Thank God I'd been reading up on the first trimester. I knew that sometimes women get an aggressive form of morning sickness and need medical attention, and I was damn glad I had ignored my concerns that maybe I was overstepping by showing up at her place without an invite.

But I had been worried. I couldn't help it. This shit was all brand-new to me, and it seemed that knowing I had a cell-dividing zygote independent from myself was as capable of fixating my attention as kinetics. The last two weeks had been hell, absolute hell. It had been clear Kylie was feeling rough and I didn't know what to do about it.

Just knowing they were pumping electrolytes into her made me feel better.

"We're going to do the ultrasound now," the nurse told Kylie. "Is it okay if your boyfriend stays?"

I chewed on my fingernail, feeling awkward and very aware of my sperm-donor status. It wasn't worth correcting the boyfriend assumption, but I still felt like a fraud. Kylie didn't answer the nurse's question.

"Is this when you do the wand thing on my stomach?" she asked.

"It's vaginal," the nurse told her, already moving a cart with some equipment over to the bed. "It's too early for the tummy."

"What?" Kylie looked horrified. "How . . ."

The nurse held up a wand.

I knew that's what she meant by vaginal ultrasound, but seeing the wand was another thing altogether. I wasn't sure how appropriate it was for me to be seeing that disappear somewhere I wasn't all that well acquainted with myself.

"Maybe I should go," I said, inching backward in my hiking boots.

"No. Don't go." Kylie reached out for my hand.

Well, fuck. How was I supposed to say no to that? I would just look at the screen not the nurse. I pushed up my glasses and stepped up next to the bed and took her hand. I massaged her palm with my thumb. "You feeling better?" I asked her. She had more color to her cheeks.

"I'm okay."

The nurse had helped put Kylie in a gown and now she draped a sheet over her knees. When the nurse's arm disappeared under there, Kylie winced and shifted on the bed. I winced, too.

"That's not really all that comfortable," she said, giving me a nervous look, her hand squeezing mine tightly.

"Just relax," the nurse reassured her. "Look at the screen."

I looked at the screen and I had no idea what I was looking at. Presumably Kylie's uterus, which was a fucking freaky thought.

"See that flickering right there?" The nurse pointed to the screen. "That's the baby's heartbeat."

"No shit, really?" I said, before I could stop myself. "Sorry. But . . . whoa."

"Whoa is right," Kylie breathed. "It's so tiny and fast. It's amazing."

It was amazing. More impressive than splitting an atom. That was our baby on TV.

It changed everything. It changed my fear of the future to a quiet awe and excitement. It changed my view of that passionate night in Kylie's cramped and dark apartment that it had been a mistake to the idea that maybe this could be one of the best things to ever happen to me. I was going to be a father.

Without even thinking about it, I bent over and kissed the top of Kylie's head. "Does everything look okay?" I asked the nurse.

"Everything looks great. There is the amniotic sac forming and I'm just doing some measurements here. It looks like your due date is August twenty-third."

For whatever reason I actually pulled out my phone and put it on my calendar. What, like I was going to forget? Kylie didn't notice, too busy staring at the screen, but the nurse gave me a look of amusement.

"Why am I so sick?" Kylie asked.

"It happens to some women. You're just lucky, I guess. The doctor will be in soon to talk to you. He'll probably admit you for a few days to stabilize you."

"So this isn't dangerous for the baby?" I asked, staring at the flickering on the screen.

"Baby will be fine, don't worry." The nurse gave me a smile. "You did the right thing bringing her in. Dehydration isn't good and she'll be much more comfortable once we get the vomiting under control."

I nodded. The nurse removed the wand, printed out the image on the screen, and handed it to me. Then she efficiently put all the equipment away and said, "Doc will be right in."

We were alone again and I held up the printout for Kylie to see. "That's pretty cool, huh?"

"It's so tiny." She touched the paper then glanced up at me. "It doesn't seem real, does it?"

"No. But then, yes." I laughed. "It's surreal, I guess. Yet so real it's terrifying."

"I'm scared, too." She sighed. "And tired."

Something tight happened in my chest when she said that, and I squeezed her hand. "Close your eyes, Kylie. You deserve to sleep. I've got this."

I did. I had it. I was somewhat amazed that I did, but it seemed once I was pried forcibly out of the lab, I could handle more than academia.

I wondered if Charles Darwin had kids.

Charlie was a good name.

Huh.

THE NEXT DAY I WAS FEELING A LITTLE BETTER, PROPPED UP in my hospital bed, my IV dripping away with many, many things that different nurses kept injecting into it. My stomach felt a little more settled and I texted Jessica and Rory, who insisted on coming up to see me. I asked them to bring dry shampoo and facial cleanser. One glance in the bathroom mirror when the nurse had helped me use the toilet had made it clear that I was a natural disaster in desperate need of a hairbrush. Jonathon had said he would stop by around four to see how I was doing between class and his lab and I was feeling recovered enough to not want to look like total ass.

My friends came in around three thirty, Jessica carrying a big satchel. "OMG, I can't believe you are in the hospital and you didn't tell us until after the fact! I almost died when I read your text."

"I didn't think it was something to go to the ER for, you know," I said, shrugging. "I mean, I'm pregnant, I figured suck it up, bitch, right? But Jonathon was worried I was dehydrated."

"Jonathon gets a thumbs-up," Jessica said, dropping the bag on the foot of the bed.

"How are you feeling?" Rory asked.

"Better. But I look like crap. I haven't showered in five days, and Jonathon is supposed to be here in thirty minutes." I held my hand out for the bag. We were short on time here.

Jessica grinned. "You like him, don't you?"

I made a face. "Of course I like him."

"No, I mean you have a crush on him. I knew it."

Probably. But it was too embarrassing to admit. "Harass me while you brush my hair, please." I pulled the rubber band out of it and shook my head a little, suddenly feeling dizzy from the motion. I gripped the handrail. "Shit. I hate this dizziness."

Jessica looked contrite. Rory had the bottle of dry shampoo in her hand and she worked it into my hair, then Jessica brushed. "I feel like a princess. A hideously greasy and pregnant princess."

"You don't look hideous," Rory said. "And FYI, Tyler and Riley are packing your bags as we speak so you can come back to our apartment. You're not going back there alone until you're feeling better because you scared us, big-time."

"You could ask me, you know," I protested. "I'm not helpless."

"No. But you're not Wonder Woman either, so quit acting like you are."

I knew their hearts were in the right place, but I felt put out. "Fine." Of course I preferred to stay with them instead of by myself, but at the same time, I wanted to make my own choices. I wasn't stupid, even though everyone seemed to think I was most of the time. But I couldn't be a total brat about it when they were grooming me.

Jessica handed me a facial cleanser wipe and it was glorious to scrub my nose free of oil. My hair felt a thousand times better after the shampoo and brushing, and Rory produced a toothbrush, getting a cup of water from the bathroom. "Don't use any toothpaste, it might make you feel queasy again. Just brush."

It did make me feel better even just to brush my teeth and my tongue and swish the water around in my mouth. Jessica even had a razor in the bag so I quickly shaved my armpits in bed and then used the stick of deodorant she handed me. Finally, unscented lip balm went on, and I felt almost human again, instead of like something dredged up from the bottom of the river. A glance in a compact mirror showed a marginal improvement in appearance but that my skin was still pale, dark circles under my eyes prominent.

The toiletries disappeared into the bag and Rory placed a stack of fashion and gossip magazines on the tray that rolled over the bed. "I thought you might get bored."

"Oh, cool, thanks. Yeah, the doctor said I'll probably be here for three days. I have like no idea what I'm going to do about my classes. I'm going to be so behind." Just the thought made me start to feel sick again.

"Hey, don't stress yourself out. Your professors will be understanding." Rory pulled out her phone. "Give me your schedule and I will go and talk to them for you."

"Really? You're awesome sauce." My friends were the best, seriously.

There was a knock on the door.

"Come in," Jessica called.

The door opened and Jonathon's head peered in. "Is this Kylie Warner's room?"

"Yep. Come on in. I'm Jessica."

He came into the room, a bouquet of flowers in his hand. Oh my God. He'd brought me flowers. That was hot. A flush came over me. "Hi," I said. "Thanks for coming. This is Jessica, like she said, and Rory. This is Jonathon."

He nodded and smiled at my friends. "Nice to meet you."

"You, too." Jessica turned and gave me a wicked smile, her eyebrows going up and down.

I ignored her, smiling back at Jonathon. He was wearing jeans and a flannel shirt.

He came up to the bed. "You look fantastic today. Seriously." He held the flowers out to me. "For you, for being such a trooper."

"Thank you." I took them and felt a little shy and in awe. I wasn't normally shy, but he made me feel less inclined to verbally vomit. They were bright big fuchsia roses. "They're beautiful."

"Pink is your favorite color, right?"

I glanced up at him, surprised. "How did you know that?" I was absolutely positive that had never been mentioned in our few conversations. "It totally is."

He shrugged, with a grin. "Lucky guess. Because your backpack is pink, your scarf and your keychain are fuzzy pink, your boots and your comforter are pink. So you know, the volume indicated a certain preference."

I laughed. "Good call, Sherlock."

"Has the doctor been in?"

"Not today." I set the flowers down and tried to reach the nightstand. "Hey, will you grab the ultrasound picture? I want to show the girls."

"Sure." He picked up the printout and held it out for Jessica and Rory. He put his index finger on the paper. "This is the heartbeat."

"No way," Jessica said. "That is a freakout."

When Jonathon set his backpack down on the floor and bent over to get something out of it, Rory grinned at me and gave a thumbs-up. Jessica mouthed that he was cute. I shook my head, grinning. They were not being totally obvious or anything.

He stood back up, his tablet in his hand. "You can use my iPad while you're here in the hospital to work on catching up on reading for school. You should have an Internet connection so you can access your e-mail, and your university account to read your course syllabi. Most of the reading material should be in your Google Drive, right?"

I nodded, stunned, as he set his iPad on my tray.

"I talked to your professors and explained that you were in the hospital. I had the papers from the ER so they knew it was legit. They all agreed to a week's extension on any assignments and know not to expect you in class."

It was like having another brain. A brain that was smarter than me and extra helpful. I was pretty sure that if I hadn't been sick as a dog and in the presence of my friends I would have had sex with him right then and there.

"Wow, thanks, Jonathon. That's super helpful."

He gave a sheepish shrug. "Hell, it's the least I can do. I feel guilty that I'm walking around perfectly fine and you're so sick. You kind of got a raw deal on this one."

"It's definitely the gift that keeps on giving," I said, wanting to tease him a little. All of this got too heavy sometimes. I wasn't a heavy or deep kind of chick, for the most part.

Jonathon laughed. "Well, I'll let you visit with your friends. I just wanted to check on you and give you the iPad. If it's okay with you, I'll stop by tomorrow."

I nodded. "Great. Thanks."

Then he was gone with a wave.

Jessica waved her arms in front of her face like she was overheated. "What the fuck?" she said in a stage whisper. "Girl, I think you hit the baby-daddy lottery."

"I wasn't even planning to play that lottery!" I protested, creeped out by the way that sounded.

"Which makes it even luckier. He's like the sweetest thing ever. It's disgusting."

"He is." I couldn't argue with that. I kept waiting for him to be a total dick, but since that night I'd told him I was pregnant and he had made a few rude remarks he had been nothing but nice and considerate. That should be awesome, right? Except it was making it harder for some reason. It was seeming like the cruelest of all ironies.

"He clearly really cares about you," Rory said.

But that made me scoff. "He doesn't care about me. He's being a decent person. He cares about the baby. I'm just the . . . what do you call it? Surrogate."

"He didn't have his sperm-fertilized egg implanted in you. He had sex with you." Jessica looked bewildered by my logic.

"So?"

"So he obviously likes you on some level. Most guys would be running like the hounds of hell or the child support lawyers were after them. I think he wants a relationship with you."

And just like that, I burst into tears.

They both went wide-eyed. "What's wrong?" Rory asked.

"Don't do that to me. I don't want to have any hope. Don't you understand? I can't have hope. I need to have strength and independence and realism, not hope." The days of rolling around my dorm bed giggling with my friends and grinning because I liked a new guy were over. There was no room in my life for that anymore, and it was a luxury I couldn't afford. I was having a hard enough time fighting the urge to swoon; I didn't need them encouraging me to be delusional. "This isn't about me," I added. "This is about the baby."

They both stared at me, and nodded, like they understood, but I could see the incomprehension in their eyes.

For the first time, I realized the gap that would grow between my friends and me as surely as my baby would grow. My life was going to be completely different from theirs and I would experience feelings, pain, responsibility, love they could only know in theory. Yes, Jessica was with Riley, and he had custody of Easton, but that wasn't a baby and he was Riley's responsibility more than hers. It was not the same as giving birth and caring for a newborn. Rory's focus was on getting into med school.

It made me sad and sorry that we wouldn't walk down the same path together anymore, but at the same time, I had no regret. When Nathan had cheated on me, I had lost something precious, a faith and trust, an innocence. I couldn't be the same fun-loving party girl anymore, and I didn't want to be. Instead of feeling aimless, hurt, unsure, I now had a focus, a future.

A reason to set aside my personal pain and work hard, graduate on time, be a good mom.

"We're just acquaintances," I said. "Tied together by accident. Jonathon is being awesome, and that's more than I ever hoped for, so it's all good." I gestured to the flowers. "Can you guys get some water to put these in? They're too pretty to wilt."

Their stunned silence said more than speaking ever could have.

CHAPTER EIGHT

GUILT WAS WRAPPED AROUND MY THROAT LIKE A NOOSE, and sitting across from Lydia only contributed to it. I felt guilty that I still wanted to see her. I felt guilty that I hadn't told her about Kylie. I felt guilty that Kylie was in the hospital hooked to an IV while I was eating pasta with someone else. There just wasn't any way not to feel like shit unless I came clean with Lydia and let it be.

It wasn't a nice restaurant, just a hole-in-wall fake Italian place, and it was appropriately dim, so hopefully if she threw a fork or something at me the other diners wouldn't notice.

Lydia paused in the middle of gushing about her PhD advisor and I dove in. "So, uh, I got an e-mail from this girl I was involved with." That was a polite way to put it.

She blinked, her bangs too long, like she had forgotten to trim them. Or brush them. Sometimes I thought Lydia's face and her body were lost in a sea of dark hair and denim. "Okay."

"It turns out she's pregnant and it's mine." That wasn't so hard. I was getting used to the idea and the words came out easily, and maybe even with just a hint of pride. "I thought you should know because I plan to be involved. With the baby. Not the mother."

There was a pause then she said without hesitation, "Thanks for letting me know. I don't think we should each other again, then."

I was a little stunned. She hadn't even taken thirty seconds to think it over. "Just like that? Why?"

Lydia gave me the look that indicated I was being what women deem an idiot man. "Darwin, the answer is obvious. Why the hell would I want to be involved with a guy who has a baby mama? That is drama I have never sought and frankly, despise. Nor do I have any interest in listening to you talk about your baby. Or worse, be with you when you have the baby. I don't like kids."

As long as she was sure about it, damn. She made it sound like I had adopted a boa constrictor. Her voice was laced with disgust.

I tried to explain. "I wouldn't expect you to be involved in any way. It's my responsibility."

"We've only been out a few times. I don't have strong enough feelings for you to risk that."

It was a good thing my feelings toward her were mostly those of intellectual curiosity, because I decided I didn't like Lydia. At all. "I see."

"I also think you're being naïve if you think that you and the mother can just be friendly without it either turning into you two duking it out in court or being involved with each other emotionally and/or physically."

Stunned, I just stared at her. "Thanks for your honest opinion. I guess."

"I've offended you."

"A little." It was insulting that she didn't think I was capable of having a respectful friendship with Kylie for the benefit of our child.

"Come on, you know I'm right. We're not hardwired to raise children in a casually friendly co-parenting arrangement. We're predisposed to either abandon our offspring or protect them to the death. And if it's the latter, either mothers do it solo in the animal kingdom or with a mate."

Why did she have to sound so much like a scientist? It was annoying as hell.

"Except we're not in the animal kingdom. We're in the Gaslight district of Cincinnati." And I was thinking that I couldn't choke down the rest of my pasta. I gestured for the waiter. "Can I get a to-go box?"

"Are we leaving?" Lydia asked.

"I think so," I told her. "I don't see any point in staying." She had basically called me a delusional idiot. I wasn't having fun. The chime on my phone dinged on the table and I fought the urge to look at the screen and lost. It was Kylie texting me.

Going home tonight, yay!

I immediately texted back: That's great! Do you need a ride?

No, Rory and her bf are on it. I'm staying at their place for a few days.

Okay, ttys.

Frowning, I thought maybe I should have offered her a place to stay. She shouldn't be alone after what had happened and I should have thought of that before her friends had to offer. Fail.

"Baby mama?" Lydia asked.

Busted.

"I told you it's impossible to stay detached," she said, smugly. "Your expression is very revealing."

"Are you a psychology or a physics PhD?" I asked, now thoroughly annoyed. "You can't 'read' my face." Yeah, I was seriously annoyed when I started using fucking air quotes.

Lydia just rolled her eyes. "Here's a little advice. Just dive in, Darwin, and try to make it work. The sooner you do, the sooner it will crash and burn, and you can get back to what matters— your research."

Why in the hell had I ever thought I liked her? Talk about misjudging someone. Throwing enough money down on the table to cover the whole bill, I stood up. "I say you put that on a greeting card, Lydia. Forget physics. You're a natural born romantic."

"You don't want to hear my opinions on romance."

"You're right. I don't, actually."

I had never considered myself a romantic but I liked to think I wasn't cold-hearted either. There were certain emotions that, while they could technically be explained by science, were too intimate to force into a formula.

It didn't require or benefit from dissection.

Romance was one of those.

BY THE TIME I GOT TO THE TOP OF THE STAIRS AND INTO Rory's, I was exhausted and gasping for breath. "Oh my God, it's like I'm ninety. This blows."

"You're malnourished. Once you start eating solids again, you'll have more energy."

In the hospital I had stuck to Jell-O, Popsicles, and crackers. They were the only things that didn't make me sick. I had a list of suggested bland foods in my purse from the discharge papers, but right now all I wanted to do was collapse on the couch.

"It's bizarre how pregnancy kicks some women's asses," Tyler commented as he opened the door.

The steep flight of stairs to the living room mocked me.

"Damn it, I still have one more flight of stairs to go. Let me sit down a minute." I sat down on the first step and took a deep breath. I did feel so much better than I had when Jonathon had found me in my apartment. But that didn't mean I felt great.

"I'm not used to seeing you like this," Tyler mused. "I never thought I'd say this, but I miss your motormouth."

I flipped him off.

He laughed. "That's better."

Heaving myself up with the handrail, I trudged the rest of the way up the stairs and sank down onto the couch. "Ah, that feels good."

"Can I get you anything?" Rory asked. "You should keep up with your fluid intake."

I thought about it. "Can I have a blanket?"

Tyler shook his head. "The way your brain works fascinates me."

"What?" I laughed. "She asked me if I needed anything."

"She meant a drink."

"I don't want a drink, I want a blanket."

"I'll tell you what. How about I get you a blanket and a drink?" he asked.

"Sure."

He went back downstairs and Rory sat on the coffee table facing me. "Is there anything else you need? Ignore Ty. You're not limited to beverages only."

I bent over and tried to take my snowy boots off. "I should have taken these off downstairs. But I'm so out of it, I didn't think about it. But no, I'm fine."

"It's hard to believe it's January, isn't it?" she asked, knit cap still on her head, a thick oatmeal-colored sweater on under her winter coat. "This time last year I was a mess. Tyler and I were split up."

I remembered. "It was really hard to watch you hurting like that."

"That's how we felt about you, after Nathan."

"I know. But at least you and Tyler worked out." I leaned back on the arm of the couch and sighed. The year before I had been blissfully in love with Nathan. Or the person I thought Nathan was. It had turned out I hadn't known him at all. Of course, looking back now there were signs that I had chosen to ignore. His willingness to let Grant hang around even after he had pushed it too far with Rory and almost raped her. Nathan's jealousy. His obsessive interest in porn. All those times when he pulled my hair in teasing, only it was just a little too hard. Individually, none of them seemed like that big of a deal, and even together I probably would have ignored them if it weren't for the cheating. That wasn't something I could ignore.

Nathan wasn't a horrible guy. He just wasn't a good guy either. Or at least not good for me. There were good parts to him. He was loyal to his friends, he had a great sense of humor, he was affectionate.

"A year ago Riley and Jessica weren't together," I said, thinking back again to all the changes. "Robin hadn't met Phoenix, she hadn't transferred yet."

"My mother was alive," Tyler said, coming back into the room and spreading a blanket over me.

"Thanks." I reached out and squeezed his hand, feeling schmaltzy. "You're a good man, Mann."

"Thanks." He ruffled my hair. "You're not so bad yourself." He unscrewed a Gatorade and set it on the coffee table next to me. "Now make sure you're drinking that, Mommy, or I'll chew your ass out."

Mommy.

Goose bumps rose all over my skin and I felt tears well up in my eyes.

"Oh, shit. What did I say?" Tyler asked, looking contrite.

I just shook my head and cuddled under the blanket. "I'm fine. I'm going to take a nap, if you don't mind."

"Sure, no problem."

They both moved off and went back downstairs to the kitchen and their bedroom, but I didn't fall asleep. I did something really weird.

I texted Nathan.

I have no idea why I did it.

Maybe it was because everything was changing so fast.

Maybe it was because I wanted to remember when things were simple and I thought I'd had the answers.

Maybe because I missed having that total understanding of what you have with someone. That easy sense of knowing what you would do on Saturday night, knowing if you touched them or if you said certain things, that you could predict their response. While it hadn't been perfect with Nathan, I'd known how each day would be, how he would be with me.

That didn't exist for me now. Everything was new, uncertain, the feeling of walking on eggshells.

So I wrote something utterly pathetic.

Why did you cheat on me?

I instantly regretted it, the very second it was too late to take it back.

I lay on the couch, exhausted yet unable to sleep, tense over the answer he would give me, only to drift off to sleep an hour later with no answer whatsoever.

Which just made me feel worse.

I REGRETTED MY IMPULSIVE TEXTING EVEN MORE THE next day.

Jonathon stopped by to pick up his iPad now that I had access to my laptop again and I invited him in, because it seemed totally wrong to just hand it to him over the doorjamb and wave good-bye after all he had done when I was in the hospital. Besides, I wanted him to hang around. I admit it.

"You look good," he told me. "You feeling better?"

"I'm still exhausted, but I do feel better." We climbed the stairs to the living room together. "I still look totally busted, but oh, well. I'm just glad it's winter and I can get away with wearing ginormous clothes and hats." I had tried to glam up before he came over but totally gave up after my shower. Cleanliness was all I could manage without needing a nap. I hadn't even been able to blow-dry my hair because I couldn't hold my arms up that long.

"You don't look busted."

"Yes, I do. I look completely wrecked, but thanks for being nice about it." I smiled and sat down on the couch. "Sit down. How are you? It seems like we always talk about me. How are you doing?"

"I'm okay." He sat down next to me and smiled.

Tucking my feet under my butt, I studied him. "You look tired, too. I guess you have a lot on your mind."

"Just a little. I keep fluctuating between wanting to explore every little detail of pregnancy and iron out a concrete life plan for the next eighteen months, but then I think it's impossible to plan every contingency and maybe I just need to let it ride for a while and see what happens. But then I think that's stupid because then I won't be prepared. Do you know what I mean?"

115

"Totally. I keep thinking that I need to figure out what I'm doing, where I'm going to live, how I'm going to have money, but all I can manage is making through one day at a time without throwing up or going all narcoleptic while I'm reading my material for class. But that will get better. I think. I hope."

"It definitely will."

I wondered what options he was contemplating. I knew that I was debating whether it was even possible for me to stay in Cincinnati or if I would have to go back to my parents temporarily. I didn't want to have to do that, but financially it probably made more sense, plus I would have free babysitters I could trust. "So when are you supposed to finish up your masters degree?"

"May."

"Oh, that's good. Congrats. That's a huge accomplishment. Are you going on for a PhD?"

"That's the debate. I don't think so. I was already on the fence about it, and now I think it would make more sense for me to get a job, and see how that goes for a few years. It will be easy to get a job because there is such a strong plastics and chemical industry here. I could make good money, which would then help you. I could probably give you at least a thousand a month. Would that be helpful?"

My mouth fell open. Like down into the cleavage. "That much? I wasn't even expecting half that. I was actually thinking maybe I would have to go live with my parents to make it work. They live in Troy."

"That's over an hour away." He didn't look happy. "It would be hard for me to see the baby."

"But if you can give me that much support, then I don't have to move back. I can stay here. I might even move in here so that Rory and Tyler can help me out if I absolutely need it. Like the whole watch-the-sick-baby-while-I-run-to-the-store-and-get-baby-Tylenol kind of thing. And then you can see her whenever you want."

I wasn't sure why I always referred to the baby as "her." But it just felt natural.

He nodded. "That would make me a lot happier. Okay, so I'll start looking for a job. I'm confident I can get a lab job as a chemist. Done."

I smiled, giddy with how rational we were with each other. We both wanted the same thing—what was best for the baby, and what was best for the baby was to have both parents in her life. "You feel marketable?"

"I feel in demand," he said, giving me a teasing shrug. "Because, you know, who wouldn't want me?"

I did. But I couldn't say that. Or could I? My expression must have revealed something of what I was thinking because his smile fell off his face and his eyes darkened behind his glasses. I shifted, moving my legs back to the floor so that my body was closer to his. I dropped my gaze to his lips. Would he bolt if I kissed him? I willed him to kiss me so that I didn't have to make that first move and risk rejection.

Fortunately, he did. Jonathon shifted on the couch and put his hand on the back of my head. "Do *you* want me?" he asked, lips very close to mine. "I want you, Kylie. I know it's a bad idea, but I can't help it. I want you so goddamn bad, I can already taste you."

"I want you, too." I put my hands on his chest and locked my fingers onto the fabric of his plaid shirt to draw him closer to me. "I think it's okay, you know. I can't get pregnant a second time."

He was kissing my neck, his touch feathery and arousing. For the first time in three weeks I didn't feel nauseous. "We don't have to have sex," he said. "I know you don't feel good. I just want to touch you, hold you."

What could possibly be hotter than that?

Jonathon kissed me softly, his lips lingering over mine in a kiss that was as sweet as it was passionate, before urging me onto my back. His hands slid under my sweatshirt and he cupped my breasts, which were straining against the fabric. "You already feel different. Your breasts are fuller."

They were also more sensitive. I bit my lip when he brushed his thumb across my nipple.

"Is this okay?" he asked.

I nodded. More than good. It felt amazing. "Oh, God, Jonathon, do that again."

"I feel so bad that you've been sick. I want you to feel good."

"You make me feel good. Really good." He did. His touch was gentle, skilled, and he was aware of every sound, every goose bump, every reaction I made.

I wanted to reach down, undo his pants, explore his naked body, but while I didn't feel in danger of losing my paltry dinner on him, I had no strength to even unzip. I just lay there and let him do what he wanted, all of which made me feel warm and delicious, and happy with my body for the first time since early December. He had slipped my oversized pajama pants down and he was using his tongue on me, the rhythm steady and dedicated. He seemed determined to compensate me for the weeks of morning sickness. I wasn't going to argue. I had been through hell, right? I was entitled to a little oral sex.

My eyes were closed and I dug my fingers into the softness of his hair, the shaggy top a good length to grip. It wasn't even two minutes before I was having a lazy, expansive orgasm, crying out loudly.

He gave me a smug grin, his head still down south. "How was that?"

"I think I needed that, thank you." My body felt more relaxed, languid.

Jonathon shifted to move up and he paused over my belly to skim his lips over the bare skin. It wasn't sexual, but sweet. "Hi, Baby," he said.

Yeah, that was my heart melting. When he moved up alongside me, giving me a soft kiss, I felt more than could possibly be wise. Like serious emotion. Beyond crush and deep into like territory.

But then I remembered something and I stopped him from kissing me again. I had a horrible and stinky rotten thought. "Aren't you dating someone?"

Oh, God, it couldn't be that Jonathon would cheat. It just couldn't be. I would literally die and become a celibate man-hater if I had just become a party to hurting some other girl.

"No. She dumped me yesterday."

"Oh." That was good. That was a relief. Yet I wasn't sure how I felt about it exactly. I mean, thank God, he wasn't a cheater. But then what did that mean? Was he upset? Was I just a substitute for this magically delicious chick I could never compete with?

The doorbell downstairs rang. I wondered if I should pull my pants up. I heard Tyler open the door and oh, shit, that was Nathan's voice. Yes, I needed to pull my pants up. I scrambled to get them on, shoving Jonathon out of the way. "That is my ex-boyfriend downstairs," I said urgently. "Oh, shit, fuck, damn, I do *not* want to see him."

"Do you want me to tell him to go away?" Jonathon asked, looking neutral. He sat up, but he made no move to either push up his glasses or take his hand off my leg.

"No, no, I'll just go and see what he wants. Maybe he's actually here to see Tyler." Which would be one serious downside to living with Rory and Tyler that I hadn't considered.

"Dude, you need to ask before you just charge up there and bug her," Tyler said, sounding annoyed.

Then Nathan was at the top of the stairs, Tyler right behind him. "Sorry," Tyler said. "Nathan can't take a hint."

Nathan's face when he saw me with Jonathon was glorious. Not that I wanted to hurt him. Okay, I kind of did. Besides, it wasn't like it could come anywhere close to what I had felt when I'd found those texts on Robin's phone. That night was a blur of tears and horrific stabbing betrayal. Fury. Anguish.

Yeah. I didn't feel bad about being seen with Jonathon months after Nathan had destroyed me.

"What the hell are you doing?" Nathan asked, glaring at me.

"What do you mean? What are you doing? Are you here to see Tyler?"

He stood there, hand going through his hair, expression still shocked as he took in how close Jonathon and I were sitting to each other. "Who are you?"

"I'm Jonathon." He stood up and offered him his hand.

I was surprised, but Nathan actually took it and shook. "Nathan."

Why were they shaking hands? Why was this happening? I actually felt a horrible sense of how far my life had spiraled out of control as they stood there, assessing each other. My past and my present eyeing each other, and ignoring me, I might add.

Finally Nathan glanced over at me. "Are you two . . ."

Yeah, no. I didn't even know what Jonathon and I were doing. I wasn't going to discuss it with the man who had begged blow jobs off my best friend. "Can I talk to you downstairs?" I asked Nathan, standing up myself.

Tyler was giving me a look that said he wasn't down with any of this, but I tilted my head toward Jonathon so he would get a hint to keep him up here while I went downstairs with Douche Canoe.

I brushed past Nathan and stomped down the stairs, assuming he would follow me, my arms over my chest. My bra was unhooked from fooling around with Jonathon and I would really rather be continuing that than doing this.

"Why are you acting pissed?" he said from behind me. "You're the one who texted me."

Oh, great. I had no doubt Jonathon had just heard that. "I didn't ask you to come over! I texted you because I'm stupid. I wanted answers you can't give."

"I already explained that to you. I did what I did because I was afraid I would lose you."

Once in the kitchen, I rounded on Nathan. "That's not an answer. That is the lamest justification I've ever heard. I'm sorry I texted you. I was feeling sorry for myself, but it won't happen again."

"Why, because now you have that guy?" He jerked his thumb toward the stairs. "Seriously, Kylie? He wears glasses."

What the hell did that have to do with anything? Half of America was nearsighted. "So? He is about a thousand times smarter than you and as far as I can tell, he's honest, which is not something you're familiar with."

"Are you trying to start a fight with me?"

"No. I'm not trying to do anything with you." All my irritation disappeared and my stomach was starting to churn ominously. "Go home. I'm sorry I bothered you. It won't happen again."

"Are you having sex with him?"

"What are you, my dad? That's none of your business!"

I tried to move past him but he actually reached out and grabbed my arm. "Just tell me. If you are, I'll go away. If there is no chance for us, I'll leave you alone."

He'd promised before to leave me alone, many times, and it had never worked. But I had texted him. I was just as much to blame for continuing our pointless interactions. My anger thawed.

I had loved him for a whole year. It was hard to look at him and feel nothing. "There is no chance. We can't fix anything at this point."

"Are you sure? You know we had something good. Before Robin threw herself at me."

Wow. Way to take responsibility. I couldn't do this anymore. I knew the best possible way to get rid of him. "I'm positive we can't be together. Nathan, I'm pregnant. Jonathon is the father."

His face froze. Then he shook his head. "You can't be serious. You're just saying that to fuck with me."

"When have I ever just fucked with you?" I snapped, annoyed. "It's true, I am pregnant. Now go home." I opened the door to the hallway and stared him down.

His jaw worked but finally he moved, going through the door. "You're a bitch," he told me. "You did this on purpose to hurt me."

Clearly. Because it made total sense to get pregnant just to piss him off. I rolled my eyes and slammed the door in his face.

When I got to the top of the stairs, still fuming, Tyler and Jonathon were hovering. Jonathon was pacing back and forth. "Everything okay?"

"Yes. I'm sorry, I told him about the baby. I know I shouldn't have, but it seemed the best way to get him to leave me alone forever."

Tyler shook his head. "Man, he has lost his mind the last six months. I don't even know what is going on with him."

"Is that what you want?" Jonathon asked. "For him to leave you alone?" His eyes were searching my face, like he could see something there that I didn't feel.

"Yes. Why?" I wasn't sure exactly what he was asking.

"Because don't feel obligated to me if you want to be with him. I don't have any claim over you."

I sucked in a breath, I couldn't help it. I didn't speak for a second, letting my eyes express how I was feeling. Stake a claim, I wanted to tell him. Conquer me for king and country, damn it. Couldn't he tell that's what I wanted? Sure, I wanted to be independent and strong and smart and not jump into a relationship and complicate things. But at the same time, since almost the first minute I had met him I had felt ooey and gooey things for him, and I wanted him, in my bed, in my heart. I couldn't help it. I could control it, I could be rational and hold him at arm's length, but that didn't stop me from wanting him to throw caution to the fucking wind and fall in love with me.

All I said was, "I don't want to be with him. Ever. Trust me."

Jonathon just nodded. "Okay. Just checking. I should head out." He kissed my forehead. "Talk to you soon."

A second later he was gone, like we hadn't been in the middle of having sex fifteen minutes ago before Nathan's interruption. I stood there, blinking. He'd actually forgotten his iPad. It was still sitting on the coffee table.

Tyler had a pained look on his face. "Well, that was awkward. I need a beer."

"I need a lobotomy," I told him, flinging myself down onto the couch.

Tyler laughed. "I'm sorry, I shouldn't have let Nathan in. He caught me off guard."

Waving my hand, I said, "Don't worry about it. This is all idiotic. Where is Rory, by the way?"

"The animal shelter."

"That's what I need, a dog. They make more sense than men."

"Don't slam my gender because of one dickhead. I seriously am going down to get a beer. Do you want anything?"

"Ice cream." The thought of its creamy coldness made my mouth water.

"We don't have any ice cream."

"Figures."

"Do you want me to go get you some?"

I hugged the throw pillow and felt sorry for myself. "Thanks, but that's okay." It would make me feel even more of a loser to have to borrow my friend's boyfriend to get me ice cream. Granted, Tyler had been my friend even before he had started dating Rory, but still. Talk about feeling pathetic when he took so much pity on me he would hoof it in a foot of snow in January to pacify me with Rocky Road.

"All right, I'll be in my room lifting weights if you need anything."

"I thought you were getting a beer."

"I am. I'm going to drink a beer, smoke a cigarette, and lift weights."

"Sounds healthy."

"It's a lifestyle, babe. Oh, and just an FYI, even though you're sleeping on the couch, this isn't a bedroom. There's no door and sound carries, if you know what I'm saying."

Excellent. So he had heard me having an orgasm. "Sorry."

"Hey, pregnant chicks need love, too, but I don't want to hear it." He gave me a grin, then jogged down the stairs.

I stared at the ceiling, a blanket pulled up to my chin.

I was mad at myself for doing it again. Not for starting to have sex with Jonathon. That I couldn't be upset about, except for the fact that we had been prevented from finishing. No, I was mad at myself for another reason. For hoping. For that little seed of hope that had taken root again, and I couldn't seem to choke out. This was when being a glass-half-full person just set me up for disappointment. I couldn't hope that Jonathon would want something, anything, with me.

I needed to be like him and realize that while the glass might be half full of liquid, the rest was vapor. I couldn't see it, touch it, feel it, smell it, hold it.

It wasn't mine.

CHAPTER NINE

"SO WHAT IS GOING ON?" MY FATHER ASKED. "WHY ARE YOU so distracted? I've never seen you have this lack of focus."

That was almost a compliment coming from the stingy Professor Kadisch. He was actually giving me credit for generally having focus. I had gone to his office to talk to him. To disappoint him, truthfully. "I'm not pursuing the PhD."

"What? Why the hell not?" He pushed his glasses up. I really thought my nearsightedness and my penchant for science were the only traits I had inherited from him, though I suppose the intelligence factor was nothing to bitch about. Otherwise, though, he was impatient, tactless, and selfish and I sincerely tried to be none of those. He was shorter than me, with a more prominent nose, and sometimes the way he looked at his attractive undergrad students was just a shade too appreciative and made me uncomfortable. I seriously thought he was a man who spent way too much time in his own head, the lab, or on his computer.

There was a lesson there.

"Because it's time to get a job. I have responsibilities and I need a legitimate income."

He scoffed at me from behind his desk. His office was neat, stark. There were no family photos or anything like that. Those things didn't interest him. "What responsibilities? Alcohol and strip clubs?"

Which proved yet again he had no basic understanding of me. "Dad, I drink occasionally and I have never been in a strip club and I have no desire to."

"So then what? You buying a car? Renting a bigger apartment?"

"It turns out I'm going to be a father in a few months. I need to help support him or her."

His eyebrows shot up. "Are you shitting me? Well, hell. Can't she get an abortion?"

I wondered if he had asked my mother that. Most likely, yes. More than once. "She wants to keep it."

He sighed. "So what does that have to do with you, really? If you're in school, the court can't mandate you pay her more than a fair wage out of what you're earning from your part-time job, and I doubt they can touch your research grant once you acquire it. You'll just have to tighten your belt a little."

"That's not exactly fair to her. I'd be giving her like two hundred bucks a month, if that."

"So? It's not fair that you don't have a choice in what she does with it."

I had known this conversation was going to be hard, but slowly anger was starting to simmer. I had a whole new appreciation for my mother as I pictured her as a scared nineteen-year-old having virtually this same conversation with my father and him being a callous dickhead then just like he was now. My mom deserved a huge thank-you and maybe some flowers because not only had she forged ahead and raised me on her own, she had done a damn good job. I was proud to be her son and proud that when Kylie had confronted me with the same scenario, my reaction had been different.

"Dad, I was there when she got pregnant. It's my responsibility. I can't stiff her the way you stiffed Mom, sorry."

Now his shoulders went up. "Hey. I did my duty. I paid your mother every month."

"You gave her a lousy fifty bucks a paycheck until I was five years old! And you never bothered to see me, not once, until I was seventeen." I had thought I was over all this shit, but suddenly it felt I was choking on my resentment.

"That's when you got interesting."

I stood up, throat tight. "You know, my mother discouraged me from coming to college here, even though it was free, and sending me somewhere else would have meant she would have to take loans to pay for it. But I couldn't figure out why I shouldn't take advantage of the free education because of your tenure position and the scholarship and why I shouldn't try to get to know you. She told me that sometimes it was better to just leave things alone and that maybe I wasn't meant to have a relationship with you because of how busy you are. I have no idea now how she managed to keep her mouth shut and not call you an asshole to my face like she had every right to."

"What the hell are you talking about?" He genuinely looked confused. "Where is all this coming from? My God, it's like you're twelve all over again and sending me that nasty letter accusing me of ruining your mother's life. That was a piece of melodrama that didn't need to happen."

I didn't want to talk about that letter. I had written it, angry and indignant, pouring out my preteen bitterness and anguish on the paper. He hadn't responded to it and right then and there I had decided he would have no emotional impact on me anymore. I had thought I could maintain that creed and spare my mother the expense of college and grad school by accepting his offer of an education.

Now I wasn't sure it was worth it. "Dad, you're a dick. You just are."

"If you say so." He didn't sound particularly worried about it. "Who is the girl, by the way?"

I debated telling him or not and decided it didn't matter if he knew the truth. He wouldn't cut Kylie slack if he knew the truth. "Kylie Warner."

Understanding dawned on him. "Ah. I see. Not very bright. But she is hot, I'll give you that."

Fuck. "Seriously, don't say stuff like that. It's inappropriate. And it really, really pisses me off."

Then I left, hands shaking, the urge to hit him more powerful than I would have thought possible. I didn't have anger issues. I had a pragmatic attitude and a sense of logic about the world.

But right then I had an anger issue. I slammed his door shut behind me but that wasn't nearly satisfying enough.

Down the hall and outside I went, fists balled up, welcoming the howling cold winter wind as it hit me in the face. I couldn't believe my father was such a prick. How did someone get like that? He had pretty much laid out straight to my face that he'd never wanted me, and he considered me a financial annoyance until he had seen potential in me. All of which I knew. But did he have to say it out loud? Couldn't we just pretend that he wasn't a selfish bastard?

No such luck.

Debating where to go since I didn't feel like heading home and dealing with Devon's opinions on Kylie, which were unfortunately similar to my father's, I paused on the street corner. I realized I never actually got my iPad from Kylie. I'd been so distracted, first by kissing her and then by her douche bag ex showing up, that I had forgotten all about it.

Maybe I should go over there and grab it. The walk would do me good. There was no point in driving two blocks and I needed to cool off. Plus I really wanted to see her, settle my nerves. All she had to do was smile and I felt better. Which I really needed. It suddenly felt like everyone I'd surrounded myself with was self-absorbed. Except my mother, that is. Surely I had friends who were compassionate and generous people. But the truth was, most of my friends were acquaintances. Probably in Cincinnati, aside my Devon, my closest friend was Miranda, who happened to be a chem major as well, along with being a lesbian. Unlike Devon, she never stuck her foot in her mouth, though she could be brutally honest. Then my best friend from high school, who was a legit decent guy, was at Carnegie Mellon studying molecular biology. I decided at the very least I was going to call him when I got back to my apartment.

I concentrated on releasing my anger, one breath at a time, feet eating up the sidewalk. I didn't want to show up at Kylie's pissed off, so I pictured the way she had looked on the couch, eyes closed, ribs more prominent from her recent weight loss, her breasts bursting out of her bra cups. That was a much better thought. I'd meant what I said—I hadn't intended to have sex with her. I didn't imagine me rocking my cock into her was going to feel all that amazing when she was constantly dizzy and nauseous. For her, anyway. I'm sure for me it would feel fantastic if I were a selfish asshole. But I reserved that role for Professor Kadisch. But I had enjoyed making her come, her body relaxed, her soft moans satisfying. She had earned the right to oral sex after what she'd been through with the morning sickness.

It still blew my mind that some guy would be interested in having sex with another chick while he was having sex with Kylie. It was totally illogical. Beyond stupid. She had the most amazing body I'd ever seen, plus she was big-time responsive. I barely touched her and she was all low moans and wet thighs. It was fucking hot. But maybe there was just something between us . . . that intriguing chemistry that most people find so unexplainable, yet is so clearly rooted in science.

Whatever it was, it was making me warm despite the winter weather.

I texted her while I walked to make sure she was still awake and that it was okay if I stopped by. She said it was fine, and since she answered right away, I decided I could trust she was telling the truth. If she didn't want to see me, she'd make up an excuse, probably one that was transparent. Kylie wasn't complicated and I liked that. She wasn't manipulative or devious. She wasn't even moody, despite what she was going through.

"Hey," I said when she opened the door. "I can't believe I forgot the iPad."

She smiled. "Come on up. We were interrupted, so I'm not that surprised."

I was. I didn't forget things. My mind was like a data spreadsheet. It seemed when I was distracted by emotion my brain forgot to hit the SAVE button. "Yeah, that was unfortunate. At least he didn't come five minutes sooner." Or she wouldn't have been coming.

She gave me a look over her shoulder that had my dick swelling again. "I'm not sure we were totally finished."

I wanted to slide my hands over her ass, but I restrained myself. I was still feeling residual anger and I didn't want to be rough with her. I had a feeling if I let go, I'd be in the push-her-against-the-wall kind of mood and you just couldn't do that with a girl who was fresh out of the hospital. "You finished. That's all that matters."

Once we got in the living room, she sat down and patted the couch next to her with a smile. "You okay? You look agitated."

She said "agitated" in a funny, goofball voice. I couldn't help but attempt a smile.

"I was just in my dad's office, and it occurred to me what a complete and total dick he is."

Her eyes widened. "Well, I've always thought he was a dick, but I just figured that's because he was flunking me."

"No, he's a dick." I kicked my boots off and put my feet on the coffee table, sinking back against the couch cushions. I felt more at ease already, just being near her. "You know, my mom got pregnant with me when she was your age by a certain chemistry grad student by the name of Ben Kadisch."

"Seriously?"

"Seriously. History is repeating itself." I gave a little laugh. "If only I believed in predestination. However, I can appreciate irony and this is certainly ironic. But the difference is, my father never saw me. He begrudgingly gave my mother a hundred dollars a month, and the first time I met him was when I was seventeen and he deemed me intelligent enough to bother with."

"Shit balls," she said. "That's harsh."

"Yeah. He's a dick." I shrugged. "I thought I was past all that, but I don't know, talking to him tonight, with everything going down . . . I just got so fucking angry."

"You have every right to be angry. None of that was fair to you."

"Or to my mom."

"No. It wasn't. I'm sorry." Her hand reached out and squeezed my thigh. "But Jonathon, you're nothing like him."

She had dug down deep to the root of my fear. I was afraid that I was like him, despite what I said. I was afraid that ultimately I would prove to be selfish and I would wind up alone, a workaholic, eyeballing girls young enough to be my daughter.

The very thought made my gut clench and my teeth set on edge. "I hope not."

"You're not."

The conviction with which she spoke made me want to do anything to live up to the belief in me she had. I could tell she trusted me, and I wanted to be worthy of that trust. "I feel guilty not liking him. He did pay for some of my education."

"So? That was the least he could do. You don't owe him anything, by the way. He lost that privilege when he turned his back on your mom. So he gave you *money*. That's easy. Any man can be a father, not every man can be a dad."

And that would be my heart crawling up my throat and cutting off my air passage. Damn. She was really something fucking special. I didn't share my feelings with women. I didn't share my feelings with anyone. That I had was amazing enough. That I had and she knew exactly what to say to me was more than amazing. It was perfection.

"Thanks, Kylie. I'm going to try to be a dad, I really am."

"You'll be awesome sauce," she said with total confidence.

I laughed. "I never imagined myself as awesome sauce. How does one measure that, precisely?"

"There's no formula for that, Darwin. Get over it."

I noticed she only called me Darwin when she was teasing or once when she'd been annoyed. I liked that she called me Jonathon. It was like she wanted to connect with me, the man, not the scientist.

"So how are you doing?" I asked. "I know it must be tough to have your ex popping up like that." Her ex who was a total tool as far as I could tell. It wasn't that he was built like a juiced-up athlete. I didn't care about that. It was the way he looked at Kylie, like he was frustrated that she didn't just fall in line with what he wanted. He seemed entitled and I didn't respond well to that.

She sighed. "Can I cuddle with you? I'm sleepy."

That. There it was. The whole reason I was so drawn to her. She was just so sweet and genuine. "Of course you can. Come here." I turned on the couch so my back was against the armrest and I drew her between my legs. She rested her head on my chest, her arms wrapped around my waist.

"Ah. That feels good. Sometimes it's like my head is too heavy for my body." She nuzzled her nose against my shirt. "I have an itch."

I snaked my hand up and scratched her nose.

"Thanks."

Maybe she didn't want to talk about Nathan. I didn't really want to talk about him either. I just wanted to relax. "What do you think of the name Charlie?"

"Girl or boy?"

"Either."

"I kind of like it. Hmm." Her fingernail played with a button on my shirt. "Are you sad you got dumped by that girl? Is it because of me, and the baby?"

"No, I'm not sad," I told her honestly. "We only went out a few times and I was only interested in her because, well, it seemed logical for me to date her. But what I think I'm learning is that sometimes logical is so safe it becomes dangerous."

It forced you into predetermined positions, whether they were right for you or not. "I'm sorry I was a jerk about it when you first told me you were pregnant."

"It's okay." Her hand traveled up to my chin and she ran her soft fingers over my beard. "Your beard is even more scratchy than it was two hours ago."

"It's a fact that a man's beard grows faster when he is anticipating sex."

She looked up at me suspiciously. "Are you making that up?"

"No. I'm totally serious. It's true."

"Did you come here anticipating sex?" The saucy smile she gave me indicated she would not be at all offended by that.

"Not specifically. I mean, I'm always hopeful, though. Basically, I've been in a heightened state of sexual arousal since the very first minute I laid eyes on you."

She laughed. "Yay."

"No. Not yay. Bad. Very bad. I shouldn't want to strip you naked when you are fighting the urge to vomit."

"I don't mind."

She was killing me. "So . . . are you saying you want to have sex right now? Or just generally speaking, as the occasion arises, literally and figuratively, you are willing to consider the possibility?"

"Oh, you're so silly sometimes."

"I'm silly?" Now that was an adjective never once used to describe me. "How am I silly?"

"You think too much."

Maybe I did. "I'll think about that."

"Haha," she murmured.

Her body felt warm, her breasts pressing against me. She had slung her ankle over my calf and I slid my hand down over her ass, deciding that I was just going to go for it. She'd tell me to stop if she wasn't into it.

Except I realized that she had fallen asleep.

Fucking-ay.

So much for sex.

And so much for me going home. I couldn't disturb her. Not after the last few weeks. So I just shifted down until I was flat on my back and she was splayed out on top of me, her breathing settling down into a tiny, steady snore, her hand spread across my chest. Stretching my arm, I pulled a blanket over her and sighed. There was a light on in the corner, but it wasn't pointing in our eyes and it wasn't all that bright.

So this wasn't comfortable. Not even close. But I figured it was a lot easier than growing a placenta and hosting a fetus, so I could suck it up and deal.

Besides, she smelled good and I liked holding her. It made me feel important. To her.

I WOKE UP WITH A START WHEN JONATHON MURMURED TO me. "Morning, Kylie."

"Oh, shit." I rubbed my mouth and tried to unglue my eyelids. "It's morning? OMG, I'm sorry. You didn't have to stay here all night."

"I didn't want to disturb you."

Sitting up, I stretched and shifted so he could maneuver himself out from under me. "Did you sleep with your glasses on?" I asked him as he rubbed the bridge of his nose under the frames.

"Yeah. Wouldn't be the first time. Nor the last, I imagine." He sat on the couch, legs apart, forearms resting on his thighs for a minute, like he was trying to wake up. "Eight a.m. classes suck."

"I haven't had one since freshman year. They're on my shit list. Like nail polish that chips after a few hours."

Jonathon laughed softly. "That made your shit list?"

"It's really annoying," I told him. "You put all this effort into your mani and then bam, it's fucked. I hate that."

"We have first-world problems, don't we?"

"Totally." I yawned. "Like where to get coffee."

"I don't think pregnant women are supposed to drink caffeine."

"Oh." It was too early in the morning to be reminded that I didn't know what the hell I was doing. "How do you know that?"

"I did a little research. It helped me cope."

Then I blurted something out that I didn't mean to, but was a huge fear rattling around in the back of my brain. "What if our baby isn't smart? What if she's a dumb blonde, like me? Will you be super disappointed?"

He looked shocked. "Kylie, you're not dumb. Don't say things like that."

"Let's face it, I'm not smart. I know that. People have been pointing it out to me my whole life. What if my DNA overpowers yours?"

"A quality of a human being isn't measured solely in his IQ. What I want most of all is a baby that is healthy, who grows up to be happy and kind and productive."

He looked sincere. He sounded sincere. He probably was sincere. But how would he feel when our kid was struggling with addition in first grade? Probably not thrilled, no matter what he said. But I couldn't exactly argue with him. So I just nodded and bit my lip.

Jonathon took my hand and squeezed it. "And you call me silly. Now you're the one being a goof." He kissed my forehead and stood up. "I'll talk to you later. Let me know if you need anything."

"Okay, thanks."

Then he took his iPad and left, still looking a little groggy, his movements slow, his shoulders hunched.

Lifting my phone off the table, I called my mother, feeling pensive. "Hi, Mommy."

"Hi, sweetie! How are you feeling?"

"Less like total crap. Now just slightly like crap."

"That's progress. Have you made your first appointment with the doctor?"

"No." I had been too busy trying not to throw up. "Is there a list for our insurance I have to pick from?"

"Yes. I'll e-mail all of that to you. But you know, if you go down to part-time this semester or next semester, you'll be dropped from our insurance."

"Fabulous. No pressure or anything." It was too early in the morning for this much reality. I was suddenly doubting my ability to handle any of this—a baby, bills, an apartment, Jonathon. Ugh.

"Don't stress about it. It's just something to be aware of."

Sure. Don't stress. I was already super behind for this semester and I was due basically when classes were starting again in August. That ought to be entertaining. "Isn't there any other way to get insurance? Because my due date is August 23. How am I supposed to give birth and go to class?"

"Not unless you use government assistance."

Those were my options? Give birth in class at McMicken Hall or go on welfare? Excellent. "I can't think about this. It's making me want to puke."

She changed the subject and talked about my brothers and my sister and something about my dad almost electrocuting himself trying to fix the dryer.

"When you're feeling better I'll come down and pick you up and bring you home for a weekend. Or maybe you can get a ride with someone."

Was she hinting that the someone should be Jonathon? I had no idea. My mother's hints were always so vague I never knew what she was talking about.

All I knew was over the next week she kept calling me and texting me about absolutely nothing and Jonathon kept texting me both questions and informational links about pregnancy and childbirth. I knew that he was trying to be helpful. He was trying not to repeat his own father's dickheadedness and I understood and appreciated that. I felt grateful that he was trying so hard. But at the same time I didn't feel like discussing my cervix with him. Or my increased blood volume, which he seemed to find endlessly fascinating.

I just wanted to be Kylie to him for a change. I just wanted to be someone he looked at and wanted—both sexually and as a friend. Not the Future Mother of His Child. Was that so much to ask for?

Apparently, because I didn't see him at all. He studiously checked in on me with texts and e-mails, but he didn't ask to see me.

Blech.

I was back to attending classes for the most part, though I was still behind. Most of my professors were understanding, but Professor Kadisch gestured to me to come to his desk after class. Great. I dragged my feet, self-conscious wearing a fuzzy pink scarf and my hair pulled up in a ponytail, no makeup. The energy to primp had only semi-returned and while I was wearing boyfriend jeans, the first pants I'd worn not made of stretchy fabric in a month, I still felt dumpy and pale.

"Yes?" I asked, giving him a weak smile. Now that I knew their connection, I could see Jonathon in his features, or I guess technically Professor Kadisch in Jonathon's features. They shared the same forehead and strong cheekbones. I had no idea what he was going to say to me. Somehow I doubted he was going to be angling for a World's Greatest Grandpa T-shirt.

"So I heard about your situation and I think you should drop this course."

Yep. No warm fuzzies there. "My situation?" I repeated because I wasn't sure what exactly I was supposed to say to that.

"Yes, that you're pregnant. Jonathon told me. Regardless of my personal opinion on the matter, as your professor I think it's only fair to recommend you drop. You barely passed chem first semester and you're too far behind already to successfully complete the course."

Except that I was only at twelve credits this semester anyway because I'd been shut out of an anthropology course I needed. If I dropped chemistry, I would be part-time and I would lose my parent's insurance. He didn't need to know that, though. Determined to be polite and not cause trouble for Jonathon, I said, "Thank you. I'll take that into consideration." Then because I was nosy, I couldn't help but ask, "What is your personal opinion on me having this baby?"

He pushed his glasses up on his nose. Funny how when Jonathon did that it was cute, endearing. When Professor Kadisch did it, it seemed angry. "I think it's selfish," he said shortly. "You're ruining Jonathon's life so you can play house."

Tears were in my eyes before I could stop them. I had known he wasn't exactly going to offer his hearty congratulations, but I hadn't expected him to accuse me of destroying Jonathon's life so I could play real-life baby dolls. "Jonathon seems okay with it so maybe you should be."

"Jonathon is humoring you because he feels guilty."

Wow.

"Well, then he's already a step ahead of you," I said. "Because at least he feels responsible for his behavior."

Then because I was crying and it made me angry that I was crying in front of him, I left, hitting a chair with my hip on my way to the door.

THE NEXT DAY WAS MY BIRTHDAY. IT WAS A THURSDAY AND I went to class, trudging through the slushy snow remnants, feeling distracted and a little sad. Usually I loved my birthday. I had always been that way, as long as I could remember. I barely slept the night before. I pranced around telling everyone that it was My Day and that they had to treat me like a princess. I either had a party or went out, depending on my age at the time, and I rapturously opened all my presents, taking my time, saving ribbons and bows and pretty wrapping paper to recycle into craft projects.

This year, my mother had sent me a pretty card with a Visa debit card in it, suggesting I use it for maternity clothes. Because there was the gift everyone wants to get for themselves—elastic-waist pants. There would be no going out clubbing. No party. Funny how I had waited my whole life for my twenty-first birthday and here it was, just a gloomy Thursday, a winter day like any other. My phone rang as I passed the University Center, debating whether I could stomach lunch or not. I glanced at the screen and saw it was Robin calling me.

"Hi," I said, suddenly grateful that she had called. It made me feel like things hadn't changed as dramatically as they had.

"Happy Birthday!"

"Thanks. Listen, Robin, I'm sorry I didn't get to see you before you and Phoenix left but I had just found out I was pregnant and

I wasn't feeling good . . . I wasn't trying to be a jerk." I ducked into the UC and decided all I wanted was a whipped cream–laden latte. Then I remembered what Jonathon had said about caffeine. Did they make decaf lattes? Did such a thing exist?

"It's okay, I understand. I'm sure you were completely in shock."

"That's definitely true."

"How are you doing now?"

"I'm okay. It's going to be fine." Then because that sounded so not enthusiastic, I asked, "How is New Orleans? Are you like all into voodoo and crawfish now?"

She laughed. "Not exactly. But I like it here. It's like sixty-five degrees, by the way, and people call me 'precious' all the time. Classes are awesome and Phoenix likes the tattoo shop he's working at. We live uptown, on the parade route, so we'll be having our first Mardi Gras in just a couple of weeks. I can't wait."

Robin sounded great. Eager, excited, happy. "That's awesome. How is Bourbon Street?"

"Not really the most exciting place for two people who don't drink. But we like to go to Frenchmen Street, where there is live jazz. It's less about the Huge-Ass Beers there."

"That's cool. No Huge-Ass Beer for me tonight either. It's not exactly how I imagined my twenty-first birthday." I sat down on a bench and felt sorry for myself. Not that I had any right to be pouting, really, but it seemed like the only party I was going to get was a pity party, so I might as well excel at it.

"Ah, I'm sorry, Ky-Ky," she said, genuine regret in her voice. "I know you always wanted a big blowout."

"It's okay." But I sighed anyway. "It wouldn't be so bad except I look like butt. My skin is dull, my hair is dull. I haven't shaved my legs or anything else in weeks and my nails looks like rats have been chewing on them while I sleep. I feel hideous."

"Go get your nails done, then. It's your birthday, you should be able to get a manicure."

There was that Visa card in my purse. How irresponsible was that? Screw the maternity jeans, I would just wear yoga pants until I split the seams. I needed pampering. I could hear the song in my head. "It's your birthday, it's your birthday."

"That is a great point. I think I will do that. Thanks, Robin."

She laughed. "My birthday gift to you—financial justification."

We talked for another ten minutes and it was an easy conversation. I didn't even think about RAN at all during that time. It seemed to matter less and less. I was never going to forget, and I likely would always hold a tiny bit of resentment, but maybe in the end, Robin's drunken fuckup had been the best thing that could have ever happened to me. It got me away from Nathan.

There was a salon on campus and I walked in and snagged a nail appointment. I let the tech massage my hands while I bitched about morning sickness. I felt all suburban housewife and it totally made me feel better. This wasn't as far off of my vision for my life as I had originally feared.

Jessica and Rory met me afterward in the UC and Jess had a fancy cupcake for me, with a candle in it. She flicked a lighter over it.

"You can't light that in here," Rory protested.

"By the time someone notices, it will be out."

I closed my eyes and made a wish. Then I blew it out before Rory's fear of campus cops descending on us with billy clubs came true.

"What did you wish for?" Jessica asked. "I know you, you totally made a wish. You've been doing that since you were thirteen."

I had. Actually, I'd been doing it since I was four. But Jessica met me in middle school. When I was thirteen I wished for my pimply complexion to clear up. At sixteen I had wished to pass my driver's test on the first try. One year I'd been convinced my parents were getting a divorce and I had wished for them to stay together. But never had I made a wish about a boy, because birthday wishes were about *me*.

Technically, I still didn't make a wish about a boy, but instead of focusing on me, I focused on the baby. Though alongside a wish for a healthy baby I crammed a wish for something else I wasn't even sure I could admit to myself.

"I'm not telling you! It won't come true then. You don't want to curse my unborn child, do you?"

"Did you wish for a girl?" Rory asked.

"No. For her to be healthy. I already know she's a girl."

"How can you know that?"

I shrugged. "I don't know. I just do." It wasn't because I wanted a girl more than a boy. I hadn't really had any gender preference going into this. It just felt . . . feminine.

"Oh, what, now you're like all wise because you're a mother?" Jessica teased.

"Totally. Don't I look wise?" I made a hair mustache.

Then I unwrapped my cupcake as we all laughed. "What flavor is this?"

"Red velvet. Your favorite."

"Yay." I sniffed it cautiously to make sure my stomach wasn't going to protest. The cocoa in it was very prominent and I could smell the butter in the frosting.

"What are you doing? You look like a drug dog."

"My sense of smell is super sensitive. I'm just making sure it's not going to smell bad to me or get my gag reflex going. The weirdest things make me feel sick. Like tacos. I usually love tacos. But I walked past that Mexican restaurant and I almost threw up in the parking lot bushes."

"That is unfortunate, and why I do not think I'm cut out for motherhood." Jessica made a face. "That's just one of them, actually. Riley and I are like total bumblefucks trying to raise Easton. I mean, he's eleven, he's half formed anyway, but still. Rory, you and Tyler are way better at it."

"That's Tyler, not me," Rory protested. "I grew up an only child, remember? I don't know anything about kids. I just hug him and bake him cookies and that seems to suffice."

I was pretty sure that counted for a lot to an eleven-year-old.

"So Professor Kadisch told me I was selfish to ruin Jonathon's life like this."

Both their jaws dropped. Jessica looked outraged. "I hope you told him to go fuck himself! If Jonathon didn't want his quote life ruined, then he should have doubled up on the birth control.

God, he seems way less of an asshole than his father. How did that happen?"

"His mother raised him."

"Well, buy that woman a beer because she deserves it."

I bit the bottom of my cupcake and, holy shit, it tasted good. It tasted like pure moist sugary magic. It was the first thing in three weeks that didn't taste like cardboard. "Oh my God, I think I just came. This is so good."

"Do you need to be alone with your cupcake?"

"Maybe. I think I need to rowboat out onto the river Seine in Paris and make out with my cupcake. God. This is like heaven in my mouth."

"So it's good?" Rory asked in amusement.

I tried to explain. "You don't understand. For a month every single thing I put in my mouth made me gag and tasted like someone dumped something metallic into it. This is the first thing that tastes like food and it's awesome. I want to make love to this cupcake."

"At least you're being romantic about your cupcake. Moonlight rowboating, Paris, making love. Your cupcake is more than just a piece of ass to you." Rory grinned at me.

"Speaking of a piece of ass, Jonathon is texting you." Jessica gestured to my phone sitting on the table.

"Hey!" I said, offended. "He's not a piece of ass."

"No?" Jessica looked pleased that she had gotten me to admit that so easily.

"No." I stuck my tongue out at her before checking to see

what he'd written. "Pieces of ass aren't so concerned with my iron count."

"He asked about your iron count?"

"Yes. He's afraid I'm anemic." Jonathon had just asked me how I was.

I wrote back, "It's my birthday today." Because, well, why not? It was my birthday.

Really? Happy Birthday! How old?

21. ☹

Ah, I'm sorry. ☹ Do you have any plans?

Just a hot date with a half-eaten cupcake.

Do you want some company?

Hell to the yeah.

If you're not busy. I'm back living at my place.

I'm never too busy for you.

If I weren't already pregnant, I would have dropped an egg at the swoon-worthy quality of that statement.

K. Thx. ☺

Rory and Jessica were both looking at me with knowing eyes. "Stop," I groaned.

"Tyler said he heard you guys messing around," Rory said.

"Tyler needs to mind his own business."

"He wasn't trying to listen, but apparently it was kind of obvious."

"So? Jonathon was just trying to make me feel better."

Jessica laughed. "How convenient for him. Let me make you feel better via penetration. And he didn't even have to use a condom. It's like he hit the sexual jackpot."

"For your information, we didn't have sex. He just got me off," I said, with as much dignity as anyone can have issuing that statement. "And I don't think it can be considered the sexual jackpot considering one, how shitty I look right now, and two, he will be paying for this for the next eighteen years." Hearing that number out loud made me feel green. I shoved the cupcake away from me. That was a long time to be involved with someone. Freak-out time.

"Hey, sorry, I wasn't being judgmental." Jessica looked like she felt guilty. "Sometimes you really should just smack me. My mouth gets carried away."

"It's okay. I just, I don't know. It's just weird to be sort of involved but not really with Jonathon. I never know what I'm supposed to do, or what I'm allowed to say. But you know what? Fuck it. It's my birthday. I'm going to say whatever I want."

"What do you want to say?"

What *did* I want to say? For me, who was never at a loss for words, I had no idea. There were too many thoughts, too many emotions. I was never good at editing my own words so now, when talking about him, it just seemed safer to not say anything at all. So I went for the generic laugh they were expecting. "That I want me some booty."

We all laughed. Hey, that wasn't a lie. I did want Jonathon.

But in what way?

CHAPTER TEN

"WHAT THE HELL ARE YOU DOING?" DEVON ASKED ME AS HE walked into our apartment.

"I'm questioning the next step in evolution because my opposable thumbs are fucking useless," I said, accidentally taping my finger to the box instead of the wrapping paper. "How do people do this?"

"They don't. They buy gift bags. Why exactly are you wrapping a present?" He dumped his messenger bag on the table next to the mess I'd made. "My birthday is in July."

"It's Kylie's birthday," I said absently, forcing the corner of the pink paper onto the box and securing it with three pounds of tape. It looked like a two-year-old had wrapped it.

"Oh yeah? Is it required to get your baby mama a birthday present? I'll make a mental note."

"Don't use that phrase, I hate it. It's demeaning." I peeled the sticky back off the bow and set it lopsided on my shitty wrap job. Feeling stress, I groaned. "This looks terrible. I give up."

Devon rooted around in the fridge and emerged with a soft drink. "You look like you're going to have an aneurysm. Calm down."

"I didn't know it was her birthday until two hours ago," I said. "The pressure is killing me. I didn't know what to get her. I can't do jewelry because that's too personal. Electronics are cold and too expensive. I can't do something pregnancy or baby related because this is about her, not the baby. I just wanted to do something small and stupid so she would know I was thinking about her but I can't just hand it to her. I needed to wrap it. And now, we have this." I gestured to my hot-mess present.

"Okay, you sound like a girl. Just wanted to point that out so maybe you can draw your balls back out of your body." He took a sip. "And saying you can't get her jewelry because it's too personal when you are having a baby together is ironic as hell. But I get it. So here." He reached over and undid the wrap job.

"Hey!"

"I'm fixing it." He balled up the paper after removing the bow and took another square of the wrapping paper. "Right angles, dude. Come on. This is basic math." He made a couple of folds to create triangles and lifted them over the top. "Give me a piece of tape."

I obeyed and he secured the fold and efficiently turned and did it to the other side. He flipped the box over and it didn't look half bad. "See?"

"Thanks, man." I took a deep breath and drummed my fingers on the table. "I don't know how to do this shit."

"What shit? Wrap presents or have a relationship with a girl you barely know?"

"Both. I think the second one is probably a bigger issue, though."

He sat down across me and studied me with his dark eyes. "You're into her, aren't you? I mean, aside from the literal interpretation of that statement, which we already know for a fact."

I laughed. "Pig." I put the bow back on the package.

"That's not really an answer."

Because I was avoiding the question. I had no idea how I felt about Kylie. Which was a lie. I knew exactly how I felt about her. I liked her. A lot. Seeing her made me . . . pleased. "I have a certain reaction to her, I'm not going to deny that."

Devon raised his eyebrows. "Seriously?"

Hey. So I wasn't used to discussing my emotions. Sue me. "What do you want me to say?"

"Nothing. I just think that if you like this chick, you should just see where it goes. Why are you making such a big deal about it?"

"It is a big deal. If I fuck things up I still have to communicate with her for the rest of our frickin' lives."

"That is heavy shit. True. But I see three possible scenarios here. One, you end up with her. Like being together raising your kid and the whole happily ever after crap. Two, you have a polite friendship with each other and you eventually both end up marrying someone else. Three, you communicate through the courts and trash-talk each other. Which one appeals to you the most?"

One. "Two is the most practical."

"I didn't ask you what is the most practical, dick face. I asked you which one you want."

"Fine. One." Why was that so hard to admit? "But two is realistic."

"Is it? If you both dig each other but you pussy out and just try to have a friendship, how is that going to work when you're both involved with someone else? Is it going to make you feel friendly and happy for her or just pissed off when she marries some dude who is with your kid all the time?"

When he put it that way . . . "I don't think I would like that." In fact, I would hate it. Sure, eventually I could learn to deal with it, but what if it happened in just a few months? What if she was with someone by the time the baby was born? The thought made me feel like my head was going to explode off my shoulders.

"Because let's face it, you may be single until you're thirty-eight, but she won't be. Chicks like that have guys lined up to marry them."

I frowned. "Thanks, asshole."

"It's true. It's part of their culture. Meet, mate, marry."

"Who is 'they'? Conversely, who are 'we'? And what is our culture?" He made us sound like aliens.

"We're nerds. We meet, we mate occasionally, we educate, then around forty we hyphenate our name with someone else's as we recognize our cells are no longer regenerating themselves and we'll eventually need someone to push our wheelchair."

"That is a ridiculous generalization." Yet three months ago that was pretty much how I had seen it going down for me.

"Is it?" He gave me a mocking grin. "Is it, really? Then fine, go for option two and see how it plays out for you. Maybe she'll invite you to her wedding as a courtesy so you can make sure your daughter doesn't jack up her flower-girl dress because she's going to be two years old when it happens, max. Trust me on this."

I decided that Devon was an evil genius. But he had forced me to see that the supposed simple reality wasn't that simple, really. Ironic.

So if taking the easy way out wasn't a guarantee of simplicity, the risk of pursuing option one wasn't actually statistically as large of a risk as originally seemed.

I stood up, grabbing the present. "Sometimes, I think you actually make sense."

"You're welcome. I expect to be named godfather."

"You're not even Christian."

"Neither are you."

"Rendering that statement even more ridiculous." I waved to him. "But thanks for the man talk. Don't wait up."

"Enjoy spreading your seed with abandon."

Now there was an utterly creepy way to look at it. I laughed. "You are a poet."

But despite Devon's warped view of the world, I did feel better. No matter what I did, there would be a risk involved, so I might as well go for what I truly wanted.

And what I truly wanted was Kylie.

SHE LOOKED AMAZING WHEN SHE OPENED THE DOOR AND stepped aside so I could enter her tiny apartment. There was color back in her face and her hair had a little more volume than in recent weeks. Her lips were shiny, her eyes bright. She was wearing a tight red sweater with a V neck, and her fuller breasts were bursting out of the top, making my mouth water. Because her chest was bigger the sweater was a little too small now, and it kept riding up on her stomach, exposing a ribbon of flesh that I wanted to lick from one side straight to the other and on down, into her jeans. While her jeans were baggy, they were a step up from the constant workout pants she'd been wearing, and I could see the physical evidence of her morning sickness receding. I was relieved. And turned on. Very turned on.

"Hi." She smiled.

Without hesitation I bent down and kissed her, for real, on the lips. She was caught off guard, but after a heartbeat, she kissed me back, her fingers hooking onto the waist of my jeans.

"Happy birthday," I murmured.

"Thanks." She was blushing a little as she took a step back and that fascinated me, pleased me. I didn't think it was nerves that made her cheeks turn pink. It was that she was attracted to me, the same way I was attracted to her. More than sexual, though that was pulsing between us. It was more than that.

I handed her the box that Devon had wrapped.

"Oh! You didn't have to do that."

I shrugged. "It's nothing big. But even on an hour's notice I wanted to get you something. Twenty-one is a big deal."

She gave me a rueful look. "So I'm a woman now, is that it?"

That would be my dick hardening. Damn. Did she have to say things like that? "Oh, I think you were a whole lot of woman before today." I kicked my shoes off and peeled my jacket down.

Tossing it on the floor, I took her free hand and went to the bed so we could sit down.

She took the bow off the box and stuck it in her hair. "How do I look?"

"Beautiful."

She rolled her eyes, but she looked pleased. "I did shower and brush my teeth today."

"What else could you possibly need?"

"An esthetician."

"I don't even know what that is."

"Really? I can't believe there is actually something I know that you don't."

She was carefully undoing each piece of tape and slowly folding back each triangle. My lame gift was going to get lamer if she put this much consideration into undoing it. "I'm sure there are plenty of things you know that I don't." Like how it was possible that she could just be sitting there with breasts like that and not want to touch them.

Finally she was into the box and she gave a laugh and shot me a big smile. "Jonathon! Hot pink chip-free nail polish? It's perfect."

"I thought maybe one less thing on your shit list would be helpful."

"Definitely." She held up her hands. "I actually went and got a manicure today with a gift card from my mom because I couldn't stand my wretched nails, but I really shouldn't have. The gift card was supposed to be for maternity clothes. But now I will be able to do my nails at home, chip-free. Excellent."

The nail color she had on was almost identical to the one I'd picked out. I felt a little smug that I had gauged her preference so accurately. "I don't think you need maternity clothes just yet. You're like a buck fifteen and your stomach is concave."

"Concave?" She tilted her head.

"Inverted." I demonstrated with my hand.

"Ah. Well, I'll be fat before you know it," she said, but she sounded pretty cheerful about the whole thing.

Feeling better was clearly improving her mood, too. Not that she had ever been grouchy, but she had just sighed a lot. "You'll be gorgeous no matter what."

"Holy crap, you are being so complimentary to me. I should have my birthday every day. Why so sweet today? Do you have an ulterior motive?"

"Well, I do want in your pants," I told her truthfully. "But every word I'm saying is the God's honest truth."

She laughed. "Speaking of God, are you Jewish?"

That was a change of subject I wasn't prepared for. I was more ready to explore the whole getting-in-her-pants thing. "Technically, yes, though neither one of my parents are practicing. I didn't even make my bar mitzvah. Why?"

"Just wondering."

Maybe she could wonder that a different day, because I did not feel like having a theological discussion at the moment. "So did you want to go somewhere? Or watch a movie?"

"Whatever."

I reached out and cupped her cheek. "Why don't you think about it while I kiss you?"

Her eyes widened. "Okay."

"I think a lot about the way you taste," I told her, running my finger over her bottom lip. "I think about you a lot in general."

"I think about you, too," she said, her chest starting to rise and fall faster.

When I gave her a soft kiss, she actually shivered. "I want to spend more time with you," I said. "I don't want to see other people. I want to see what there is between us, because it's starting to feel like something real."

Then because I didn't want her to reject the idea, I didn't give her time to respond. I kissed her again, insistently sliding my tongue between her lips, while my hand cupped her breast and teased her nipple. Her arms came around my neck and I tilted her down onto the bed. She stared up at me, her eyes soft and filled with desire.

"It *is* real," she said, with complete confidence.

That was all I needed to hear. I had her shirt and my shirt off in about thirty seconds. "If anything hurts just tell me to stop."

She laughed breathlessly, her hair sticking up a little from where I had yanked her sweater. "I'm not a virgin. Obviously."

"But things might be . . . tender." I brushed my mouth across the satin-smooth curves that her bra couldn't even come close to containing. I sucked the flesh. She gave me a soft moan of approval.

"I'll tell you if it does," she said. "But I feel more achy than tender. I can't wait to feel you inside me." Her hips lifted in invitation to accompany her words.

And that would be the sound of all my blood going south and

my brain atrophying instantly. Holy fucking shit. Could she be any hotter?

"I had planned to take this slow, but maybe I shouldn't." Even as I spoke I was stripping my jeans off.

Given that she was wiggling out of her own jeans, she seemed to agree. "I promise when the morning sickness is totally gone I'll give you head," she said, breathless, breasts jiggling enticingly as she worked the pants down.

And she did it again. Rendered me a complete drooling idiot with her words. "You're not required to give me head," I said, voice gruff as I threw both our jeans off the bed. "You can if you want at some point, but only ever do what you want. Do you understand me? Seriously." I didn't want her to feel obligated to suck me or anything else.

For a second, her eyes shuttered and I remembered that her asshole ex had cheated on her. Did she doubt her ability to hold a guy's interest? That was insane. Beyond insane. Incomprehensible.

I would just have to prove to her that if I was with her, I was never going to be tempted to stray. "How's my beard?" I asked, because it was clear the conversation made her uncomfortable.

She giggled. "The longest yet, I think."

"See what you do to me? You make me a beast." I rubbed my chin lightly over her shoulder and chest.

"That tickles."

I slipped my hand inside her panties and stroked her. "How about that? Does that tickle?"

"I'm not laughing, so what do you think?"

"I think you're already wet, that's what I think." She had also clearly not been shaving. She had wispy hair that I gave a playful tug to.

But she was instantly apologizing. "Sorry, I should have shaved. But grooming is so much work and I've been so tired . . . I'm sorry."

"I don't care, seriously. Either way is fine with me." I absolutely meant that. "All I care about is access, I don't worry about the finer details. It's your business, not mine."

"Really?" She arched up to meet my touch, push my finger deeper. "I'm not sure I should believe you."

"Then just let me show you." She started to speak, but I put my finger on her mouth. "Shh. Just let me make love to you, Kylie."

Her eyes widened in surprise. I was next to her but our bodies weren't touching except for my thumb sliding across her clitoris. I moved my hand so that I could roll her onto me, our skin touching from toe to tip. "This okay? You're not dizzy?"

"It's fine. Actually, it's more than fine."

I would agree with that assessment. Her body was warm and smooth, her ass high and tight as I ran my hands over it. She put her hands on either side of my head to kiss me, her hair surrounding me, a soft golden curtain cocooning us. When she kissed me it wasn't just a couple of mouths mashing together. There was an odd vulnerability about her, like she was waiting for the sincerity between us to evaporate, for something different, something I couldn't even fathom. Her arms trembled a little from holding herself up and her eyes were glassy, filled with passion and a certain shyness.

She was the most beautiful girl I'd ever been in bed with and I traced her cheek, her nose, her lips, brushing my palm across her long eyelashes. "I hope our baby looks like you. You're so pretty."

"If she has your brain, she'll rule the world."

"We complement each other, you know," I told her, kissing her softly. "We're a good fit."

She sighed in anticipation as I moved my hands down and lifted her waist up, angling her hips.

"Do you like to be on top?" I asked her, teasing between her legs with my fingers. She shifted anxiously.

"It's my favorite."

"The birthday girl should definitely get her favorite."

I moved my hand so that I could push inside her and we both groaned. Yeah. No condom was better. No question about it.

"I'm so glad I'm pregnant," she breathed.

"What? Why?" I lay there for a second, just feeling the tight squeeze of her moist passage around me. Hot thick saliva was in my mouth and I gripped her waist tightly, urging her to sit up so I could see her moving on me.

"Because we don't have to use condoms, silly."

"Totally worth it," I told her solemnly, and as she started to rock up and down on me, I basically believed it. Damn. That was amazing.

The view was stellar as she started to find her rhythm, hands on my chest, her breasts heavy and full as they rocked with her body. I reached up and skimmed my hands over her nipples as she bit her lip in pleasure, hair swinging forward. I could see my cock disappearing into her each time she pumped her hips and I watched it intently, fascinated and aroused and seriously, crazy infatuated with her. I wanted to stay in that little room, with her, forever. I would survive on sex, I was sure it was possible.

Sex and love.

I was starting to fall in love with her. It was the way she looked at me, so sensual, yet guileless, and like she thought I was really something very impressive. Like she was a little in awe of me. I wanted to be worthy of that.

It wasn't possible to fall in love with someone you didn't know all that well.

But then again, she was no longer a stranger.

And it was easy to fall for someone who embraced such a huge responsibility and change with a smile. Who was so genuinely kind, sweet.

Chemistry was about reactions and that first night we'd met, she had responded to my scent, and here we were. Having the best sex ever. And a baby.

"Oh, Jonathon," she breathed, her skin dewy, her clavicle area a deep pink from heat and arousal. Goose bumps rose on her skin as she moved, arching her back, hands buried in her hair. She was going freestyle. I loved it.

When she came, I watched her, just appreciating the shudder of her shoulders, the glassy ecstasy in her eyes, the tightness of her grip on the roots of her hair. I was holding her so tight I was probably bruising her, but it kept me in control, let me stay still so she could do whatever she wanted, so she could take her pleasure.

She collapsed forward onto my chest with a moan. "OMG. That was . . . immense."

"It's not over yet." Holding her carefully, I turned her onto her back and I slid back out. Not giving her time to protest I went down on her. And immediately noticed she had changed there, too. "You're so . . . swollen. Holy shit, it's the hottest thing ever."

"It feels different, too," she said. "Oh, God . . ."

This would be the side effect of increased blood flow. I liked it. I sucked on her soft flesh and worked her with my tongue. Her piercing was endlessly fascinating to me and I played with it, tugging with my teeth. But as her wiggling increased and her moans grew more raw, I stopped indulging myself with exploring and got down to business. I liked the sound she made when she had an orgasm. It was a soft cry of surprise every time, like she couldn't believe something could feel so good.

It made me pull back, wiping my mouth as I moved over her. She was breathing hard and reaching for me. It did something weird to my gut, to see her like that, so sexy, looking up at me, hand out. I felt connected to her then, in a way I had never had before with another girl. Woman. This was going to be an adult relationship. Not a fantastical high school crush that flared and died. Not a casual companionship or a college, drama-filled disaster. But a real thing, where we shared a life.

I waited for it to be terrifying, to shock me into losing my erection, to make me say something stupid and asshole-ish so she wouldn't assume too much.

But it wasn't.

And I didn't.

And she couldn't. Because there wasn't too much.

As I pushed inside her, enjoying the freedom of no protection,

I pulled her leg over my hip so we were locked even closer together. "I may be getting addicted to you," I told her.

Her nails dug in to my back. "You can have me whenever you want."

Hell, yeah.

For the first time since that life-altering moment when she had sat across the table and told me she was pregnant, I felt at peace. More than at peace. I felt lucky.

This.

It was right.

CHAPTER ELEVEN

MY TWIN BED WAS TOO SMALL FOR TWO PEOPLE, BUT IT WAS better than the couch at Rory and Tyler's, and I liked cuddling up close to Jonathon, our naked bodies still moist and warm. I felt post-orgasm satisfied and I trailed my fingers over the marks and numbers of his tattoo, content. He was a generous guy in bed, focusing on me, and I felt a little guilty for letting him do that, but at the same time, duh, I enjoyed it. There was something so easy about being with him. I didn't worry that I wasn't sexy enough, or kinky enough, or that at an important moment in the action, he would suggest how hot it would be if I did another chick in front of him, ruining my orgasm with the self-doubt that raised.

I didn't think for one minute that Jonathon would want me making out with a girl in front of him. He was definitely a one-on-one guy. He made eye contact the whole time he was inside me and it was so foreign to me sometimes I had to fight the urge to look away, afraid he would see how hard I was falling for him. I didn't want to scare him off, but I didn't know how to play the game with someone like him, because I didn't think that he knew that games existed. He was straightforward, logical.

Yet there was something wonderfully romantic about him. The fact that he had given any thought to a birthday present for me made my heart squeeze. Any other guy would've gone for a desperate last-ditch box of chocolates or worse, a helium balloon. But he had given me something that showed that even coffee- and sleep-deprived, he listened. I kissed his shoulder on that thought and in response he squeezed my butt, his hand resting comfortably there.

"What are you thinking about?" I asked him, because he had his thinking face on, the one that said he was calculating.

"You don't want to know."

I sat up, not liking the sound of that. "Why? What are you thinking?"

"I don't think I should say. You might misconstrue."

He didn't want to see me anymore. He found me boring. He wanted a DNA test done. "I'm going to think up so many horrible things, that whatever you say can't possibly be as bad. Don't torment me."

Glancing over at me, he looked surprised. "Kylie, it's nothing horrible. No. Sorry. It's just my creepy science mind at work. I was thinking how bizarre it is that a parasite is growing in you and will eventually explode from your body through an extremely narrow opening, and yet you will both survive."

My jaw dropped. "Jonathon, oh my God!" The things he said . . . and he actually looked amused at the thought. I was not amused. Exploding anything out of my vagina was just not something I wanted to think about. It was a horrible word choice.

"Told you that you wouldn't want to know."

"Our baby is not a parasite!"

"Technically, it is. You're the host." He gave me an amused look. "It's just the way my mind works, I can't help it. I had to take it there because it's a curious process if you think about it."

"I'd rather not." But he was honest, I had to give him that. "And here I was just thinking how romantic you can be."

Now he laughed out loud. "Shit. I ruined that, didn't I?"

"Totally. I'm sure you'll figure out how to make it up to me."

"Oh yeah?" He gave me a sexy smile. "Does it involve this?" He kissed me, his tongue slipping into my mouth.

"Mmm." I loved the way he kissed. It was exploratory, slow, like he had all the time in the world to taste me.

Fingers walked down my ass and between my legs. "Does it involve this?"

He was stroking me from behind and I felt lazy, my arousal less urgent than it had been before. "Mmm," I repeated, before kissing him again, tracing the muscles of his chest and down his abs.

After a few minutes I buried my mouth on his shoulder and let the pulsating reverberate through my whole body. "Oh, you're so good at that." He always knew right where to touch and the perfect pressure.

"I like seeing you enjoying yourself."

I actually believed him. "You know what else I would enjoy?"

"I would enjoy that, too, trust me, but I need a couple more minutes, babe."

Oops. Too bad that wasn't what I was talking about. "I was actually going to say I would like some ice cream."

"What?" He patted my butt. "And here I thought you were as hot for me as I am for you."

"I am! But I'm hungry. I can't help it. Today I actually ate half of a bagel and half a cupcake, and didn't feel sick. Now for some reason, my stomach is growling and I really, really want ice cream."

"You're the birthday girl. Ice cream it is." Jonathon pulled his phone off the nightstand and squinted at it. "It's only eight. There should be an ice cream place open still. Unless you want a pickle to go with it. Then we can just go to the grocery store."

"I don't want a pickle." I peeled myself off his chest, shivering a little as the cool air hit my breasts. "Ick."

"I thought that was de rigueur for pregnant women."

"I don't know what de rigueur even means but pickles are like slimy cucumbers. Gross."

"They are pickled cucumbers."

"Well, I know that. I just mean . . . never mind. The thought of pickles is icking me out."

"We definitely don't want to ick you out."

Yawning, I found my bra wedged under Jonathon's hip and I yanked it out. "I think I need new bras." Stuffing my boobs back in was like forcing cats into a carrier—they just didn't want to go.

"I would agree. You look like you're about to sever all your circulation." Jonathon was on his back pulling his briefs and his jeans up his legs. "Like I said, use the gift card from your mom for that."

"How exciting. Bra shopping for my birthday. Yay, me. And why are my boobs getting so big anyway? It's not like I'm lactating yet. It seems unnecessary. And, ew, did I just say lactating? That is a gross word."

"Lactating is slightly mammalian sounding, I will admit. As to why they are swelling, that I don't know. But I'm not going to complain."

"You don't have to carry them around." I wiggled into my panties.

"I can if you want me to. I'll just hold them whenever you're tired of relying on your bra."

I laughed. "Weirdo."

"My secret is out." He pushed his glasses up his nose and sat up, reaching for his shirt.

The room was dim, like it always was, but I could still see all the lines of his body. His hoodies and plaid shirts hid a lean but muscular body. I liked seeing him naked, butt tight, tattoo sleeve so intricate and black against his light skin. He had slight olive undertones to his skin, but he was fair, and his little beard scruff on his chin grew quickly, a stubbly shock of caramel-colored hair. I didn't know if he was bullshitting me about the whole sexual-anticipation-causing-his-hair-to-grow thing, but I did know that it was soft and I liked the way it tickled my thighs when he was down there.

When I stood up and went to the bathroom before getting dressed, I felt him watching me, too. A glance back showed his stare was appreciative. I felt sexy again, for him, and I blew him a kiss before retreating into the bathroom.

But in a minute my contentment evaporated when I saw there was blood on the toilet paper. It wasn't a lot, just some spotting, but it was enough to shock me. Pulling my panties back up I threw open the door and called to him. "Jonathon, I'm spotting. Oh my God."

My heart was racing, my palms clammy. He looked instantly alarmed but then he stood up and came over to me, his voice reassuring. "Spotting is normal in the first trimester. It's okay. It's not heavy, is it? It's not like a period?"

"No. It was just a pinkish smear."

"That could be from sex even, from your cervix being bumped."

I knew he was right. Sometimes I spotted after a pap but it still scared the shit out of me. I let him hug me, burying my head into his shirt he'd put back on. "Are you sure?"

"What, that I might bump your cervix? Well, I don't mean to brag but . . ."

I smacked his chest. "I'm being serious."

"I am, too. Look." He pulled his phone out of his pocket and started typing one-handed. A few seconds later, he read off his screen. "'Bleeding during pregnancy is common, especially during the first trimester, and usually it's no cause for alarm. About 20 percent of women experience some bleeding in the first twelve weeks of pregnancy.'"

My shoulder relaxed slightly. "Where are you reading that?"

"The Mayo Clinic. I think we can trust them."

I stared up at him, my chin still on his chest. "Everything is okay, right?"

"Absolutely. Now let's go get some ice cream. Though you probably need to put on some clothes first. It is almost February." He tilted my chin up with his index finger and gave me a kiss.

I let out the breath I'd been holding. Funny how five weeks

ago I had been panicked at the thought of being pregnant, now I was panicked at the thought of not being pregnant. Pulling on my clothes, I tried to put it out of my head. It was nothing. Jonathon was right. It was my birthday and we were getting ice cream.

As we stepped outside, it was lightly snowing and Jonathon stuck out his elbow for me to hook my arm through. The air was still, the night quiet. I blinked as the snow softly dropped onto my eyelashes, and the cold filled my lungs and made me feel clean, alive. I was glad to be having my first trimester during winter. The thought of that sour stomach during the heat of July was horrifying. The crisp air always seemed to help calm my icky stomach.

Jonathon let go of me for a minute to slide across the snowy sidewalk, surfer style. I laughed. "You're going to fall."

"Nah." He did it again, his arms flailing as he momentarily lost his balance.

"So how do you get all those muscles?" I asked him. "Are you a secret gym fan? Are you really pumping iron when you say you're in the lab?"

"Pumping some Fe, you mean?" He gave me a grin as he stopped and waited for me, reaching for my hand.

"Seriously?" I laughed. "Not that I can say anything because I think I started the stupid chemistry jokes."

"I think you did. But no, I don't spend hours in the gym. I work for a moving company on Saturdays and Wednesdays. Hauling boxes and furniture keeps me in decent shape. How about you?" He leaned down and whispered in my ear, "You have some amazing thigh strength."

How was it he could make me blush like that? He could be so

truly nerdy, yet he made me feel way more shy than Nathan or any other cocky douche bag I'd dated before. "I played volleyball, remember?"

"Oh, right. Bump. I should start calling you that. It really applies now."

I was sorry I had reminded him. "But now I do zumba and Pilates, though not since before Christmas. No energy."

"Maybe you should try yoga instead for the next few months."

It was a good idea. "Will you go with me?" I don't know why I asked that. It was something I would ask Jessica or Rory, not a guy. Nathan would have told me no, then asked to see my legs over my head, if I had asked him that.

But Jonathon just shrugged. "Sure. If I can fit it in my schedule. I've never tried it because it's a bit of a challenge for me to quiet my mind."

Pleased that he was willing to go with me, I nudged him with my hip. "You can just think about the parasite quality of our baby while you meditate."

"Fair enough." Jonathon held the door of the ice cream shop open for me.

It was one of those places where you pile on your own toppings and they weigh the final creation. Jonathon got chocolate ice cream and then loaded it with gummy worms, sprinkles, cookie crumbles, chocolate sauce, and a cherry on top. It looked like something an eight-year-old boy with a gift card to burn would have gotten. I got cookie dough with whipped cream. Keep it simple.

We sat down in the warm shop across from each other, Jonathon clearly enjoying his massive mess of sugar. He pulled a worm out and sucked some chocolate sauce off and chewed the head aggressively.

"Oh, gross." For some reason it sparked a memory of the Christmas green bean casserole, which had reminded me of real worms. My cheeks puffed out as my gag reflex started.

Contrite, he popped it all the way into his mouth. "Sorry."

"It's okay. Eventually this will go away, right?" I took a teeny bit of my ice cream. The cold did taste good in my mouth. "I do feel a lot better. And, thank you, by the way, for the ice cream. And everything."

His eyes were warm. "You don't have to thank me."

There were so many things I wanted to say to him. To ask him. Feelings I wanted to share, feelings I wanted to earn. But instead, I just said, "Your dad suggested I drop his class."

Jonathon pulled a face. "Whatever. I know you can pass it if you study."

I wanted to tell him what Professor Kadisch had said to me, but I knew I couldn't. It would just hurt him. "That would be satisfying to pass the class, I have to admit. I need to get back to normal."

"I can study with you if you want. I have it on authority that I'm a really good tutor."

True that. "Will we really study?" I asked him, suspicious. "Or will you distract me?"

"I don't know what you're talking about, Bump." He gave me a grin. "If anyone did the distracting, it was you."

"Me?" I went for indignant, but the truth was, he was probably right. I moved my tongue down my spoon slowly, up and down, enjoying the way his expression changed, his own spoon pausing halfway to his mouth. "I don't know what *you're* talking about." Reaching over I stole his cherry and sucked on the tip.

"Flirt. You know exactly what you're talking about."

I laughed. I hadn't felt this good, this easy, with someone since long before RAN. He was right—I was flirting with him. And enjoying every second of it. "What's your favorite Disney movie?" I asked him.

"My favorite Disney movie? And Kylie gets the award for the most random question ever."

I laughed. "I'm serious. I think it says a lot about who you are. I'm trying to get to know you."

"Via cartoon?" He licked his spoon. "I'm not sure I've seen a whole lot of Disney movies. I was more a Harry Potter kind of kid."

"Okay. So which house would you be at Hogwarts?"

"Ravenclaw." There was zero hesitation in his voice.

"Why?"

"Because they value intelligence. You have to answer a riddle to enter the dorms, how freaking cool is that?"

It was a good fit for him. "I agree, you're totally Ravenclaw. I think I'm Hufflepuff."

"I don't know. I see a lot of Gryffindor in you. You're brave and resourceful."

I wasn't sure how true that was. "That's a stretch. I think I fit more with the Hufflepuff loyalty-and-hard-work kind of attitude."

"We'll have to ask the sorting hat."

Jonathon's ice cream was almost gone. I wasn't sure how he

had consumed that much in the same time I'd had three small bites. "I guess you like chocolate."

"I guess I do. And you like whipped cream. That's the majority of what you've eaten."

"Don't hate. I like dairy."

"Honey, the whole thing is dairy."

"Which is why I like it."

He laughed. "I have a hard time following your logic."

"That's because it's the world according to Kylie. I just say whatever is in my head, whether it makes sense or not." I might as well make that clear while he still had time to escape. Not that he could escape entirely, but he didn't have to be involved with me.

The thought that he might not want to made me more determined than ever that he would. I wanted to laugh and cuddle and spend more and more time with him.

"I find you to be super cute," he told me. "And as long as your logic makes sense to you, then I see nothing wrong with it. Just be patient with me if I stare blankly at you."

"It's a deal."

"Your ice cream is melting."

"I think I'm finished." I actually felt full from a few spoonfuls of whip and ice cream. Geez.

"Can I have it?"

"Go for it."

His eyes lit up in pleasure. I laughed. "And here I thought I was the ice cream whore."

"Now who's hating?"

I pushed it over and watched him pack away the rest of my dessert, looking very satisfied.

I knew the feeling. I was very satisfied.

And falling in love with him.

I was. I could deny it all I wanted. I could tell myself not to hope for something permanent and wonderful with Jonathon, but I couldn't help myself.

I was falling in love with him.

When we got back to my place he made love to me again, slowly, deliciously, and I didn't have to ask if he was planning to spend the night. I'd never thought of sex as making love, not once, until Jonathon had referred to it that way. It seemed so retro, and while before I might have thought it was cheesy, now it seemed right. It wasn't fucking, it wasn't just sex, something you could do with anyone. It was intimate and warm and emotional.

Jonathon pulled the blankets up over our naked bodies and set his glasses on the nightstand. "Mm. Happy birthday, Kylie."

"Thank you." I kissed him and felt my heart swell knowing that my wish had already come true.

I had wished on my cupcake candle to be with Jonathon and here I was. Here we were. A couple. He had said he didn't want to see other people. Just me.

He+Me= We.

I sighed, feeling goofy and happy and more than a little bit in love.

But then I woke up at three in the morning feeling like the sheet below me was wet, and that perfect night was over in an instant.

CHAPTER TWELVE

I'D NEVER BEEN ONE TO REMEMBER MY DREAMS BUT I KNOW
that I was dreaming that my head was under water, a hand holding me down in the warm silent bath, drowning me. I couldn't
breathe, yet I wasn't scared. I was warm and focused, curious. I
could see Kylie's reflection in the porcelain of the tub . . .

Waking up with a jerk, I sucked in a breath and tried to focus
in the dark.

"Jonathon." Kylie was turned toward me, shaking me.

"What? What's wrong?" I couldn't see well, between the lack
of light and lack of glasses, but her voice sounded urgent.

"I think I'm bleeding."

Even as she said it, I became aware of a hot sticky feeling on
the sheet beneath my thigh and her. I scrambled up, grabbing for
my glasses and the light switch on the lamp. "I'm turning the
light on."

I did, and before I could even turn back around and see, she gave a cry of dismay.

"Oh, God!" Then she started crying.

Shit.

When I faced her and stared down below her waist, it was worse than I expected. "Holy fuck . . ."

There was blood everywhere. It formed a dark circle underneath her and was smeared over her legs, my knee, her hands where she had obviously reached down to feel between her thighs. It was shocking red on her pale pink floral sheets, and the air smelled tinny and sharp. My stomach turned when I saw that there were clots in the puddle. Since Kylie had been sleeping naked, it was clear to me what I was looking at.

For a second, I couldn't think, couldn't breathe. It was gruesome. It was obvious.

She was trying to sit up, weeping, her nose running. When she wiped it she got blood on herself. The sight of that, the sharp red on her petite nose jerked me out of my frozen horror. "Shh, shh, okay." I helped her up, scooting her back out of the mess. "Do you have any of those, um, what are they called?" Damn, my mind was like river mud. I couldn't think of the word I was searching for. "Those things with wings when you have your period."

Kylie shook her head. "No. I just have tampons."

"I don't think you should use one of those. We can stop at the store on the way to the ER."

"You think I should go to the ER?"

"Yes, definitely." I was already out of bed and getting dressed.

"I had a miscarriage, didn't I?" she asked.

The look on her face, holy shit. It cut me. She looked devastated, raw, her eyes huge, shiny with her tears that hadn't fallen yet. "I don't know, sweetheart, but it doesn't look so good. But we'll have to see what the doctor says." Though I couldn't imagine the doctor was going to say anything other than that she'd miscarried. There was just so much blood. "Do you have any cramps or anything?"

She shook her head. "My back hurts, but that's it."

Tearing through her dresser I found her panties and yoga pants plus a T-shirt and sweatshirt. Screw the bra. She pulled everything on with shaking fingers while I crammed my feet in my shoes and yanked on my coat. I wasn't sure what I was feeling. When she had said she was spotting earlier, I honestly hadn't thought that it was a big deal. This was a big deal.

I took her hand and led her to the door. She walked tentatively, her legs clamped together. I put her coat over her shoulders like a cape and she shuffled to my car, her hand squeezing mine tightly.

Then it was a tense two hours, a blur of the drugstore, the waiting room, the bed where she removed her pants at the nurse's request and I saw the rust-colored stains all over her thighs, the fresh red spot on her panties. The moment when the technician had shook her head, ultrasound wand going, and murmured, "Oh, sweetie, I'm so sorry. I can't find a heartbeat."

So that was that. No heartbeat. No baby. The baby was back on the bedsheet.

I wasn't sure what I felt. Numb. In shock. I murmured to Kylie words I didn't remember later, words that I meant to be comforting, and I ran my hand over the back of her hair when she turned her head into my chest to cry. I held her while the doctor came in and there was a discussion of whether or not to conduct a D&C to ensure all tissue had been removed from her uterus, but I didn't feel anything. It was like I was still trapped in my dream, under water, head moving slowly, oxygen gone from my lungs.

I heard Kylie ask if we shouldn't have been having sex and the nurse assuring her that intercourse never caused a miscarriage.

I spoke. I had a whole conversation with the doctor where I discussed that Kylie was otherwise healthy, that she'd been ten weeks along, that it was the first time she'd had bleeding, but I wasn't sure how I spoke because I didn't feel like I was there. "I think that would be better," I agreed, when he said he would prefer to just give her medication to evacuate her uterus as opposed to the more invasive D&C. That he suspected she was mostly cleaned out given the volume of blood we had described.

Cleaned out.

Maybe that was an apt description for my own insides. I felt cleaned out.

"What time is it?" Kylie asked suddenly, her skin blotchy from crying, eyes swollen. She seemed calmer.

"It's almost six."

"I want to call my mom."

I looked to the nurse for permission and she nodded. "Go ahead. I won't tell."

Kylie had left her purse at the apartment so I handed her my phone and she dialed the number manually.

It wasn't until her mother answered that all of my emotion came roaring back to life.

"Mommy?" Kylie said, voice shaky. "I lost the baby."

Her face crumpled and she broke down in sobs and I had to leave. I couldn't hear her pain. I couldn't listen to how young and heartbroken she sounded, or see the agony on her face. My own sorrow appeared out of nowhere and I felt tears in my eyes. I grabbed blindly at the curtain, desperate to escape, muttering to the nurse, "I'll be right back."

The look of sympathy she gave me only made it worse and I walked out of the ER and straight outside to the cold parking lot. Dawn was breaking and I paced back and forth in front of the doors, making them open and shut as I tripped the sensors. I swiped at my eyes, angry. Sad.

So there was to be no Baby Charlie.

There was to be no piece of me and Kylie.

It hurt more than I could have ever imagined.

I TOOK HER HOME TO MY APARTMENT, WHERE THERE WAS NO blood. I tugged off her clothes and mine and I took her into the shower with me. I held her under the warm stream of water, taking a washcloth to her skin as gently as possible to get rid of the stains. She just stood there, against me, face swollen, fingers shaking as she covered her breasts, like she was cold. Getting out, I wrapped a towel around her and led her to my bed, holding her tight in my arms, because I didn't know what else to do. What else to say.

She had been given a sleeping pill at the hospital, and it surprised me but within a few minutes of lying down, she had fallen into a restless sleep. I could hear Devon get up and start to move around the kitchen. I waited until I heard him leave before I carefully slipped out of bed and pulled on a clean pair of jeans. Grabbing my phone I went into the other room and dumped some coffee in the machine. I wasn't going to be able to sleep.

I'd never given much thought to being a father until Kylie and her surprise news. Devon was right. Researchers, academics, a lot of us tended to wait until almost forty and even beyond to think about a family, children. I had relegated the thought to later, much later. But then I had warmed up to the idea, the concept of an infant alien but intriguing. I felt betrayed. Like fate had yanked my chain. What kind of a mind-fuck was that? Hey, take this, you'll like it, and when you do . . . oh, never mind.

Except I didn't believe in fate. I never had. Nothing happened for any particular reason other than one which could be explained by science, facts. Kylie didn't miscarry because the joke was on me, she miscarried because there was a chromosomal abnormality in the fetus and her body had done as nature intended. But that sounded so harsh, so awful. Like we had failed somehow to create a perfect fetus and that her body was the host I had mused about, expelling the parasite. All of it sounded horrible to me, the science of procreation, and it didn't account or explain how I could feel the way I did. Sure, I could argue that nature intended a male to bond with a female to ensure the survival of his offspring, and therefore his species. Logically, you could break it all down to DNA.

But sitting there, barefoot in the cold kitchen, coffee steaming up in front of my nose as I drank it, I couldn't believe that the nebulous heart that everyone discussed was purely the result of animal instinct and the need to survive. This didn't feel like instinct. This felt like pure emotion. Pain. That's what it was.

A tight, angry despair.

Scrolling through my phone, I hit SEND on the last number that had been called.

"Kylie, honey, how are you?" her mom answered immediately, sounding anxious.

"It's not Kylie, Mrs. Warner, it's Jonathon Kadisch."

"Oh! Hi, Jonathon. Is Kylie okay?"

"We're back at my apartment and she's sleeping. They gave her a sleeping pill at the hospital. I was wondering if you know Jessica's phone number. We left Kylie's phone at her place and I don't know Jessica's number. I wanted to call her and see if she can come here and stay with Kylie while I go take care of . . ." I wasn't sure how to say it. "The bed and stuff at her place."

There was no way I could take Kylie home with the bed looking like a crime scene. And I didn't want to leave her alone in my apartment.

"I see." Her voice was thoughtful. "I think it's very sweet that you're thinking about her, but maybe Kylie needs to see that, to help her process. She is stronger than she looks."

Her response made me uncertain. She thought I was doing it wrong? She should know. She was Kylie's mother, she knew her inside and out. I didn't. "Are you sure?"

"I think so. Kylie is resilient but she does better if she's not allowed to bury her head in the sand. I do have Jessica's number, though, if you have class or work. I think you're right not to leave her alone. She'll probably have a lot of cramping today."

She promised to text me the number and added, "We appreciate everything you're doing for her, Jonathon. You're obviously a good man."

"Thanks. Of course." I almost added that it was the least I could do, but I stopped myself. What did I mean by that? That the whole thing was my fault? That I was obligated to her? That our relationship was one of dependency and stoicism? The thought was so unappealing, I banished it immediately.

Dropping my phone on the table after we said good-bye, I rubbed my forehead with the heel of my hand. What now?

It was a greater question than I was prepared to answer. So I called Jessica.

Then I settled on a compromise between my own opinion and Kylie's mother's and I went to her apartment after Jessica showed up to sit with Kylie, who was still sleeping hard. Stepping inside, the air felt warm, hushed, an unpleasant smell in the air. The bed looked even more stark in the morning light than it had in the dark, the covers hanging half onto the floor, the pillows askew. The large dark stain.

Stripping the sheet off the bed, I carefully folded it over and over until it was the size of a piece of paper, and set it down on the counter of her kitchenette. Something told me she would want it.

Then I remade the bed methodically, with sheets I found in a little plastic storage container in the closet, whose drawers were filled with linens and towels. Under the bathroom sink I found air freshener and sprayed the shit out of the place.

With a final glance back at the room, I left quickly, needing to get out of there, convinced the smell of blood was still in my nostrils. It was merely an olfactory memory, of course, but it was giving me a headache, a pounding starting behind my eyes.

As I walked to class, I wished I had a vice. Heavy drinking. Smoking. A drawer with a secret stash of marijuana.

But my only vices were science and self-absorption.

So I went to the lab, where I felt in control, and where the numbers always added up.

Where the equation could always be solved.

WAKING UP CAME SLOWLY, A GROGGY SENSATION OF WANT-ing to focus, but being unable to keep my eyes open. When I did manage to push off the need to slide back into unconsciousness, I wasn't sure where I was. It was a bedroom I'd never seen before, and for a second, given how sluggish I felt I wondered if I were hungover, if I'd passed out in some random dude's bed.

But then I realized that I wasn't partying the night before, that it wasn't last year. That I had been with Jonathon and I'd woken up bleeding. He'd taken me to the hospital. Then to his place.

I was in his bed, alone, and I was no longer pregnant.

Tears stung the back of my eyelids and I squeezed my nose, which felt swollen. Then I ran my hands down over my flat stomach, unable to comprehend that what had been there no longer was. I'd gotten used to thinking of it as a little seed inside me, growing, and while I hadn't felt anything, obviously, I had mentally imagined it there. Now . . . nothing.

I didn't want to be alone. I wanted Jonathon. Pushing the blankets back, I sat up and swung my legs around. I felt a little cramping, but nothing bad. Nothing like what I imagined I should feel. I could feel the sticky trickle of blood, though, down onto the pad I was wearing, and it skeeved me out. I would never take tampons for granted again. Yanking the blanket around me and tucking it under my armpits so I was wearing it like a dress I went into the other room.

And found Jessica, not Jonathon. "Jess? What are you doing here?"

She was sitting at the kitchen table, books spread out in front of her, though she was playing with her phone. "Oh, hey." She stood up and came over, wrapping her arms around me. "I'm sorry, Kylie bug. I'm so sorry."

I nodded, throat tight. "Where's Jonathon?"

"He had some nerd alert uber urgent lab thing to do so he called me. He didn't think you should be here by yourself in case the bleeding got worse."

"He left?" I pulled out the chair next to her and sat down, surprised, then annoyed with myself for being surprised. "What time is it?"

"It's after eleven."

"Oh." My stomach growled. I was hungry. Seriously, ravenously hungry. It seemed so absolutely cruel and wrong that eight hours after a trauma and suddenly my body was all over it.

Almost like the baby had never happened. I wasn't over it. Not even close. "I'm hungry."

Jessica looked surprised. "We can either go back to my house or we can go out to eat. I don't want to go digging through Jonathon's fridge. Unless you're comfortable with that."

"No. Not really. He has a roommate. I don't know whose food is whose." In fact, this was my first time at his apartment. It was small, but it was definitely a notch up from an average undergrad guy place. He had real furniture, a stylish white table with trendy red chairs. The sofa was low and modern, a charcoal gray, and there was a graphic print hanging on the wall over it.

"Are you up for eating out? That doesn't seem like a good idea."

But I shook my head. "No, it's fine. I feel . . . fine." Which was a lie. I felt empty. My stomach empty. Uterus empty. Heart empty.

But my stomach I could fill. "I'm starving. I want waffles and eggs. Let's go to the pancake house."

Jessica looked dubious, but she nodded. "Okay, sure. If that's what you want."

"Just let me go to the bathroom. Oh, and I don't have my purse. Can I pay you back?"

"I'll just treat you. Think of it as a birthday gift."

I paused, standing up, pain slicing through the numbness I'd been feeling. "I'd forgotten it was my birthday. Well, I guess I'll always remember my twenty-first. Unlike most people who will only have pictures but no memory of what happened. Mine is burned into my brain." I gave a little laugh that sounded hollow and bitter. "Ironic, isn't it?"

"Oh, honey. This sucks."

Jessica clearly didn't know what to say. What was there to say? "Yes. It does." I went into the bathroom and used the toilet, surprised at how little bleeding there actually was now. Washing my hands, I stared at myself in the mirror.

A year ago I was in love with Nathan, giddy, confident that life would always offer me what I needed and wanted. I believed in happy endings and that kindness was always rewarded. Now, seeing my face pale, skin bruised under my eyes, mouth down-turned, I wasn't sure what I believed in any more. Why did I keep getting kicked in the gut? It was like every time I got back on my bike and started pedaling again, a car hit me.

This time I wasn't sure I could get back on.

I SUCKED DOWN THE COFFEE GREEDILY WHILE I WAITED FOR the breakfast I had ordered. Waffles, eggs, bacon, orange juice, and hash browns was probably overkill but my mouth had watered as I studied the menu so I went for it.

"We had sex twice last night," I told Jessica. "I know they say it doesn't matter, but I feel guilty."

Jessica was dumping sugar into her coffee. "That can't have anything to do with it. Thousands of babies are born every day healthy and I seriously doubt all of those parents are remaining celibate. I seriously doubt any of them are. You can't do this to yourself."

Oh, I could. And I was. I knew Jessica was right, but I couldn't help it. I just felt guilty, like I shouldn't have had those cups of coffee, like I should have eaten more, shouldn't have had sex, especially not again after that spotting. Maybe I wasn't qualified to be a mother. Maybe I wasn't qualified to be with Jonathon, who was smart enough to know I shouldn't drink coffee.

"I just feel like there aren't a lot of things I'm good at, you know? But kids I'm good with. I've always felt confident that I'll be a good teacher, and a good mother. But now it's like I've failed at the one thing I should be able to do."

"You're lucky that you just got out of the ER or I would kick your ass for saying something like that. You did *not* fail. And there are a lot of things you're good at. Jesus Christ." She threw her balled-up empty sugar packet on the table. "You will be an amaze balls mother when the time comes. If Mother Teresa had a miscarriage would you say she was a bad mother?"

That made me smile. "Mother Teresa was a nun. She wasn't supposed to be getting preggers."

"Whatever. You get my point."

"I do get your point. And I know you're right. But I need to feel sorry for myself today."

"You're allowed to do that. But you can't trash-talk yourself."

An enormous plate of food was placed in front of me. "I'm going to eat this like it's my job."

"And you should totally do that."

"Don't you have class today?" I asked her as I shoveled a forkful of hash browns into my mouth.

"Yeah, but I skipped for my best friend. She's kind of a big deal to me."

That made me feel a little less sucky. "Thanks. You're a big deal to me, too."

"I didn't tell Rory. I thought you might want to tell her yourself. But I did tell Riley."

"Okay." Everyone was going to know anyway. "I'll call her once I get my phone back. It's at my apartment and Jonathon has the keys."

"He's being great, you know. In case you hadn't noticed that," Jessica said, pouring nine thousand pounds of syrup onto her waffle. She seemed to be on a sugar kick. Being with Riley was good for her. She didn't worry about every single calorie that went into her mouth like she had before. "Jonathon's a keeper."

Grateful my mouth was crammed full of eggs, I just nodded. I knew that Jonathon was a keeper but I also wasn't sure what this would do to our relationship. We were together because of the baby and now there was no baby. Would he still want to be with me? I was a burden to him. I had been from the beginning. It was an unequal relationship, with him being responsible for caring for me. He had been the giver, me the taker.

"Speak of the devil." Jessica picked up her phone. "He's calling me."

"Why is Jonathon calling you?"

"Let me ask my spirit guides for psychic direction." She made a face at me. "I don't know, but I'm guessing it's because he wants to talk to you." She swiped her phone and put it to her ear. "Hello?"

I held my hand out automatically but she sat still, listening to whatever he was saying. Finally she said, "We're at the pancake house. She was hungry. Sorry, I didn't think to text you. I thought you were going to be gone for a while still."

He obviously said something else because she said, "Uh-huh," but then mouthed to me, "talk to him?"

I shook my head rapidly, having a sudden adverse reaction to the thought. I didn't want to talk to him. He would ask me how I was feeling and I would tell him fine and then what? I had nothing to say right now and I didn't want to come across like an asshole by being blah when he had been so amazing the last five weeks.

"Oh, sorry, she's in the restroom. I'll have her call you a little later."

Her eyes widened as he responded. "I think she can go the john by herself. It's okay. I'll have her call her later. Bye." Jessica hung up the phone, looking horrified.

I wasn't that surprised actually. He was hands-on and usually that was a good thing. But at the moment I was feeling a little too helpless, like I needed to reassert my independence.

"WTF. Does he think your uterus is going to drop into the toilet? I'm not accompanying you to the bathroom."

"For which I thank you."

"I guess I can't fault the guy for caring, especially since I live with a guy who refuses to buy my tampons when he goes grocery shopping."

"He is a nice guy." I sighed as I cut my waffle. "He's going to stay with me because he feels guilty," I told her. "Then eventually he'll get sick of me and he'll dump me and it will all be a waste of time that utterly breaks my heart."

Her fork paused halfway to her mouth. "Honestly, I have never heard you talk like this. It's freaking me out. When did you become such a pessimist?"

Was that what had happened? "I'm having a bad day," I said pathetically, tears springing up.

Her face softened. "Of course you are. Do you want me to sing 'The Sun Will Come Out Tomorrow' to you? That's what you always do to me when I'm upset and I end up so annoyed with your cheerfulness that I forget to be sad."

I gave a watery laugh. "Yes. That's exactly what I want you to do."

She did. It was off-key and she had the words almost completely wrong, but she sang her heart out to me, until I was laughing, amazed and grateful that I could.

"Thanks," I told her. "That was the best thing I've heard since I saw a video of Kermit the Frog covering a Bee Gees song."

"I aim to please." Then she started laughing, too, when she held up her phone to show me the screen. It said "Kylie's john." "OMG, your boyfriend is calling again. I guess he figures that was sufficient time to pee."

"I can't believe you saved his number as my john. That does not sound okay."

She shrugged. "It's funny. Now you better answer or he might show up here with a medical team."

Jessica had a point. I took the phone. "Hello?"

"Kylie?"

"Yes. Hi. Sorry I missed your call before." Lie. Total lie.

"That's okay. I just stopped back home to check on you between classes and you weren't there and I started to worry."

"I got hungry so Jess is buying me brunch."

"Okay. That's good that you're eating."

"Yeah."

Awkward silence.

"So you're okay?"

No. "Yeah. How are you? With everything?" I asked, because it wasn't like this, the big *this*, had happened to just me.

"Me? I'm okay." He sounded surprised by the question.

"Can you pick me up later at Jessica's?" I didn't want to go back to his apartment. It was too unfamiliar. "I can text you her address."

"Sure. What time?"

"Whenever you're done for the day. I don't want to interfere with your schedule."

"That will probably be about seven. I have to tutor a student at five."

Why did that suddenly make me completely and irrationally jealous? Had he ever slept with any of his other tutoring students? "Okay, that sounds fine."

"Unless you want me there sooner. I can cancel the tutoring."

"No, no, it's fine." My God, we were being so fucking polite and courteous with each other. It felt weird and it sounded even weirder. Given the expression on Jessica's face, she agreed.

There was a pause and he made a sound, like he was about to say something, but then changed his mind. "Okay, see you later."

"Bye." I handed the phone to Jessica.

"There has to be an ecard for this moment," she said.

Ack. "If there is, please don't send it to me."

CHAPTER THIRTEEN

IT FELT GOOD TO BE AT RILEY AND JESSICA'S HOUSE, LYING on the couch on my side, watching old episodes of *Downton Abbey*. It felt crowded and noisy with all the people moving around the house, and most of the time I couldn't even make out the dialogue on the TV, but it didn't matter. I just wanted to be distracted, and this worked. Jayden was listening to his headphones and shaking his butt.

"What the hell is he doing?" Riley asked as he came down the hall in his workout clothes, probably headed down into their basement to do some boxing.

"He's trying to twerk," Jessica said, sitting in the chair next to the couch, feet on the coffee table as she painted her toenails.

"Oh, Jesus Christ." Riley went to his brother and pulled one of his earbuds out. "Hey, dudes don't shake their asses like that. Knock it off."

"Hey!" Jayden smacked at him, grabbing to reinsert the earbud. "Mind your own business! You're just jealous because you can't dance."

Riley made a face.

"He's right, you can't dance," Jessica said.

"Thanks for the support, babe. And what the hell do I need to dance for? This isn't a movie where dance is my only way out of poverty under the guidance of a well-meaning and spirited teacher. We're not poor enough for that, ironically enough. In this neighborhood the reality is being able to dance just means better tips for you at The Rusty Pole."

"What is The Rusty Pole?" I asked.

"Strip club. Technically it's just called The Pole, but if you saw the staff there you'd understand the nickname."

Ew.

"Why are we suddenly talking about strippers?" Jessica asked. "This isn't an appropriate conversation." She gestured to Easton, who was rolling around on the floor for no apparent reason.

"I can't wait until he's eighteen and I can say whatever the fuck I want," Riley mused.

"I think you already do, sweetie," Jessica said, glancing up and smiling at him.

He laughed. "You're probably right." He bent over and gave her a kiss. "I'm going to get sweaty now."

"Yay."

Then he reached over and ruffled my hair like I was a terrier. "You look good, Kylie."

In Riley World, that was a pretty significant display of sympathy for me. I was touched. Yet it was weird to me that I was here and life was just going on as normal. Easton rolled and Jayden twerked and Riley bitched. This could have been any day.

But it wasn't.

I felt cold, like I couldn't keep the heat inside my body, and I shivered as I burrowed further down into my blanket.

"Hey, let's do a sleepover at Rory's this weekend," Jessica said.

Riley paused on his way to the basement. "What does that even mean?"

"I wasn't talking to you. I meant a girls' sleepover. Tyler can crash here and me and Kylie and Rory can have a sleepover."

I knew what she was trying to do and I was torn between liking the idea of not being alone but at the same time, not sure I could do the whole Girls' Night thing.

"I really do wish Easton was eighteen because there are all sorts of inappropriate comments dying to come out of my mouth."

"Why do girls have sleepovers?" Jayden asked. "What do you do?"

"That's what I'd like to know," Riley said, his thoughts obviously running in an extremely dirty direction.

"We watch movies and eat ice cream and paint our nails."

"You do that all the time," Jayden said, looking confused.

Riley snorted. "He's got a point."

Jessica frowned. "Maybe you have to be female to understand."

There was a knock on the front door. I glanced at my phone and saw it was quarter to seven. "That's probably Jonathon."

Riley went and opened the door and a gust of cold air and flurries came blasting into the living room. I shivered again, pulling the blanket up to my nostrils. There were introductions and the door closing and Jonathon standing in the entry looking a little overwhelmed by how many people were in the room. Jayden waved and Easton glanced up at him but didn't say anything as Jessica introduced him.

"Hey," he said, locking eyes with me. "You cold?"

I nodded, speaking through the holes of the afghan. "I wish I could take a hot bath but my apartment only has a shower."

"I have a tub, but I'm not sure that's a good idea. You should probably wait a few days . . . bacteria and stuff."

Oh, God. I wrinkled my nose. Why did he always have to be so freakin' practical? I just wanted to complain that I wanted a bath. I wasn't actually going to take one. But no, he had to take it to bacteria. Besides, he had reminded me that I had miscarried. Not that the very sight of him wasn't going to do that but still. Don't shove it in my face.

Riley obviously felt the same way. He was grimacing. "Uh, I'm going downstairs to work out now. Nice to meet you, Jonathon." Then he disappeared.

"You ready?" Jonathon asked. "Or should I take my shoes off?"

"Wow. A well-trained male who takes his wet shoes off." Jessica shot me a grin. "I am so jelly of you right now."

I gave her a weak smile then pushed back the blanket and stood up, uncomfortable with her words. Uncomfortable with everything. I wanted to leave, be in private space with Jonathon. I wasn't sure how to bring him into my friendships. That had been Nathan's place. It seemed like an odd fit to have Jonathon here, with the Mann brothers.

"You can borrow the blanket," Jessica said. "I'll get it back from you later."

"Thanks." I wore it like a cape, stuffing my feet in my boots by the door. Jonathon put his hand on the small of my back, but I barely felt it through all the layers.

"Thanks, Jessica," he told her.

"Call me if you need anything."

I nodded, and shuffled with my five pounds of fleece out to the car. In the driveway I paused for a second, startled by how black the night sky actually looked. "There's so many stars out tonight," I said, staring straight up.

"It's beautiful," Jonathon said, but when I glanced at him he wasn't looking at the sky, but at me.

My heart thawed a little. "You said once that I got a raw deal," I whispered to him. "But the truth is, you're the one who got the raw deal. You never wanted any of this and you're stuck with it. But you don't have to be if you don't want to. Not anymore."

He shook his head. "How do you figure I was shafted? I got a gorgeous and sweet woman. That doesn't sound like the short straw to me."

"I'm really confused," I said, trying to be honest, but my thoughts not translating into words. "I feel really sad."

"So do I. Come on, let's get in the car and go to bed."

We went back to my apartment and when I walked in, I saw that he had been there already. That he had changed the sheets on the bed. "Is this . . ." I picked up the sheet he had folded and set on the counter.

"Yes."

I held it to my chest, which might seem gross and more than a little dysfunctional, but it seemed right. Necessary. I wanted to feel it against me, to hold it against my heart. "I wanted this baby," I said, because it seemed important to let him and the baby know that. That while it had caught me off guard, and scared the shit out of me, I had wanted this baby and now I would never get to hold her. I ached for a weight to the sheet, for the solid feel of a living, breathy infant, her mewling yawns, and jerky hands awe-inspiring.

The blanket fell off my shoulders and I closed my eyes and kept them closed, tears trickling down my cheeks, even when Jonathon wrapped his arms around me from behind.

"I know," he whispered, his lips brushing the side of my head. "I know. I wanted it, too, and it hurts."

"It hurts a lot."

We slept spooning that night, my arms around the pathetic little sheet bundle, his arms around me.

When I woke up, he was gone.

I DIDN'T KNOW HOW TO DEAL WITH KYLIE. WITH HER GRIEF. Hell, with my grief. She was avoiding me. And I was avoiding her. I did try, in a way that would allow her an easy out. So when she always took it, and gave me excuses or suggested alternate times she knew I wouldn't be free, part of me was relieved.

There was something so intense and intimate about what we had been through, how I had seen her, that was too much. I had held her hand in the hospital twice now, I had cleaned up her puke, her blood, our baby. We shared a bed, a shower, a seat in the waiting room, fear, and tears. I needed the space, the time to avoid all of it for a few days.

A few days that turned into fourteen.

I hadn't meant for that to happen. I had just wanted to take two, three days tops to sort through my emotions, to tell my mother and father and Devon that Kylie had a miscarriage and deal with their various reactions. Which were as predicted. Horror and sorrow from Mom. Relief from Dad. Sympathy from Devon, who understood my own conflicted feelings.

Go underground, study, work, exhaust myself so I could sleep, that was the plan. I was okay with her avoiding me for a minute. But then I wasn't okay with her avoiding me because I started to think that maybe she meant to permanently avoid me and I didn't mean for her to take *that* way out. I didn't want any out from anyone.

It had been two weeks and she still didn't have a minute to see me? She couldn't meet me at the coffee shop? What the fuck? But I was willing to accept that it had everything to do with her depression, and nothing to do with me. I refused to believe that it had something to do with me, because that would suck.

Except my delusions couldn't continue when I saw a short video she uploaded on Saturday night that featured her, Jessica, and Rory in pajamas dancing suggestively. Or really, more just shaking their asses and laughing.

She didn't look particularly depressed.

At one point she turned directly to the camera and winked. The expression on her face made me both hard and annoyed. She looked fucking flirty and hot as hell. But damn it, why did she look flirty and hot?

And why was she winking at some unknown cameraperson on a Saturday night when I sitting alone in my apartment watching a horror movie? I might as well just move my furniture into my mother's basement right then.

Screw this. I wasn't sitting there worrying about her health, emotional and physical, when she was having a twerking slumber party and had been blowing me off for two weeks straight. I called my friend Miranda. "What are you doing? Want to go out?"

"Like, go out how?"

"Let's go to a bar and shoot some pool."

"Are you serious? Darwin Does Dive Bar? I love it."

"I'm game." I was. Turning off the TV, I stood up. "Can you meet me there in half an hour?"

"You okay?" she asked curiously.

"Of course I'm okay. Why wouldn't I be okay?" Because that didn't sound defensive at all.

"It's just you haven't been interested in the bar scene in like a year."

"Sometimes you have to change it up. What place did you have in mind?"

"There's The Church, but it's a gay bar. Do you care?"

"No. I'm not going to hit on anyone." I may have been put out with Kylie but I wasn't looking to replace her.

Even if she didn't want me. Which she obviously didn't.

"Okay, see you in twenty. And Darwin, walk, don't drive. I have a feeling you are going to tie one on tonight."

"Pfft." I had no idea what she was talking about.

Ninety minutes later, I did. She was right. I had walked in, sucked down my first rum and Coke and went from there. It wasn't like I set out to get drunk, but I guess emotional volatility and liquor are a frantic combination. They feed off of each other. Miranda and I shot pool and laughed and joked around, and then there came that moment where I realized with perfect clarity that I was fucked up.

It happened when I went to reach for my fresh drink on the bar and missed it. My hand just skidded straight past the glass. "Shit."

Miranda laughed and plopped down onto the stroll next to me. "So what's really going on, D?"

I hadn't talked to her since before Christmas so she didn't know. "I got one of my tutoring students pregnant."

She dropped her phone. It clattered on the bartop. "What?"

"Yeah. And then I was like just starting to really dig her and think maybe everything would be okay, and then she miscarried."

Miranda grabbed the lime wedge out of my drink for whatever random reason and started sucking on it, like she needed the sour kick to distract her. Her right eye twitched. Miranda had thick brown curls and oversized red glasses, which she matched her lipstick to. She always wore lacy clothes and florals, yet managed to not look too cutesy by adding something tough to the outfit. Tonight she had on a floral dress but combat boots and a motocross jacket. She peeled off her jacket like the whole notion of my disastrous life had her overheated.

"I'm sorry. For the whole thing."

Feeling suddenly morose, I stared at the ice melting in my drink. "Me, too. Especially now that she's blowing me off. I mean, I was giving her space because I thought she was upset, but then tonight she posted a video of her and her friends dancing."

"Ah, so that's why I got the sudden phone call." She held out her hand. "Show me the video."

"Why do you have your hand out?" I asked. "I'm not giving you my phone."

She stuck her tongue out at me. "Just show me the video so I can assess the situation. You're probably overreacting."

"Fine." I shifted on the stool and pulled my phone out of my pocket. The bar was dim and reasonably quiet, with only a dozen people in it. The atmosphere met my mood. Dark and exhausted. "See?" I held the screen up for her.

"D, she's wearing pajamas and a tank top. This is hardly sexy wear." Miranda turned my phone so the image got bigger. "Though I have to say, well done. She's hot. I wouldn't mind getting to know her better. Naked. Rawr."

Really? I was just drunk enough to call her out. "You're giving lesbians a bad name. You sound like a sexual predator. You are not exempt from the friend code, you know," I said. "If you were a dude and said that to me, I would be pissed, and this isn't any different. What if I said that about a chick you were dating?"

"I would probably punch you."

"Exactly. So stop eye fucking my girlfriend."

Miranda had been taking a sip of her gin and tonic and at my words, she sprayed gin all over the bar. "Oh my God, I'm dying." She choked and laughed and choked some more.

I thumped her on the back, feeling more charitable toward her.

She held her hand up. "I'm okay. And fine, I'll stop eye fucking your girlfriend. Who, I'm sorry, I wasn't aware was your *girlfriend*."

"I told you she was pregnant with my kid! I didn't realize that meant she was fair game."

"Okay, okay. I was just giving you shit because it's not every day you use the word 'girlfriend.' Especially not when you're discussing someone you just said you're giving space to. There is a bit of a disconnect there, you have to admit."

She had a point. "So maybe we never defined it in those words but we agreed not to see anyone else."

"Ah. I see." She hit PLAY and together we watched Kylie and her friends drop it down low and shake it. Then the wink. "It just looks like tipsy friends having good, clean fun. It's not even particularly suggestive."

"She's been avoiding me," I admitted. "I haven't seen her in two weeks."

"*Oh*."

"She told me it was movie night, not vodka night."

"So obviously you want to be with her."

Was that obvious? "Yeah."

"So poke a little. I'll tag you here at the bar. Let her see you're not sitting at home pining for her."

I was just drunk enough that this made sense. "Okay."

Miranda complied immediately and while we were talking about her love life, which was even more complicated than mine, my phone buzzed. "It's a text from Kylie." I was actually surprised, and okay, smug. So she wasn't as eager to be away from me as she was acting if she was aware of my check-ins.

Thought you were staying home 2nite.

Got bored.

Oh. K. Have fun.

Huh. Did she mean have fun for real? Or was she annoyed? Because, frankly, I wanted her to be annoyed. "What now?" I asked Miranda.

"So the goal is to get her thinking about you, right?" When I nodded she pulled out her phone. "Pic of you and me. Now."

"Brilliant," said the Rum and Coke. But before I did that, I texted back, *Love the dance moves.*

Miranda took at least seven shots of us leaning in together. After each take she would study it and attempt improvement. "You need to be closer to me. Oh, fuck, my eyes are closed in this one. Put your arm around me."

"Why is this so damn complicated? And why is my drink empty?"

"The mysteries of life." She showed a picture to me. "Okay, I'm posting this one now."

I barely saw the picture before she yanked her phone away again.

My phone went off.

Thx. Who are you with?

A friend.

She's cute.

That should have been a warning. Like a really big fat-ass warning. Instead, I just felt triumphant. Kylie was paying attention. Kylie was jealous. Therefore, she cared what I was doing and about me.

Normally, I could follow the line of reasoning beyond the obvious and conclude that fanning the flames resulted in a big fucking fire. But my brain was clouded by alcohol and didn't realize that I was in danger of being caught by a relationship flashover, the near-simultaneous ignition of most of the directly exposed combustible material in an enclosed area. I.e., pissing off your girl by waving pictures of you with a woman she doesn't know in her face via social media.

What I actually typed was, *She's a chem grad student, too. Super smart.*

Which was basically like taking a container of gasoline and tossing it on top of a burning campfire.

You'll never escape without getting burned.

And I was too stupid and drunk to run anyway.

CHAPTER FOURTEEN

I HADN'T HAD A DRINK SINCE NOVEMBER, SO WHEN WE finally got together for our Girls' Night pj party two weeks after Jessica suggested it, one martini was enough to go to my head. Two had me agreeing to twerk on camera. I liked to think I had rhythm. Rory claimed she could only dance when she was drunk and I would never tell her, but it was true. It was like her hips couldn't move independently of the rest of her body. I could do all right in zumba and swing dance, and when I've had some vodka in me, my hipbones seemed to disconnect from my legs and I could do some amazing moves. That looked ridiculous when I watched them sober.

But in the moment, I was hot, and damn it, I needed to feel hot. Jonathon was avoiding me, it was so obvious. Now that I was nothing but the stupid girl flunking chemistry, he clearly had lost interest. Which totally wasn't fair, I knew that. He texted me every day and he had asked me to do things with him, but I was drunk. I was allowed to be irrational.

My pajamas were enormous, pink and blue plaid, and when I was dancing, at one point I stepped on the pant leg and ended up pulling them down and flashing the top of my ass to my friends.

Jessica laughed so hard she snorted. "You are lucky I wasn't taping right then."

"I would kill you if you posted that," I said, breathless, collapsing on the sofa. I hadn't had this much exercise since before Thanksgiving. Glancing at my notifications on my phone I saw Jonathon was out at a bar according to his check-in. With a girl named Miranda. I clicked on her name to see her profile picture. She was cute in a nerdy chic way. What the hell?

"Jonathon is out with a girl," I said, my amusement evaporating.

"What?" Rory turned down the booty-grinding music. "I thought you said he was staying home tonight."

"That's what he said he was doing." My cheeks suddenly felt hot. "Is he on a date?"

"She's probably a friend."

"I'm texting him." I tapped quickly, my heart rate high and not from dancing. He answered immediately. "He says he got bored so he went out with a friend."

I hated myself for doing it, but I felt dissatisfied with his casual response so I added, *She's cute.* Which was stupid, because now he would know I clicked on her name. But then a picture of them was posted.

Looking very, very cozy. A hot, sick sensation filled my mouth. "Oh my God, look at this." I shoved my phone at Rory.

"He said they're just friends, right? You should trust him."

"How can I trust him? I haven't seen him in two weeks!"

"Yeah, but wasn't that your choice?"

Because that's what I wanted—someone to point out it was my fault. Not. "He could have tried harder."

"Kylie bug, he texted you like five times a day. He asked you to dinner, to the movies, to just hang out at his place, to hang out at your place. I'm not sure what else he could have done."

I threw a pillow at Jessica. "You guys suck."

Jessica laughed. "Why are you mad at us? I think it's perfectly normal and understandable that you needed time to yourself the last two weeks, but you can't act like he was a shit who blew you off."

"Jonathon is probably wondering where you stand," Rory added.

"So if he's wondering where we stand he goes off and nails some other chick?"

"Whoa. Now you're jumping to conclusions. Big time."

I knew I was. I could feel my anxiety rising and my childish need to finger-point increasing. I wanted to blame the vodka, but the alcohol wasn't entirely to blame. Every day I had been struggling more and more to understand what I wanted and why I kept refusing to see Jonathon. I cared about him a lot. I missed him. I wanted to see his smile, hear his laugh, feel his mouth on mine.

But for some reason every time he suggested we see each other, I froze. I panicked. I had no idea why. Well, maybe I did. For one thing, I was feeling sad and not ready to talk about the miscarriage. I also felt like I would be letting him down if I didn't have my shit together, that it was finally time for me to offer him a genuine display of gratitude and cheerfulness. That he would think me exhausting or pathetic or annoying if I was bummed out in front of him or if I wanted to talk endlessly. I felt like I needed to be happy Kylie and I wasn't ready to be happy Kylie. I was starting to worry I wouldn't ever be ready to be happy Kylie again.

At least sober.

None of that meant I didn't want to be with him. Totally the opposite. I didn't want to see him and give him reasons to not want me. Which was all I was accomplishing anyway, because he clearly didn't want me. He wanted Miranda of the cute red glasses and bouncy hair and freckles. I felt my lower lip start to tremble.

"Oh no. We're not doing that."

I was pretty sure I was and Jessica couldn't stop me. Except that I got another text from Jonathon. She's a chem grad student, too. Super smart.

There was one thing that could shift my emotion from upset to anger and that was it. He was saying I was stupid. I could read between the lines and that was my hot button, no doubt about it.

"Oh, hell, no," I said, hand coming up. "No and no." I showed the text to Rory.

"I don't think he means . . ."

I cut her off. "Rory, I need to borrow a pair of jeans. I'm going to The Church."

"Um . . . Kylie, you're like four inches taller than me."

"Who cares? I have cowboy boots. No one will know my

pants are too short." I stood up and glanced around for my overnight bag. I had a clean tank top in there that I could pair with one of Rory's sweaters. "I need makeup, stat."

"Is this a good idea?" Jessica asked me.

"Yes."

"Is this a good idea?" Jessica asked Rory.

"I suppose it depends on what the goal is."

Wasn't that obvious? "The goal is to show Jonathon that while I may not be a chemistry genius I'm not an idiot."

"So enlighten me as to how showing up at the bar he's at after you told him you couldn't see him tonight is going to accomplish that." Jessica held her hands out. "I'm serious, not trying to be a bitch."

I didn't have time to debate my highly intelligent point. "I want to show him that he wants to be with me, not some hipster."

"Why? Because you want to be with him?"

"Of course I want to be with him!" I said, exasperated. "When did I ever say I didn't?" Why were they having such a hard time keeping up?

"I guess you didn't."

"Now are you going to go with me or what?"

"Can I suggest a text to him first?" Rory asked. "You know, sort of like a 'hey, we're going out, maybe we'll stop by The Church,' and see what he says?"

I looked to Jessica. "Tell her how naïve that is."

"That's naïve."

"What? Isn't it better to be honest? What if he's gone by the time you get there? Then you'll really be pissed."

"He'll still be there if we get our shit together." I started down the stairs to the bedroom Rory shared with Tyler. When I opened their closet, it was a sea of band T-shirts and floral dresses. "Oh my God, Tyler hangs up his T-shirts? Who does that? And where are all your jeans?"

"He doesn't like the wrinkles when you fold the shirts in drawers." Rory pulled out a dresser drawer. "My jeans are in here. But I have mostly colored denim. Do you want pink?"

"My cowboy boots are brown. That sounds like an ick combo." I pawed through her dresses to reach the cardigan section. Her closet was very organized. Mine looked like the discount bin at Walmart. "How about red or blue?"

"I'm going to tell Riley and Tyler what we're doing," Jessica said.

"Okay, cool." Rory skimmed off her pajama pants and put on the pink jeans I had rejected.

She was definitely someone who proved that redheads could wear pink. She looked adorbs in pink.

Jessica dumped out her overnight bag. "Good thing I actually packed jeans. I could never fit in Rory's. My butt is way more bootylicious than Rory's dainty ass."

I didn't think I would have fit in Rory's pants either before the pregnancy, but I had lost at least five pounds, maybe more, so it might be a squeeze, but it should work. I took the pastel blue jeans Rory handed me and decided to just wear my ribbed white tank top with a chambray shirt from the closet over it. It was a tight squeeze in the jeans, but the stretchy fabric helped. And the butt cuppage gave me a boost.

"Your ass looks great," Jessica said.

"Thanks. But my hair looks like shit. I need a hat." I found a beanie and after aggressively brushing my hair, I put the hat on. Rifling through Rory's jewelry, I found mostly broaches and weird shit with feathers and pearls, but I did find a long necklace with lots of things hanging from it so I put that on.

"I love how we're just raiding Rory's stuff," Jessica said, snagging a headband and putting it in her hair. She had picked a floral sweater out of Rory's closet to pair with her own jeans.

"I don't care," Rory said. "It's actually kind of fun. And I'm absolutely convinced that we'll get to the bar and this misunderstanding will be resolved."

"Are you sure you don't want to be a lawyer instead of a doctor?" I asked her. "Though you're far too cute to be either. I love those jeans on you, BTW. And who has red lipstick I can borrow? I look like I died last Friday."

"Riley wants to know if he and Tyler are allowed to crash Girls' Night since we are leaving the confines of the apartment to go to the bar. He wants a beer."

"I can't really say no since I'm going up there to try and bust up Jonathon's date with Chem Cutie." What amazed me was how productive anger could be in creating focus. I was methodical in getting ready, swiping on eye shadow and lipstick and doing another butt check of my booty in the jeans. I piled on a bunch of bracelets from the drawer where Rory kept her jewelry and I was ready. "Let's roll."

I hadn't gone out in months and I hadn't wanted to. Yet I had to admit, I felt a little of my old confidence returning. I felt attractive.

Maybe it was the vodka acting as liquid courage, but I felt full of sass and ready to fight for my man.

Because damn it, he *was* my man.

Whether he liked it or not.

Well. I hoped he liked it.

Otherwise that was kind of counterproductive.

Anyway, point being, I had to tell Jonathon how I felt. I had to show him that despite me making up bullshit excuses for two weeks, I wanted to be with him. That I couldn't explain why I had done that, not exactly, but that it had been super hard to lose our baby and I hadn't known how to deal with it. I hadn't known how to deal with him given the origin of our relationship.

For one of the few times in my life, I hadn't wanted to talk about it.

Plus, I wanted to show him that I was hotter than Miranda.

Duh.

"I CAN'T BELIEVE THIS ISN'T A GAY BAR ANYMORE," MIRANDA said, looking around and clearly lamenting the lack of lesbians. "You know, if a bar is going to shift clientele it should be advertised."

Since I had no stake in it, I wasn't bothered either way. "I don't think the bar determines it. The crowd does. If this is no longer a gay hangout, it must be because they found somewhere better." I was on my seven hundredth Captain Morgan and Coke and I was still logical. Damn, I was good. "I mean, this place isn't exactly upscale or trendy in its décor."

"There's mostly men in here," Miranda complained. "And douchey men on top of it all. Like men who chew tobacco."

"You'd better redneckanize," I said then laughed, because I cracked myself up.

"Oh, Lord." She rolled her eyes. "Darwin, you are drunk."

"I am aware of that fact, thank you very much." There was a buzzing in my ears and my tongue felt too large for my mouth. I kept glancing at my phone. "Why doesn't Kylie want to be with me?" I asked, because that question kept popping into my head and making me feel like shit. And I didn't want to feel like shit. "I mean, she has a lot of nerve, really, if you think about it. There's nothing objectionable about me."

"Let's put that on your online dating profile. 'There's nothing objectionable about me.' Way to sell yourself, D."

"Do you think I'm too nice? Do I need to be a dick for chicks to like me?"

"I've never actually thought you were super nice. I mean, you're certainly not a dick, but you are fairly self-absorbed."

Well, that was helpful. "I disagree. I tried really hard to be there for Kylie. Like . . . I tried." My thoughts were slower than normal and my vocabulary seemed to have shrunk dramatically.

"Did she answer your text? And please, God, tell me, you didn't ask her what you just asked me."

"No. To both." I may have been drunk but I still had a modicum of self-respect.

"Then fuck her. There's nothing you can do about it tonight. Let's shoot some pool." She stood up. Her skirt was flipped up, exposing her butt, obviously crumpled from when she had been sitting.

"Hey," I said, grabbing at the skirt to fix it. I didn't imagine she wanted all the douchey guys in the bar to see her ass and her red lace panties.

"What?" She smacked backward at me. "Hello. Three hot chicks just walked in."

"I'm fixing your skirt; stop hitting me! Your underwear is showing." God, that was a lot of fabric for a drunk man to deal with. I felt like my thumbs had disappeared into a flower garden.

"I would show my panties to these chicks."

I glanced over her shoulder to the door to see who had attracted her attention and slipped on my stool, crashing forward into Miranda, who also stumbled. I grabbed her waist, ass, legs for support. "That's Kylie," I said, shock turning to pleasure. Kylie looked so good. So pretty. So sexy.

She was wearing tight jeans and a denim shirt she had tied in a knot under her breasts, a white tank top showing how narrow her waist was. There was a little beanie on her head that just made me want to cuddle in a corner with her. Then on her feet were cowboy boots that made me want to fuck her with nothing on but those.

"That's your girlfriend?" Miranda glanced back at me. "She looks even better in person than she did on camera in pajamas. Now you might want to take your hands off my ass before she raises the question of what the hell you're doing."

Good point. I dropped my hands and moved around Miranda to meet Kylie, smile on my face. I had really, really missed her. "Hey, what—"

"What the hell are you doing?" Kylie asked me, hands on her hips.

"Having a drink." Or twelve. Why did she look so angry? I tried to lean over and kiss her, but she dodged my touch.

Huh. I waved to Rory and Jessica. "How is Girls' Night?"

Jessica raised her eyebrows. "Drama filled, as always." She leaned around me and held her hand out to Miranda. "Hi, I'm Jessica."

"Miranda. Darwin's very gay friend."

"You're gay?" Jessica asked, glancing over at Kylie. "That's awesome to hear."

Miranda was still holding her hand and her smile grew flirtatious. "Really? Glad to hear we're on the same page."

"Oh." Jessica laughed. "No, sorry, that's not what I meant. I have a boyfriend. I meant that I'm sure Kylie is happy to hear that you're not creeping on Jonathon."

Was that true? Did she actually care? Was she jealous? The thought made me ridiculously pleased.

"I am so not creeping on Darwin. We've been friends since our freshmen year as undergrads. He's a great guy, but not my type. You know, not being a girl and all."

"But you would totally want me if you were straight, right?" I asked, joking.

"Of course. No question about it. You are a man among men." She rolled her eyes.

Kylie was just looking at me, her mouth set in a hard line. "I thought you were on a date. If you are, just fucking tell me."

"Nope. No date. I would never do that to you."

"Because you know, I wasn't sure what was going on between us."

Were we doing this right now, right here? Okay. And you know, I was offended, damn it. "I wasn't either, but that doesn't mean I would be such a gigantic asshole that I would start seeing someone else without discussing it with you first."

"The thought made me very, very angry." She still looked angry. Her eyes were burning with emotion, her hands on her hips.

"I see that." Rory, Jessica, and Miranda had taken seats at the bar and were talking. I fought the urge to smile. I really liked where this was going. "Why do you think it made you angry?"

"Because I don't want you with another girl. It pisses me off."

"Can I tell you what I want?" I asked.

For a second, her confidence wavered, but then she raised her chin. "Absolutely. What do you want?"

"You." I put my arm around her waist and drew her closer to me. She dug her heels in, and kept her arms crossed. She leaned away from me, head turned slightly. I was undeterred. The fact that she had shown up at the bar told me everything I needed to know. I ran my lips over her ear, across her cheek. "I want you and no one else. I've missed you. A lot."

Her shoulders relaxed, her arms going slack. "I needed space. I was confused and upset and I didn't know if you would still want to be with me."

"I know." I wanted to point out that we could have just had a conversation about this, but I didn't want to set her back up again. So instead I said what rum and my heart were telling me to say. "Kylie, there is no one else I want to be with. Not seeing you, not being sure where we stood, it was killing me."

"Really?"

"Really. Because the thing is, I'm pretty damn sure that I'm in love with you."

It was out. In the open. No taking it back. I didn't regret it. It felt strong and right and honest. I was in love with her.

This was different. She was different. I wanted to spend every night on her twin bed in her micro-apartment holding her against me. I wanted to make her laugh. I wanted to hear her stupid chemistry jokes and answer every one of her random and out-of-context questions. I wanted it to be her and me. For real. Not because we had to be but because we *wanted* to be together.

Her eyes had widened, her arms had dropped. "You are?"

I nodded, solemnly, wanting to make it clear that this wasn't a casual statement. My fingers brushed her hair behind her ear and my gaze drank in her features as greedily as my mouth had the rum. Her pert nose, her lengthy eyelashes, her high cheekbones, her soft, plump lips. "Yes. I love you." I kissed the corner of her mouth. "They say it happens when you least expect it. When I showed up to tutor you, I had no idea that anything was missing from my life. Then I met you and I knew what was missing was *you*."

Her fingers gripped the front of my shirt. "Oh, Jonathon. I love you, too. I don't know when or how I knew it. It just feels like I always have. Like I've always belonged to you."

Hearing that had me kissing her, hard, intensely. She kissed me back, eagerly, her mouth hungry for mine. She loved me. Kylie loved me. She saw something beyond the self-absorbed science guy. When we broke away, both breathing hard, she looked at me with shiny eyes, a grin splitting her face.

"Yay."

That about summed it up.

I laughed. "Come sit down and we can have a drink with our friends. Then they can figure out Girls' Night without you because I'm taking you home and I'm not going to take no for an answer. I'm not going to be polite, I'm not going to be nice. I'm not giving you any more space or time. I want you and I'm taking you."

"Oh, shit, I like the sound of that." Her hips moved against mine suggestively and her eyes darkened. "By the way, I have a buzz. I haven't had a drink in so long the vodka went straight to my head."

"Then we're buzzing together because I drank enough rum to disinfect a small hospital."

She kissed me again, gripping my face. "I was so mad at you!"

Her particular brand of anger seemed to work in my favor. "Tell me again."

Kylie kissed me again. "I really was pissed."

"Uh-huh." I led her to a stool, sat down, and pulled her onto my lap. She felt amazing in my arms. "You feel so good, gorgeous."

She was all long legs and tight ass, tiny waist and perky breasts. Her hair hung straight down, falling over my arm, and when she wiggled to get more comfortable on her perch, I wanted to groan. Damn, fucking damn, I had never stood a chance. From that very first night when she had smiled at me so sweetly, her head propped up on her hand, I had been sunk.

"Mm. You feel good, too." Her arms came around my neck and we kissed some more. And then some more again.

Someone kicked my stool and I could pretty much guarantee it was Miranda. "Yeah?" I asked her, turning to see her glaring at me.

"Dude, like show a little decorum. You're in public." Then she promptly got distracted when someone walked in the front door. "Oh, hello. That's Chastity, and believe me, her name is an oxymoron. I'll be right back."

"Your friend seems nice," Kylie said, snuggling up against me.

I laughed. "That is something I love about you—you're very generous."

"Wait until you see how generous I am later."

And she said that.

Damn. I think I groaned. "You're killing me. It's been a long-ass two weeks."

"I know."

"Is everything okay down there? No, uh, bleeding?" Why did I feel self-conscious using that word? We were way past the point of needing to give a shit about modesty. "You feel okay?"

"No bleeding. And yes, I feel okay."

I locked eyes with her, my hands tight on her waist. I wanted her to understand what I didn't have the words to say. "I'm sorry," I said gruffly. For being irresponsible and getting her pregnant. For the morning sickness and the heartache of the miscarriage. For not pushing harder afterward to see her.

"Me, too," she whispered. "But I just want you to know that when I'm with you, my glass is full."

Ah, shit, now she was being downright romantic. She'd remembered our glass-half-full conversation where I had insisted on the logic of a full glass. I drank in the sight of her, nestled on my lap, her face close to mine, the smell and feel of her wrapping around me, and I wanted to capture the moment, hold on to it.

I'd always thought I was pragmatic, methodical, but Kylie had drawn something out of me that I hadn't even noticed existed. I wanted to say something epic but I didn't know how to convey the enormity of the emotion I felt for her. Maybe it was the rum. Most likely it was just that I didn't have any experience with this feeling of not being whole without someone else.

So instead I gave her a soft kiss then said, "Hey, Kylie. So a neutron walks into a bar."

She laughed. "Oh yeah? What did he do in the bar?"

"He asks the bartender, 'How much for a beer?' The bartender gives him a smile and says, 'For you, no charge.'"

"Oh, Darwin." Laughing, she lost her balance on my lap and almost fell off the stool. "Ack!"

"What are you two doing over there?"

I turned and saw that Miranda was still talking to her potential hookup, but that Jessica and Rory were watching us, Rory smiling knowingly, Jessica looking a little put out.

"We're making up," Kylie told her.

"Making out is more like it."

"Jessica," Kylie said, "a neutron walked into a bar. He asked the bartender how much is a beer and the bartender said, 'For you, no charge.'"

Jessica's eyebrows shot up.

Rory laughed. "Nice. I see you've been studying hard."

"You are drunk," Jessica said, a grin splitting her face. "Since when do you tell chemistry jokes?"

"I'm a bad influence," I said. "Hey, Tyler and Riley just came in." Jessica and Rory's boyfriends had paused in the doorway and nodded when they saw us. "It's a party."

They both looked mildly curious to see Kylie sitting on me, but mostly interested in ordering a couple of beers.

"I can deal with this kind of Girls' Night," Riley said, giving Jessica a kiss hello. "Though I'm not sure how you all went from pajama dancing to this place."

"Kylie and Jonathon needed to talk," Jessica told him.

"Looks like it." He eyed us and gave me a grin.

"Rory, we need to talk, too," Tyler told her, nudging her so that he could slide under her on the seat and pull her down onto his lap. He kissed her. "See? I had to say that."

"I have to pee," Kylie announced, because that's what Kylie did. She announced things. "Rory and Jess, you need to come with me."

She hopped off my lap and grabbed both of them by the hand and dragged them away from their boyfriends and toward the restroom.

"Why do chicks do that?" Riley asked. "They move in unison like schools of fish. I have never once needed company when I went to take a piss. In fact, I can't stand it when some asshole tries to talk to me at the urinal."

"That is weird," I agreed. "But I think girls do it for two reasons. First, they can't wait to communicate their thoughts and emotions. Two, they don't want anything of importance to happen while they're gone, so by taking their friends with them, they ensure it won't."

"I think you're exactly right," Tyler said. "They're afraid they'll miss some gossip or their friend will get hit on while they're gone."

"The three of us are right here; who is going to hit on them?" Riley asked.

"I don't mean specifically now. I think it's a learned behavior," Tyler said.

"I imagine they get hit on a lot when they go out solo," I said.

"Yeah, thanks for reminding me." Riley shook his head and took his beer from the bartender. "Thanks. God, I hate these Girls' Nights. Something fucked up always happens."

"Looks like tonight is going to end on a high note for all of us, though," Tyler said, expression pleased. "It's the best Girls' Night they've ever had, in my opinion."

"Way better ending than I would have thought two hours ago," I admitted. "I thought Kylie and I were done."

"Are you pretty hot for her?" Riley asked. "Like deep feelings and shit?"

"Yeah." I would say there were definitely deep feelings and shit.

"Then trust me on this. It's not done until they say it is."

"Amen to that," Tyler said.

"We're putty in their fucking hands, bro." Riley saluted me with his beer.

I nodded, feeling the wisdom of that statement. I raised my glass.

I would drink to that.

CHAPTER FIFTEEN

"SO . . ." JESSICA SAID WITH A GRIN AS WE PUSHED INTO THE restroom. "Things look pretty steamy out here with you and Jonathon."

I totally didn't have to pee. I just needed to share with my friends or I was going to burst. "He told me loves me!"

"Really? That's awesome!" Rory grinned. "I guess you were right not to text him first. I stand corrected."

"Ah, I know! I'm like so happy!" I couldn't contain my excitement so I did the cabbage patch in front of the mirror. "He loves me, he loves me." I capped it off with a few fist-pump, hip-thrust moves.

Jessica snorted. "Oh my God. That's the most ridiculous thing I've ever seen and I have sex with my boyfriend on a waterbed, so that's saying a lot."

"I don't care what you say." I did a cupid shuffle. Two stomps.

"I feel good. I look good. Though I need more lipstick. Jonathon kissed it off."

Rory pulled out a lipstick. "Here. And I want you to know that it makes me super happy to see you happy. The last six months have been a suckfest for you."

They had been. But maybe I could appreciate this more because things had been so hard. "Thanks, Rory Bory. That means a lot to me. It did suck."

"The last Girls' Night was—"

I held my free hand up to stop Jessica. "OMG! Don't bring that up. I am still not able to forgive Nathan, but the thing is, he no longer deserves any of my attention. I don't love him. I never loved the real him. He was someone totally different from who I thought he was so it doesn't count."

"I like that you're able to use his name instead of calling him Voldemort."

"That's giving him too much power." I shrugged. "The thing is, he's just not a nice person. Jonathon is more than a nice person. He's a good man." Suddenly I felt tears in my eyes. "I'm really, really lucky that he was there through all of this with me. Most guys . . ." I couldn't keep going because I was choked up.

"Oh, honey." Jessica pulled me into her arms and Rory joined us in a group hug. "I'm sorry that you've been through so much."

Rory said, "You're right. Most guys wouldn't have stuck by you. The *right* guy isn't most guys, though. That's how you know he's worth keeping. He sticks."

I nodded. "Totally. Now I need to stop or I'm going to eff up my makeup. I don't want to be puffy and streaky." I pulled back and wiped at my eyes, sniffling and blinking hard. I fanned myself. "Oh, shit. I think I'm done with the vodka for tonight. My buzz is wearing off and I'm okay with that. I just want to go home and climb Jonathon like a tree."

"Hello." Jessica laughed. "Someone's feeling better."

Rory said, "I have the absolute worst visuals now. Jess flopping around a waterbed, you in a lumberjack outfit climbing Jonathon . . . I'm going to need to see my boyfriend naked sooner than later to eradicate those bizarre images."

"And now you just put the thought of your boyfriend naked into *my* head. Ew."

"Hey, what do you mean ew? Tyler is—"

"Fabulously hot and hung, I know," I laughed. "But our oversharing hour ended when we showed up here. You guys don't mind if I go home with Jonathon, do you?"

"Of course not." Jessica rubbed her teeth in the mirror. "I think Riley is relieved. He's going through a bit of an insecure phase. He's convinced every man within twenty feet of me is hitting on me."

"What do you think that's all about?" I asked, adjusting my hat.

"I think he is worried now that we've been together for nine months that I'll decide I don't want all the baggage he comes with—the house, the mortgage, Jayden and Easton, my dad's disapproval, etc. So I've been working hard to reassure him without coming right out and saying, hey, don't worry. Because he doesn't have any reason to worry. I love my life and I love my life with him."

"Okay, we really do have to get out of this restroom," Rory

said. "Or I'm going to get emotional myself. Tyler doesn't worry about other men hitting on me. He worries that he doesn't make enough money and that I'll be embarrassed of him. Like I give a shit about money. What I give a shit about is that he's a great guy."

"The male ego. We must treat it like it's glass."

"Hmm." I decided to go pee after all and as I went into the stall I wondered what Jonathon's ego trigger was. So far I didn't think I could pinpoint what was his real or imagined flaw. My only issue, which was more observation than issue, was that he could be very literal sometimes.

On that thought I flushed and decided I wasn't going to think about any of that stuff tonight. I could worry about that when I was where Jessica and Rory were with their boyfriends, nine months and over a year in.

"I find it quite adorable that you are dating a genius," Rory said as I washed my hands. "He looks at you so bewildered, like he can't crack the equation on why you're into him."

I laughed. "He does not."

When we came back out of the restroom and went up to the bar, all three guys turned to watch our approach. I didn't bother to look and see how Tyler and Riley ogled my friends, I was too busy sticking my hands in my front pockets and putting a sway in my hips to impress Jonathon, enjoying the hungry look on his face as he stared at me.

"You took forever in there," Riley complained.

I ignored him and Jessica's response and stepped right between Jonathon's legs when he turned his stool completely. He widened his legs to accommodate me and then closed them again, clamping me between his knees.

"Got you."

Laughing, I put my arms around his neck. "Yes, you have me. Will Miranda be upset if we leave? Do you need to give her a ride?"

"I walked and I think Miranda is just fine." He gestured with his head.

A glance back showed his friend making out with the girl with the short spiked blond hair. "Oh. Excellent."

"Do you mind walking?" he asked.

"No. It's just a few blocks to my place. I left my bag at Rory's but there's nothing in it I need tonight."

"Perfect. Let's go then." He leaned closer and murmured in my ear, "We need to stop for condoms on the way."

My cheeks got hot. I nodded, not wanting to talk about it. I knew we needed to discuss more reliable birth control, and we really needed to share our emotions about what I couldn't even bring myself to think about right at that moment, but I wasn't ready. It would ruin my mood, ruin the joy I felt in looking at him and feeling that swell of love rise in my chest every single time my gaze locked with his.

"Let me pay my tab and tell Miranda we're leaving."

Suddenly I changed my mind about wanting another drink. "Let's have one last drink and then we can go, 'kay?" I cupped his face and gave him a kiss. "Mm. I love smooching you."

"Smooching?" He laughed. "You are so damn cute, I really

can't even stand it. If you want a drink you can have a drink. What would you like?"

"I would like a vodka martini now that I am legally twenty-one, the last of all my friends. I want to sit here and sip from a glass like a big girl." Sure, that was part of it. But maybe part of it was that I didn't want to freeze up and panic when it came time to get naked, not because I didn't desperately want to have sex with him, but because I was terrified that I'd lost the baby, terrified that we could go through that again.

I didn't want to think about it right then. So I found my own stool next to him and I talked and laughed with my friends and Jonathon and drank my martini. I'd been avoiding the situation for two weeks and I knew I couldn't avoid it forever, but just for tonight, while I was feeling the giddiness of knowing Jonathon cared about me, I was going to keep on with the ignoring.

Which meant the buzz that had been dulled came roaring back and by the time we left the bar, I was feeling sassy. It took three times as long to walk back as it should have because Jonathon and I kept stopping in doorways to make out.

"Oh, God, I want you so much," he murmured as we grinded on each other in the alcove in front of the record exchange shop.

I saw the retro LP album cover posters on either side of us, the cold wind whipping behind us, but neither really registered. My head was spinning, with vodka and love and desire, and I wrapped my leg around his, wanting closer. "Take me."

His fingers had popped the button on Rory's jeans and were already down my pants. He was stroking me while we kissed and

I couldn't believe how good it felt, how hot and wet I was for him. "Oh," I moaned. "Don't stop. I'm going to come."

"Really? Now that is fucking hot."

It was. I let my head fall back and there on the sidewalk, with Jonathon shielding me from view, ears cold, yet body feverishly hot, I had an orgasm from his talented touch. I bit my lip and shuddered, forehead on his shoulder. "Shit." My mouth felt thick and hot.

He pulled his hand out of my pants and redid the button. With a smile he said, "Let's keep going. We may not be feeling the cold but it's only twenty-five degrees outside."

"I guess we don't want frostbite in important parts." I took his hand, his fingers warm and slick. Knowing what that was made me aroused all over again, and walking only reminded me of how wet and aching my inner thighs were.

When we went into the gas station to buy condoms, the fluorescent lights were harsh and I blinked, the warmth and the sudden need to act normal subduing. Jonathon picked up a twelve-count box and got himself a cup of coffee. I knew that I had a naughty little smile on my face. I couldn't help it. I was very aware of me and Jonathon and I couldn't wait until our bodies were perfectly aligned with each other.

He offered me a sip of his coffee as we stood in line behind a guy buying cigarettes. "Blow on it first," he said.

I raised my eyebrows. He cracked me up. Because I couldn't see it was hot? "Thanks." I took a sip and then we were paying, the clerk trying not to react to our purchase, but doing a lousy job. He shook his head and said, "Man, I am so jealous of you right now. I'm stuck here until six."

"Sorry," Jonathon said. "But I guess there's always morning sex."

The clerk was big, like six foot five, with short curly hair. It shook when he laughed. "Except you need a girl, bro. Have fun." He smiled at me. "Make him work."

I laughed. It should have been creepy, but it wasn't. He just seemed friendly and conversational, and, hey, who would want to be stuck behind the gas station counter on a Saturday night watching everyone come in, clearly out having fun? Not me. "Thanks." I never needed to make Jonathon work. He just did. It was always way more about me than it was about him. I decided I needed to give him a little more tonight.

"So what is your favorite position?" I asked him as we left. "What is your fantasy for when we walk in the door?"

He gave me a sideways look. "Actually, I want you in nothing but that shirt and cowboy boots, right up against your door."

I sucked in my breath. "Oh." I was sorry I hadn't waited until we were back to ask him. Because now my anticipation was only heightened. But we were already turning up the walk to my building.

Jonathon shoved the door open the minute I turned the key, grabbing my hand and dragging me up the stairs. I laughed. "Slow down!"

"Easy for you to say. You're one up on me."

True. I was already yanking my coat off as we entered the apartment and reaching down to yank my boots off. I undid my jeans and shoved them down as fast as I could. But he had already noticed how short they were.

"Why are your pants mid-calf? Is that a new style?"

"No, they're Rory's. I didn't bring any jeans with me and when I decided we should come up to the bar, I wasn't going to do it in pajamas."

Jonathon was taking his coat and shoes off, too, but his eyes were trained on me. "I wouldn't have cared if you had. I'm just glad to see you."

I bent over a little, turning sideways, to drag down the jeans.

"On second thought, no, I prefer these." His hands were suddenly on me everywhere, brushing over my front, my back, my breasts.

I reached for the button on his pants but he pulled away, his hand covering mine to stop it. "No. I want to make sure I'm wearing a condom first, before we go any further."

I flinched inwardly, though I just nodded. He was right, he was being smart. But it definitely killed the mood, the spontaneity, just a little. While he was taking care of that business, I put the boots back on after skimming my panties off. Then I unbuttoned my shirt, removed the tank and my bra, then slid the shirt back on, leaving it flapping loosely open.

"Oh. My. God." Jonathon stared at me, his eyes sweeping up and down. He had removed his shirt, but his pants were still loosely hanging around his hips, his erection rising enticingly toward me.

Yum. He looked seriously hot.

"You are like off-the-fucking-hook gorgeous." His hands

came up but he didn't touch me, just moved down in front of me like he was tracing the outline of my body. "How did I get so damn lucky?"

"As a man of science I wouldn't think you would believe in luck."

He laughed softly. "Then thank God for whatever came out of my mouth that night that convinced you to give me the time of day."

"I think it was more that you felt sorry for me." I leaned against the door, putting my feet a little apart, gripping the lapels of the shirt.

He shook his head slowly, taking a step toward me. "I feel sorry for every man who isn't me right now."

Then he lifted my left leg and wrapped it around the back of his thigh, and he gripped my ass with one hand, the other arm on the wall behind my head. The first push of him inside me sent me up on my toes, a soft moan escaping my mouth. Jonathon didn't hold back. It was hard, it was fast, my back slamming into the door with each rough thrust. This was what he hadn't been willing to do before, when I was sick and still pregnant, and while I had mixed feelings about the reason, I was definitely enjoying it. I was also shocked to have an orgasm, in a good way. I didn't think I could even do that, but suddenly bam, there it was and I was whimpering and clinging to him.

He was getting a little louder, his expression fierce, but then suddenly he pulled out and came with his hand on himself, over the condom.

"What . . . are you okay?"

He nodded. "Just making sure."

Well, that was deflating. I had wanted him to have full satisfaction, and I immediately felt bad. "I'm sorry, you should have said something. I could have . . ." I covered his hand with mine, dropping back down onto my heels.

"It's okay. It was amazing." He kissed me. "I love you."

My heart squeezed. Aw. "I love you, too." His arms were around my waist inside the soft shirt, and his chest was warm against mine.

"I forgot to take my pants off," he said.

I laughed. "Well, why don't you do that and we can get in bed and snuggle?"

"Is snuggling the polite word for it?"

"I was talking about cuddling. What were you talking about?" I sat on the edge of the bed and bent my knee to pull one of the boots off.

He groaned, his hand going into his hair. "See, when you do things like that, it's impossible to imagine just rolling over and going to sleep yet."

The amazing thing was that he found me sexy without any particular effort on my part. That seemed almost too good to be true. He had taken off the condom and tossed it in the wastebasket and was already reaching for another one. I yanked off boot number two and watched him ditch his pants.

"So that was your first fantasy. What position would you like now? Doggie style?" I asked, because I was pretty sure every guy on the planet would choose that as his number one position.

But Jonathon shook his head as he came over to me. "As much

as I can appreciate that position, I want to see your beautiful face tonight."

How could I do anything but melt when he said things like that? I took his hand and lay back as he moved over me. "For a scientist, you prove yet again that you are actually quite romantic."

"Let's just keep that between the two of us."

It was all just between the two of us. It was an intimacy, a bond, I had never experienced. He had seen me at my worst, my most vulnerable, and he had never wavered. He'd fallen in love with me. I could see it in his eyes, feel it in his touch, and I was in awe of it. I didn't feel like I deserved it. Wasn't sure I knew how to keep it.

But for right then, I was going to enjoy it. Suddenly, it felt like the scariest thing I could do was tell him how I felt. Sure, I'd already said it in the bar, but this was different. Here, in my bed, where both good and bad had happened between us, it meant more to me. So as he urged my legs apart, I stared up at him. "I am so in love with you."

His response was to lean down and kiss me, his glasses slipping and smooshing between us. "Kylie Ann, I am so in love with you, too. And it only has a little bit to do with how you smell."

I laughed. "Good to know. And how do you know my middle name?"

"I listen to everything you say."

That right there was what made him so sexy hot.

He listened to me.

To my words, to my actions, to my body.

When we finally drifted off to sleep an hour later, I already felt different, like the anxiety of the last six months were a bal-loon that had a pinprick, and all the air was finally out. Like I could close my eyes and sleep in peace, shoulders relaxed, mind clear and free of worry.

Happiness. I'd missed that crazy and elusive bitch.

WHEN I WOKE UP, KYLIE WAS STILL ASLEEP, HER NAKED BODY draped across mine. I reached for my phone to see what time it was and noted the date. That was ironic. Kissing the top of her head, I questioned how it was statistically possible for a guy like me to end up with a girl like her. I could account for it if I were rich, in the tradition of nerds who change the world and get a hot chick to boot. But I was just a grad student with a possibly unhealthy interest in kinetics. I wasn't exactly sure what she saw in me, but I wasn't going to question it any further.

She gave a little sigh as she woke up, wiggling against me.

"Guess what today is?" I asked her.

"Sunday?"

"It's Valentine's Day." A holiday I frankly despised, given that it had morphed into a commercial marketing ploy to sell flowers and chocolates under the pressure of being a romantic failure if you didn't comply. Yet no one seemed to discuss the fact that St. Valentine had been beheaded, hardly a well from which romance should spring. But it was fascinating to note that now that I was head over ass for Kylie, I was perfectly willing to believe the bull-shit surrounding February fourteenth.

"Really? Aw." She strained to give me a kiss. "That's perfect."

It was. "Happy Valentine's Day." But now that I was fully awake and she was moving around, I was starting to get hard, which made me nervous. I held her around the waist, but I rolled to the side to snag my underwear off the floor. When I started to stick my feet through them, she blinked at me.

"What are you doing?"

"Putting my underwear on. It makes me nervous when we're naked and parts are touching without protection."

She looked annoyed, but she had to know it only made sense. She didn't say anything, though.

"Can you maybe go on the pill?" I asked her. "I know you had reasons you didn't want to, but I think it would alleviate a lot of stress for both of us if you did."

"Do we have to talk about this right now?"

"We have to talk about it sometime." Yesterday wouldn't be too soon for me. I wasn't going to be able to be stress-free until she was on some serious hard-core birth control. "If you don't want to take hormones, you can get an IUD. That's hormone-free."

She sighed. "Fine. I'll go to the doctor and talk to her."

Why was she making me feel like a dick? It wasn't something we could ignore. A little voice in the back of my head reminded me that she was barely twenty-one, and that a five-year age gap may not seem like much, but maybe it was when it came to certain things. Then I felt like a dick for real for thinking that.

"Did you have any plans for today?"

"Nope. Just a shit ton of studying. I'm doing awful in all my classes. Better than last month, but it's hard to catch back up."

"Is there anything I can help you with?"

"You can give me a portion of your brain."

"That might be counterproductive given that once it leaves my body all parts of my brain will be non-functioning. But I can take you to the library or the coffee shop and pump you full of caffeine. I can also answer any chem questions you might have."

"Okay." She yawned. "Can we go out for breakfast?"

"Of course. Where do you want to go?"

"Somewhere that has pancakes. I heart pancakes." She made a little heart with her fingers.

"Done." I felt guilty for starting the day off with the touchy birth control topic. Then was annoyed with myself for feeling guilty. "I'm surprised I don't have a hangover today. I drank way too much rum last night before you showed up."

"I have a slight headache, I'm not going to lie." She sat up and rolled her neck. "But I think coffee will fix it."

I watched Kylie as she climbed over me and walked across the room in nothing but the shirt she had never bothered to take off. It was unbuttoned and flapped open as she went into the bathroom. She didn't close the door, just sat down on the toilet right in my line of view. I'd never had a girlfriend who was so comfortable with her body and it was actually pretty awesome. Granted, I didn't need or particularly want to see Kylie peeing, but I didn't object to it, and the plus side of that liberated attitude was I got to see her strolling around naked.

Like when she flushed then stood up and stretched, her arms going over her head. "Should I take a shower?"

The questions she asked sometimes. They defied logic. But it was part of her charm. "Do you feel dirty?"

She grinned. "I always feel dirty when I'm with you."

"I completely understand." My hands were behind my head and I had put my glasses on so I could fully appreciate the view of her in that doorway. "Take a two-minute shower. No hair washing. That will keep us from breakfast for an hour."

"Okay." She yawned again and dropped her shirt.

Turning back to the bathroom, she leaned into the shower and turned on the water, giving me a shot that I would have loved to capture on film, except that I know full well no electronic source is ever fully secure and nothing is ever truly deleted. So I would just have to commit her image to memory, remember this day, this moment.

And there she was out of the shower just a couple of minutes later, toweling herself off. My God. I needed to remind myself a hundred times a day I was a lucky bastard.

While she got dressed I took a quick shower myself, then, holding hands and still groggy, we trudged off to the pancake house, where I saw a whole new side of Kylie. I'd never seen her eat much of anything, and watching her tear up breakfast was a different perspective. I liked how she smiled the whole time as we talked and laughed and ate, how she closed her eyes when she took particularly delightful bites, and how she bounced in her seat a little with excitement when they brought her extra whipped butter. There must be something completely freeing about being comfortable expressing your genuine emotions all the time. I would feel ridiculous showing that kind of enthusiasm.

Maybe that was why we were drawn to each other.

"You're so good for me," I told her. "You complement me."

She made a face. "Well, everyone likes to be complimented. Didn't your other girlfriends tell you were hot? Or that you have a fab penis?"

I choked on my coffee. "No, not that compliment. Complement, as in a our personalities together create a perfect balance."

She started laughing. "Oh. Well, they sound exactly the same spoken."

"Very true, they do." And I appreciated that she could laugh at the mistake, one anyone could have made in that context. "But now that you mention it, no, no one has ever told me I have a fab penis."

"Bitches," she teased.

"Seriously. What's a guy have to do to get a compliment around here?"

"A guy just needs me." She gave me a sunny smile behind her coffee mug. "Your penis is glorious."

"Yeah." My laughter died out. "He does need you."

I did.

CHAPTER SIXTEEN

"JONATHON IS HARASSING ME TO GO ON BIRTH CONTROL," I told Jessica as she fiddled with giving me false bangs as practice for school.

"This doesn't look right," she said, frowning at me.

"Did you hear me?" This was becoming like the biggest obstacle in an otherwise perfect relationship. Jonathon pretty much wouldn't walk into a private room with me without wearing a condom. I was starting to suspect he wore a condom when we went to the coffee shop to study, and it seemed to be getting worse not better as the weeks went by.

"Yes, I heard you. But I mean, I kind of see his point. It's not like condoms worked out so great for you guys." She yanked the fringe out, clearly discontent with it.

"Ow. That hurt."

"Sorry. So why don't you go on the pill? I'm on it. Rory is on it. Even Robin is on it, and she's like homeopathic and vegan and like whatever else you can be now that is hippie-ish. The modern version of the pill is supposed to be perfectly safe to take for years and years."

"I'll never remember to take it every day. You know this about me. Condoms are actually safer."

"Then tell Jonathon that."

"I did. He told me to set an alarm on my phone and we'll use condoms as a backup plan."

"That's a good idea."

"Why are you taking his side?" I pushed my chair back, annoyed with her hands in my face. We were in her kitchen, the chili that was their dinner simmering on the stove.

"I'm not taking sides. But if I was forced to, I would always be on your side. However, I don't see anything wrong with being extra cautious." She folded her arms over her chest and reread the directions on her tablet screen. "I'm going to be a beauty school dropout."

"So you think I should go on the pill?"

Riley walked into the kitchen right then, headed for the fridge. He heard my words, froze, then promptly turned around and tried to leave without getting whatever it was he had come in the room for.

"Hey! Riley!" I wanted someone to validate I wasn't being unreasonable. "Don't you think it's my decision whether or not I go on the pill?"

"Yes," he said so quickly I wondered if he had even really heard the question.

"Do you think Jonathon should have a say in it?"

"Yes. Can I have a beer now?"

Jessica laughed when I made a face. "You asked him." She turned to her boyfriend. "Yes, you can have a beer."

"Why should he have a say in it?" I pushed.

"Because if you get pregnant, it's fifty-fifty his responsibility. So even though the pill is going in your body, he should at least be entitled to say he would prefer that you use a more reliable source of birth control." Riley got his beer. "Now don't throw that wig thing at me. I'm just being honest from a guy's perspective. Condoms can cramp our style. Not because they're messy and whatever else, but because you always worry that something will go horribly wrong from a hole to a slip. And there's nothing sexy about that."

"Wig thing?" Jessica asked him. "But otherwise, I totally agree with you."

I wasn't entirely sure why I was so resistant to the idea of going on the pill. I just knew I didn't want to. Part of me wondered if it made me feel immature to have Jonathon suggesting what I do and even giving me helpful hints on how to be successful at it, like using my phone as an alarm. Part of me also wondered if I actually wanted to get pregnant again. That couldn't be, though. Who would be insane enough to want that, right?

Clearly not Jonathon.

Which was most likely the root of the whole issue for me. He was so clearly terrified of another accidental pregnancy that it made me oddly sad. It made me wonder what would have happened if I hadn't miscarried. It was an absolutely pointless line of thinking, but for some reason I couldn't seem to stop it. I was preoccupied with thoughts of Jonathon finding someone smarter than me who had an IUD and didn't want children until she was thirty-five. Someone nothing like me.

I wasn't even sure why I had those insecurities. It wasn't like he wasn't saying and doing to the right things. It had been three weeks since Valentine's Day and he was awesome, a wonderful boyfriend. I didn't see him as much as I would have liked, but he had classes and a job and tutoring and lab time. Real stuff. But he always managed to text and call and see me whenever he could. But he was just so mature. He was applying for real jobs and had even gone on an interview with a plastics company for a chemist position. It made me feel immature and more than a little bit like a loser. I was barely passing the semester and he was being called for interviews for jobs with salaries that made my head spin.

Part of me also wondered if maybe, instead of college, my calling was to be a mother.

I found myself fantasizing as I walked past those baby gym classes and I knew that was bad. Really bad. Nothing I could share with Jonathon or he would take off so fast he would make a running vampire look like a slowpoke.

Sighing, I put my head in my hand and rested my elbow on the table. "You're probably both right."

"Look, I would shit myself if Jessica got pregnant and I'm the same age as Jonathon. The fact that he didn't bolt tells you he's a good guy. Throw him a bone, ease his anxiety for him, you know?"

"Are you saying you would bolt if I got pregnant?" Jessica asked, the corner of her mouth turning up in amusement as she refastened the bangs to my hair.

"No, I'm saying I would shit myself. That is hard-core responsibility."

Said the guy who had been taking care of his brothers and a house and mortgage for years. It was weird what people considered their capacity.

"Okay. Thanks, Riley." I looked in the mirror at Jessica's second attempt. "I look like a drunk Christina Aguilera."

"Nothing wrong with that. I bet she's fun to party with."

"I have a bigger problem."

Riley was in the middle of lifting the lid on the chili to sniff it, but he paused. "Crap. Why do I have a feeling this is going to be even more awkward? Can you just let me leave right now?"

"No. I'm pretty sure Jonathon's father hit on me and I don't know what to do about it." Talk about awkward.

"Oh, shit, for real?" Riley looked horrified, and then immediately pissed. "You tell Jonathon, that's what you do. Christ, Kylie. That is so not cool."

"I can't tell Jonathon! What if he doesn't believe me?"

"Why wouldn't he believe you? What happened exactly?" Jessica asked.

"He asked to see me after class so I went up to his desk and he suggested again that I drop his class. I said Jonathon was helping me study. He said unless Jonathon took the midterm for me there was no way I was going to pass. Then he said that if I like the son, maybe I would appreciate the father even more, and that if I went back to his place and was very nice to him, he would see what he could do to help me pass." The words all came out on a rush, and frankly, sounded even worse in retelling that they had at the time. I had been upset, and disgusted, but I hadn't been afraid. Mostly annoyed that I had to deal with this kind of bullshit. But now I felt more than annoyed. I felt downright pissed.

"No, I guess there is no mistaking that." Jessica made a face. "God, what an asshole. A creepy asshole. First of all, the breach of power is disgusting. Second of all, he's your boyfriend's father. Third of all, doesn't he know he's just an old nerd? Why would anyone want to have sex with him?"

Riley gave her a look. "Jess, if the dude thought chicks would voluntarily nail him, he wouldn't be blackmailing them. Side note—taste this chili. I don't think I put enough cayenne in it."

"You made the chili?" I asked Riley.

"Of course I did. You don't think Jess cooks, do you?"

"No, I guess not."

"She heats stuff up, that's about it. But she can vacuum the shit out of this house. We split the household stuff."

He looked proud of that fact, as he should be.

I knew that right now Riley made way more money than Jessica did waitressing, because she worked limited hours because of school. But once she graduated and got a job in a salon, she would probably come pretty close to equaling his income, and they would continue on the same path. That had to make it easier. Rory and Tyler, on the other hand, were going to flip completely once Rory graduated med school and I wondered what that would do to their relationship. It seemed Tyler wondered, too. Now, Tyler made the money and she made absolutely nothing, living off him and loans and her dad's willingness to pay her tuition. They seemed to be equal in terms of who did what around the apartment, and the same went for Robin and Phoenix. He was paying all their bills while she went to school.

Jonathon and I would never be equals. He would always make way more money than I would and he would hang with uber smart colleagues every day while I would be with five-year-olds.

"Definitely more pepper. Anyway, you have to tell Jonathon about his dad." Jessica looked at me in concern. "I actually think you should complain to the university but I know you and I know you won't do that."

"No, I'm not going to do that. It's his father! How can I do that?" The thought made my stomach clench. "I don't think this is a common occurrence. I just think he thinks I'm easy because I got pregnant."

But even as I spoke the words, I worried that maybe he had pulled this with other students. God, how could I stay quiet and risk some other girl getting pressured by him? "Maybe I should try to get his threats in writing before I go to the dean of the department."

"I doubt he'll put anything in writing. He's too smart for that, don't you think?" Riley asked.

"Men are not smart when it comes to getting busted misbehaving," Jessica scoffed. "Hello, Anthony Weiner. John Edwards. Bill Clinton. Arnold Schwarzenegger. Tiger Woods. Should I continue?"

"I get the point."

"That's what I need to do, then," I said, feeling empowered. "I can't let him get away with this." My thought was that I would confront him with the evidence and make him repent and agree to never do it again. That way Jonathon wouldn't have to know his father was a pervert. Professor Kadisch wouldn't lose his job. I wouldn't lose Jonathon. If he wasn't contrite, I would go to the dean.

It seemed simple. Plausible.

It was stupid.

So totally stupid.

And when that became apparent, all I could think was that I was as dumb as everyone had always insisted I was.

SOMETIMES I LOOKED AT MY GIRLFRIEND AND I KNEW EXACTLY what she was thinking or what she was going to say. Granted, I couldn't always predict the particular Kylie spin she might put on phrasing, but I knew the general idea of what she was going to say, or the emotion behind it.

But then other times, I realized I had no clue what went on in that gorgeous head of hers.

Such was the case when I came out of my room post-sex to get a drink and Devon was sitting at the kitchen table, biting his fingernail and eyeing me nervously. "What?" I asked. He looked guilty.

"I didn't mean to look," he said. "I swear. But her phone was just sitting here on the table while you two were doing your thing and I glanced at it automatically when it buzzed because we are essentially programmed to do that. It's Pavlovian."

"Okay." I popped the top on my soft drink and came over to the table. "What did you see on her phone?" I had a feeling it was Nathan sending her some lame vow of love. I suspected he still texted her from time to time, though I trusted that she was completely not interested.

"Your dad texted her."

I choked on the sip I had just taken. "My *dad*? What the fuck? Are you kidding me? How did you know it was him?"

"It came up as Professor Kadisch." Devon looked horrified. "Dude, I'm sorry, I wasn't trying to creep. But when I saw that, I couldn't help it. I read it. He's trying to get your girlfriend alone and I don't think he has extra credit in mind, unless extra credit is a new euphemism for blowing him."

My face felt instantly hot, my gut tight. I squeezed the can in my hand so hard liquid sloshed over the side. Kylie was half asleep back in my bedroom. The fact that she had left her phone out on the table with no lock indicated she had nothing to hide, right? Yet I still glanced back down the hallway as I reached for the phone.

There it was. Professor Kadisch.

Make sure you have at least an hour.

"He could be planning to help tutor her." Not that my father was big into helping his students. He was of the camp that you either sank or swam.

"Oh, look at the one before that. The one before the text from Jessica asking her to let her wax her eyebrows for practice. It's a picture, you know, which when small like that is hard to decipher but shows certain characteristics of . . ."

I was already opening it, figuring the hell with it. She could be pissed at me if she wanted for invading her privacy. But it was my father and his . . . "Oh my God! It's his fucking dick!"

"Shh!" Devon shot a frantic look down the hall. "I know! What the hell? Who sends a picture of his junk to a student?"

"I'm not sure which is worse! That she's his student or his son's girlfriend. Oh my God, I'm going to lose it." I paced back and forth, shaking with anger. "Oh my god, oh my God, oh my God."

"It's not even good junk," Devon said. "From what I can tell, he's only semi-erect."

I held my hand out. "No. Just no. We are not going to study the junk in question and evaluate it, for fuck's sake. I'm going to throw up, seriously. Never under any circumstances should a guy's girlfriend see his father's semi-erection unless the bathroom door lock is busted and she accidentally walks in. This is just beyond wrong."

"Sorry." Devon looked contrite. "I think I need a drink. Want to do a shot with me?"

"No. Yes. No." I started scrolling back through the text exchange. "He has been texting her for three days. Three days. And every single one is an exercise in dirty old man."

We can work something out. You just have to use your assets to advantage and you have some serious assets.

The only thing that would be better would be if you had a uniform. Haha.

The more you're willing to do, the better the grade. Since you're failing, you're going to have to work hard at it, from all angles.

I tossed the phone down, hand shaking. "I'm going to kill him. I'm seriously going to kill him. That is my girlfriend he is sexually harassing."

"So why didn't she say anything to you?"

"I don't know." Maybe because who wants to tell someone their father is a pervert? "But the truth is, until the penis pic, he didn't said anything that was technically inappropriate."

"Oh, come on. You'd have to be a moron not to read the truth there. It's screaming innuendo."

"Kylie's answers are just in response to his. There is nothing suggesting she realizes what is happening. I don't think she knows he is being disgusting."

"Oh, come on!" Devon looked at me in disbelief. "Seriously, Darwin? Look, I know Kylie isn't the brightest bulb in the pack. Far from it. But a girl like her knows when a perv is hitting on her."

Now my anger shifted to Devon. "And what kind of girl is that, can I ask?"

"Don't get all worked up. You know I like Kylie just fine, and I'm jealous as hell that you get to sleep with her. But come on, she is not a smart girl, plain and simple. She can't understand basic math and science. She thinks the Big Bang Theory is just a TV show and that a tomato is a vegetable. Her whole life has been about her looks, and she knows when a guy is looking to click her LIKE button."

"Shut the fuck up. Seriously." I was so angry I couldn't even see straight. I'd never felt rage like that. Between my father and Devon, I was barely containing a tight, raw, explosive anger.

"So that's what you think of me?" Kylie asked, in the doorway, in my sweatshirt and basketball shorts. "I guess I can tell you honestly, then, Devon, that I've always thought you were an arrogant asshole who was compensating for a small penis."

"Hey, hey, now!" Devon protested. "Don't be pissed, Kylie. I wasn't saying anything negative about you."

"Calling me a moron isn't negative?" Her eyes snapped and she glared at him, then me. "What the hell is going on?"

"My father sent you a picture of his dick." I waved her phone in the air. "And you're right. Devon is an asshole." I glared at him. "Don't ever talk about Kylie like that again."

"If you are both going to persist in ignoring the obvious, which is the IQ elephant in the room, go ahead. Be my guest." He stood up.

Which was when I shoved him. It wasn't premeditated. It just happened. But seriously. Enough was enough.

He shoved me back but I had better balance and stayed mostly in place.

"Stop it!" Kylie yelled at him, and maybe me, I don't know, inserting herself between us. "Just knock it off. Devon, keep your opinions about my IQ to yourself, please, since Jonathon is your friend. And Jonathon, what are you doing? Why are you going through my phone?"

"Because it was sitting on the table and we saw that my dad texted you. So we looked and, lo and behold, Professor Penis. A picture of his junk."

"No. He couldn't have." She reached for her phone. "Let me see."

"Hell, no!" We had a bit of a thumb wrestling match for her

phone, which I won. "You are not looking at my father's nasty text!"

"He's only semi-erect, anyway," Devon said. "You're not missing much."

"You're not helping!" I turned my back so Kylie couldn't snag her phone back. "And I'm deleting this."

"Don't delete it! Don't you think the department should see that?"

I paused. "The department? What do you mean?"

"Well, I suspected that he was hitting on me, offering to bump up my grade in exchange for sexual favors, but I couldn't prove it. I figured if he texted me, then people would have to believe me."

"So you knew? You knew and you let it keep going?" Was she for real? Was she insane? "My God, Kylie, how could you be so fucking stupid?"

I knew it was the worst possible thing to say the minute the words left my mouth. I didn't mean that she was stupid, stupid. I meant that entrapping my father was a serious lapse in judgment.

But immediately her face froze then crumpled, before tears sprung to her eyes.

"Kylie, I'm sorry, that's not what I meant . . ."

She smacked at me when I reached for her. God, why did I use that word? It was her personal Achilles' heel, her insecurity, and there I had just blasted her for it.

"You're right," she said. "I am stupid. Stupid for believing that you could love me for who I am."

"Aw, baby, come on, you're not stupid. I do love you exactly as you are. I love everything about you."

"But you think I'm too dumb to figure out your dad is hitting on me?"

Kylie grabbed at me until I either had to drop the phone or push her aside, which I wasn't going to do. She triumphed in gaining her phone, then turned, tossing her hair over her shoulder. She was heading for the door.

Shit. Shit. And shit.

"Come on, don't leave like this!" I was starting to panic. She wasn't really going to just walk out. It was eleven at night and it was March. The temperature was thirty degrees out and there was snow sludge that had been melting during the day, but very possibly could be refreezing now, rendering the sidewalks slick. "There is no way I'm letting you walk home."

She rounded on me. "You are not my father, okay? You may think I'm an idiot and you may think that I need your big brain to take care of me, but I managed to survive until twenty-one years old without your handling of me, so just go suck it."

I wasn't even sure what the hell to say to that. She completely caught me off guard. Her father? She thought I acted like her father?

"I'm not letting you walk home alone at night," I insisted, ignoring all that other shit.

"Devon can drive me home."

"What?" Both Devon and I recoiled. "I'll drive you home!"

"No. Devon can do it as an apology." Kylie was stuffing her feet into her boots.

"But if he can as an apology, why can't I?" There was no logic to that.

"Don't get all fucking logical on me!" she shrieked. "I'm furious with you. So unless you want me to walk, Devon is driving me."

Oh my God, and then some. Jesus. Since I didn't want her walking alone, I would bow to her wishes. Now. But then we were going to have a conversation about this and she was going to understand that I hadn't meant to insult her. I had just been totally caught off guard by my father's nastiness.

And just what was she doing trying to create some sort of sting operation all on her own? What the hell?

"Fine. Devon, drive her home."

"But . . ."

"Drive her home!" I paced back and forth, completely pissed off. I scratched at my new tattoo, the numbers indicating the date I'd met her, the same date we had conceived the baby we'd lost, on my forearm, where I could always see them.

It was healing and it was itchy.

"Fine." Devon made a face but he went for his car keys and his shoes. "This wasn't my fault. I just want to confirm that everyone knows that."

"Stop being a selfish douche bag for about two seconds," was all I could manage to say to him. "Kylie, baby, are you sure you don't want to stay? Let's talk this through."

"What's there to say? I'm stupid and I'm going home. If you follow me, I will never speak to you ever again."

That left me so many options. Not.

So I just threw my hands up and sat back down at the kitchen table to grind my teeth and twitch.

The minute they left I called my father and told him precisely what I thought of him. I finished it with, "If you ever even look at Kylie again, I swear, I will rip your fucking nuts off and stuff them down your throat."

It seemed even I was capable of rage when the woman I loved was a target.

CHAPTER SEVENTEEN

STUPID. THE WORD JUST ECHOED IN MY HEAD. I KNEW I WAS overreacting. I knew that Jonathon didn't mean to insult me but it was just that word that made me crazy. Especially since I had been starting to suspect Jonathon was right. It was stupid to be messing around with trying to get his father to put something suggestive in a text. It had made me feel nauseous, deceptive, and violated in some way. It made me feel like even though I was doing it for the right reasons, I was a participant, a flirt.

Doing something wrong.

Which I was, by keeping it a secret.

There was nothing deceptive about my personality and I was lying, plain and simple. It made me feel super uncomfortable. So what do you do when you know you're wrong? You get defensive.

But I was telling the truth about Jonathon treating me like a kid. He did that. I was not okay with it.

"This is it," Devon said, unlocking his car on the street.

I got in the passenger side, and slammed the door shut behind me, shivering in Jonathon's shorts, sweatshirt, and my fuzzy boots. Spring hadn't arrived yet. "I live on McMillan. That way."

I pointed, still annoyed with Devon for calling me an idiot.

"Look, I'm sorry about what I said. That was rude."

"You're right. It was." Sorry, but I wasn't feeling generous.

"But you know, Jonathon's father is going to get fired if this comes out. There will be a huge scandal. You probably should have mentioned your concerns to him."

He was right. "I wasn't trying to cause a scandal. I was trying to prevent Professor Kadisch from doing this to someone else. Someone who would be afraid to speak out. But I honestly didn't think he would get this creepy." And I knew what happened to girls who spoke up without proof. They got dragged through the mud. "I didn't think anyone would believe me without something in writing."

"Well, you are right about that. Sad, but true."

"That's my building." I gestured to the right. My shitty, sucky apartment building that was going to feel empty and dark without Jonathon in it with me. I sighed.

"You know he's a good guy, right? I mean, you're just pissed right now and you'll work all this out."

Tears filled my eyes. "To be totally honest with you, I am starting to think that Jonathon and I keep trying to force our relationship to work when we were never meant to be together in the first place. My stupidity and a cheating ex-boyfriend are the reason we hooked up, you know."

"Don't discount attraction and affection."

"Affection? Yes, he has affection for me. Sort of like you do with your Yorkie." I opened the door and climbed out. "Thanks for the ride."

"Sure. Kylie, listen . . ."

But I was already slamming the door shut. When I had gone to the coffee shop and told Jonathon I was pregnant, I had also told him that I wasn't stupid, that I didn't expect him to fall in love with me and marry me. But somewhere along the way, I had expected exactly that. Sometimes I was optimistic and sometimes that moved straight on into unrealistic.

It hadn't been fair to him.

I was still doing it.

I hadn't even gone to the doctor to get birth control, the one thing he had been asking me to do. Even after hearing Riley and Jessica say it was a reasonable expectation on his part.

Running to the front door, I quickly opened it and jogged up the stairs. By the time I was inside my apartment, I knew what I had to do. I had to stop seeing Jonathon. Maybe not forever, but for now. I hadn't even been over Nathan when I had hooked up with him. Then the pregnancy, the morning sickness, the miscarriage, the tension between us, the constant changing of my perception of what the future would hold . . . when had I ever had time to just reflect, grow, mature?

When had I given him time to decide if he really wanted to be with me?

After the miscarriage I had ambushed him drunk at the bar and coaxed him home with me. That was fair. Not.

Flopping onto my bed, I pulled my boots off and dumped them on the floor. Then I slid in under my comforter and lifted the neck of his sweatshirt up to my nose so I could smell Jonathon. I started crying. I couldn't help it. I knew every inch of him, every gesture he made, every tilt of his head, every smile. Yet I didn't know what ninety percent of those numbers on his tattoo meant, and I would never understand what he was actually studying or what he planned to do post–graduate school. I didn't know what was in his head.

My phone rang in my pocket. It was him.

"Hello?"

"Kylie, I'm so glad you answered. You know I don't think you're stupid, I was just totally disgusted by my father."

"Jonathon, you graduate in two months."

"What? Uh, yeah, so?" His voice was gruff, confused.

"What are you doing after graduation?"

"Getting a job."

"Is that what you were going to do before you met me?"

"I wasn't sure yet."

I closed my eyes, right hand holding my phone up to my ear, left on my forehead. "I need you to do whatever you were going to do before you met me."

"What do you mean?"

"I mean, I don't want to be the dumb blonde who held you back."

"You're not. Don't say that."

"I am. And I won't do that to you. I want you to plan your life without me in it."

"Are you breaking up with me?" he asked in disbelief.

"Yes. And when you are done with school and have a plan, if you still want me to be part of your life, if you think I will fit into it, let me know." I tried to prevent a sob, but it slipped out anyway. "I'll be here."

"Kylie, no, come on. Don't overreact. This isn't necessary."

"Yes, it is," I insisted. "I want to know, no, I *need* to know that you chose me. That without the responsibility of me guiding you, you want me as your girlfriend, as your partner. Equal partner."

"I do," he said, his voice emphatic.

"You haven't even thought about it. We both need to think about it." Suddenly I just felt exhausted. Like the last nine months of my life just pressed down on top of me and squeezed every last ounce of energy out of me.

"I don't see why we can't think and still be together. I think all the time."

That almost made me want to laugh, except that my heart was breaking. I didn't want to trap Jonathon. I wanted him to come back to me all on his own because he loved me. Me. "I speak before I think a lot, Jonathon. I react. So I really believe that I need time to get myself together before we move forward with our relationship. Two months. Let's talk when you graduate."

"This is pointless and, frankly, it feels manipulative. Do you want me to beg?"

"What? No, of course not." Why was it that when I was trying to be mature guys assumed it was a game? "I just think we need some time and space."

"Space sucks," was his opinion.

I'd never heard Jonathon sound immature, but right then, he did. "I have one question—do you want me to say anything about your dad to the university or should I let it drop?" It felt like it was his right to decide. It would be his family affected by an investigation.

There was no hesitation in his voice. "I want you to turn him in. It's worse that it was you, but honestly, if it were any one of his students, I would want them to speak out. That is not okay. He should be fired, as far as I'm concerned."

"Okay." I was glad he felt that way. I was uncomfortable with the thought of his father doing to a vulnerable freshman what he had done to me.

Silence grew between us. I had so many things to say, but no coherent thoughts. How did I explain to him that I loved him with every breath in my body, but that I didn't think I was good for him? That I was worried he would grow to resent me? That the things he found cute about me now would be the things he would grow to despise as the years went by?

How did I explain that I needed to be kinder to myself, more honest? That I had never allowed myself any time to stop and listen to my thoughts. That if we were going to be together, I wanted it to be forever, not a pit stop in my life. That when I looked at him, I felt my heart swell with the most amazing sense of love and contentment and that I wanted to be his wife some day, raise his children, greet him at the front door with a baby on my hip and a smile on my lips.

You don't say those things to guys. You're not even supposed to think them. You're not supposed to admit that your greatest ambition in life is to have a family.

And lying in the dark of my lame apartment, barely passing my classes, it was all just ridiculous, a stupid dream. A future that I didn't have the right to claim, an expectation I couldn't put on Jonathon. He had to choose it.

"Jonathon . . ."

"Don't do this, Kylie. Please." His voice was tight. "I've been nothing but reasonable, you know. I've tried so fucking hard . . . it's not fair that you just get to walk away."

My tears came faster. "I don't want you to be reasonable."

"So you want me to be irrational? A dick? Yell and scream and make demands? Throw you over my shoulder?"

"No . . ." I wasn't sure how to make him understand.

But he wasn't going to give me a chance to explain. "If you want to talk in two months, you can call me. Because now *I'm* done."

And he hung up.

I cried myself to sleep, hugging his sweatshirt to me.

AFTER I GOT OFF THE PHONE WITH KYLIE, I WALKED BACK and forth across my kitchen, my fists clenched, my chest tight. When Devon tried to talk to me, I decided I had to leave. Grabbing my coat and keys, I went out onto the street, walking past the late night pizza place and the coffee shop that was open until midnight. Past the hipster club that hosted indie music acts, crowds of people hovering around outside smoking. I walked and walked, not sure where I was going, not sure that I cared. It was cold and that strange dark that you get in urban areas, where the dark is a cloudy shadow, murky and intermittent.

It felt sinister, like my mood.

I couldn't believe that Kylie had broken up with me. Sure, she said it was a break, space, time, two months. Fuck two months. Fuck all of it. Good relationships don't need a break or space. A break is a stop on the road to never seeing each other. It's a pause where you feel free to fuck other people. Then you attempt to get back together and it's all awful, it's misunderstandings and baggage and bullshit and fuck that. Fuck it.

I kicked a rock with my boot.

My whole life was falling apart. My father was a pervert. He was also my advisor so there would be scrambling to redo my thesis panel. How was I supposed to tell my mother? It was just disgusting. Now I knew there was no way I was going to stay at UC for my post-doc. There wouldn't be any point.

In the past few months, I had re-envisioned my life multiple times and I was sick of having to readjust, picture new realities. I wanted to know where I was going, what I was doing. Who I was doing it with. If I were honest with myself in the past few weeks I had been allowing myself to picture that future that Devon said guys like me weren't supposed to want. Settling down with Kylie. Having a family.

I started to call her again then stopped myself.

It had only been two hours, not two months.

How could she stand the thought of going two whole months without speaking, without seeing each other? I already felt lonely, empty. My arms already missed her. I was already spinning logical arguments I could present to her.

But she didn't want me to be logical to her.

She wanted me to proceed with my life as I had been planning to before I had met her that night.

I wasn't sure what that was supposed to prove.

And as I sat on the steps of the Corryville church-turned-rental-hall, I knew that it was impossible to stand in that same spot with the same motivations and knowledge. Everything had changed that night she had walked into the coffee shop with her pink fuzzy scarf wrapped around her neck and when she sent me that text about having my ion you. I couldn't undo any of the emotions our relationship had created. I couldn't just wipe it clean and go back to being the guy who was only thinking about himself when he thought about his future.

The date was even on my arm.

It had changed everything.

And now she didn't want it. She didn't want me.

CHAPTER EIGHTEEN

WHAT I LEARNED WAS THAT I COULD BE ALONE BUT NOT lonely. I still preferred the company of my friends and my family, but if I had to be alone in my apartment, I didn't feel depressed and like I needed to text and call and crank up music. I found that it wasn't such a frightening thing, being alone in my head, with my thoughts. I found that sometimes I even had interesting things to tell myself.

I also found, in those weeks after Jonathon hung up on me, that I was stronger than I thought I was as I threw myself into studying and recovering my grades. When I told Jessica I was amazed that I could be so strong, she laughed.

"Kylie, you had your ex cheat on you with one of your best friends and you recovered. You got pregnant and were fully prepared to make that work. You lost your baby and your boyfriend and accused a professor of sexual harassment and you're still here, smiling. You've always been strong even if you do it wearing a cute outfit and mascara. That's *you*."

And I actually believed her.

Even when the nights were long and quiet.

Even when the equations swam in front of my eyes as I tried desperately to understand chemistry and when I typed on my laptop late into the night on my essay for my British Literature class, words running together.

Even when the university interviewed me for hours about Professor Kadisch and the police were called.

Even when they suggested that I had an interest in ruining his career because he was flunking me.

Even when I got no texts from Jonathon, which, despite what I had told him, I desperately wanted.

Though I did get a phone call from his mother, who asked to meet with me. I had no idea what she wanted but I said yes, of course, too curious not to. We met at a Mexican restaurant right off campus and as soon as I walked in, I recognized her. Jonathon actually looked more like her than he did his father, and I felt an affinity toward her because she was the one who had raised him, nurtured him into the man he'd become.

"Hi, it's so nice to meet you," I said, sticking my hand out. "I'm sorry, I just realized I don't know your last name."

"It's Fagenbaum, but please don't be formal. Just call me Debbie." She smiled warmly at me and squeezed my hand, gesturing for me to sit down across from her.

I dropped my bag on the floor. It was spring and I was wearing flip-flops with my skinnies for the first time, a decorative scarf my only concession to the fact that it was still only sixty-five degrees.

"Jonathon didn't lie—you are very pretty," she said with a smile. She had salt-and-pepper hair in a pixie cut and it was very flattering.

"Thanks," I said, wondering why I had never made an effort to meet her when Jonathon and I were dating.

"I'm sure you're wondering why I asked you here. It's not to interfere, honestly. Whatever you and Jonathon are doing is your own business, though I do feel comfortable saying that I think you were good for each other."

I wasn't sure what to say. Mostly, I thought she was right. "I just needed to be sure, you know, that Jonathon didn't feel trapped by me. That this is what he wants."

"Oh, it's definitely what he wants. You're all he talks about."

My cheeks felt warm. "He talks about me?"

"Constantly. But that is for the two of you to discuss, not you and I. He doesn't even know I asked to see you."

I wasn't sure what that meant, and I accepted the water the waitress brought me right then. "Okay."

"I wanted to say that I'm impressed and proud of you for blowing the whistle on Ben. It takes a brave girl to stand up and say what her professor is doing is unethical and inappropriate and I know it's been a huge headache for you."

Immense relief washed over me. "I wasn't sure how you would feel. I felt horrible turning him in, but, honestly, I didn't want a girl to find herself trapped or pressured or feel like she had to either drop the class or do what he wanted." Professor Kadisch had been suspended for the rest of the semester pending the investigation and Jonathon's mother was right—it had been time-consuming and embarrassing at times as they had picked through my texts and cell records, including that penis picture. Once they had gone through Professor Kadisch's phone and computer, they had found I was not the only student he was talking to, which was shocking and made me glad I had gone ahead with contacting the university.

"But I worry about Jonathon," I told her. "It must be horrible for him. All the talk. Knowing that this is his father. It's such a betrayal."

"It is horrible and I feel partly responsible for that." She sipped her iced tea. "I should have told him the truth when he wanted to come to school here. He thought he was doing me a favor financially, and he was, but I would have preferred he had never seen his father. Ever. Because I never told him the truth, that I was one of those naïve undergrads who was flunking my class and Ben offered to help me study and, well, he raped me. He wouldn't think of it that way, he would say I came there willingly, that I didn't stop him, but I tried to stop him. Then I just froze and let it happen. I let it happen because I was eighteen and I was scared and I just wanted it to be over with. It felt easier."

"Oh, God, I'm so sorry." I reached across the table and took her hand in mine.

"Then I found out I was pregnant and I decided to fight for child support, but I wasn't brave, Kylie. I didn't stop him and I didn't speak out. I kept my mouth shut and I kept the peace and I raised my son alone, thinking that was the end of it. I never dreamed that he was, well, a sexual predator. I just thought that I had given him signals, I had been in awe of him and attracted to him. Not that I'm suggesting I deserved what he did, because I didn't, but I thought I should have been more forceful in making it clear that I didn't want to have sex with him."

"I'm so sorry. You didn't do anything wrong. We all deal with situations differently, and it pisses me off that people shift blame to the victim. I wasn't personally violated here. It was much easier for me to speak out, and even that was hard, because I knew I would be hurting people I care about. Everyone is going to have an opinion and I'm sure there are people right now on campus saying terrible things about me, calling me a slut, with every guy I've ever been involved with crawling out of the woodwork, but that's okay. I know the truth. And you know the truth about what happened to you and you don't have to keep that burden to yourself anymore."

She nodded, her grip still in mine. The corner of her mouth turned up. "And here I thought that Jonathon said what worries you is that you're not smart enough for him."

"I do."

"Honey, there are all kinds of smart, and you just spoke the wisdom of compassion. Give yourself a little more credit."

I sucked in a breath. She was right. I did need to give myself more credit.

"And I also want to point out that like you, I was failing chemistry, and Jonathon has never made me feel stupid or inferior to him. He loves me for the whole package, for being his mother, not for my ability to do equations. That's the thing, Kylie—we have different people in our lives for different reasons."

"I never thought of it that way. I think you have the wisdom of compassion yourself."

She laughed. "Maybe I can flatter myself that Jonathon chose a woman like his mother."

We ordered lunch and ate, talking about random things, her telling me stories about Jonathon as a little boy, and it was nice to get to know her, to see where Jonathon had gotten his personality, his warmth. When it was time to leave, she gave me a hug.

"I'm having a graduation dinner for Jonathon on Thursday. Why don't you surprise him and come?"

"Oh, that's probably a bad idea to surprise him." It was ridiculously tempting, but wow. Talk about blindsiding him.

"Just think about it. You can come early before my family arrives."

I nodded. "I'll think about it."

But it turned out I didn't have to think about it.

As I left my final exam for chemistry on Thursday morning, palms sweating, temples throbbing, shoulders tense, but feeling like I had passed, Jonathon was in the hallway.

"Oh!" I stopped, confused, not sure why he was there. Probably to speak to the interim professor. "Hi."

I started to move away, down the hall, but he touched my arm. "Kylie."

"Yes?"

"How did the exam go?"

I couldn't read his expression. I nodded. "Okay. I think I passed."

"Good. I knew you could do it." His eyes swept over me. "You look good."

"Thanks." I wasn't sure I could say the same about him. He looked tired, with dark circles under his eyes. He was wearing a T-shirt that said, "Mm . . ." then had the symbol for pi next to it. It showed that he had started a second tattoo sleeve on the opposite arm, with something that looked like coding.

I wanted to hug him. I wanted to breathe him in. I had missed him so much, painfully so, but never more than right then, when he was in front of me and I had no right to touch him. I ached.

"Congratulations on passing your thesis."

"Thanks. How did you know about that?"

His mother. "I just assumed you would pass."

He gave a soft laugh. "Do you have another exam now? Can I walk with you?"

"No. And yes. I was just going to go sit outside for a while. The warm sun feels good."

He put his hand on the small of my back as we went down the stairs and out the door. I sat on the concrete steps outside and leaned against the retaining wall. He dropped down beside me, digging in his messenger bag for his phone. He held it up to me.

"I'm not sure what I'm looking at," I told him. It was an e-mail, some kind of acceptance letter.

"I got accepted to Northwestern's post-doc program. It's one of the best in the country for theoretical chemistry."

"Wow, then definitely congratulations." My heart started to race. He was here to say good-bye. This was it. For real. He was here to tell me I was never going to see him again. "That's a huge accomplishment. You should be proud of yourself." I meant that genuinely, even when I was suddenly gripping the knees of my jeans with my fingernails. "Where is Northwestern?" I tried to sound casual, but my voice sounded far away, tight.

"Evanston, Illinois. Just north of Chicago."

That was far away. Not the other side of the country, but seven hours by car. Two states away. Near Chicago, where all the attractions of the city, where being twenty-six and trendy and smart, with the potential for making a large income, was all within his reach.

"It's beautiful there. Right on Lake Michigan. You couldn't ask for a better place to live, really. Conveniences of Chicago, but more of a small-town feel."

"Oh, wow. It sounds . . . wonderful." Far away. It sounded far away. I felt sick. This was what I wanted for him. I did. I wanted him to choose the path that would make him happy. But it still hurt. I widened my eyes so I wouldn't start crying.

"So you asked me to think and I thought. I decided I wanted to complete my post-doc. And Northwestern is where I want to do it. It's a great program. A fresh start. A beautiful town."

"Uh-huh." My lip started to tremble. Damn it. I bit it to stop the trembling.

"But what I want to know, what I came to you to discuss, is if you would be willing to come with me. Because none of it means very much to me if I don't have you."

"What?" I stared at him blankly. I wasn't expecting him to say that.

He took my hand and he swore under his breath. "You really didn't think that I would want to be without you, did you? You thought that you were giving me some goddamn gift of freedom from you, didn't you?"

I nodded.

"Except that's not what I want. It's never what I wanted." He took my hand. "Kylie, I did spend the last two months respecting your wishes and thinking about the rest of my life and you know what I realized?"

I shook my head.

"That I want to spend it with you. I want to live with you. I want to go to bed with you every night and wake up every morning with you. I want to marry you someday, with you in a white dress and our families there. I want babies and a house and you building a *home* with me. What is so wrong with that?"

"Nothing. God. Nothing." I was crying now, my vision blurry. "That's what I want. I want nothing more than that. I just needed to be sure that you wouldn't regret it."

"I want a life partner, not a lab partner, do you understand? The day I met you was the best day of my life." He cupped my chin and stared into my eyes. "I never believed in destiny, fate, soul mates. It was illogical to me. Then I met you. And I realized that in this infinite universe with its massive complexity of matter, that two people could be destined to find one another and make sense out of what is otherwise a meaningless microexistence, a mere nanosecond of cosmic time. That you and I were drawn to each other not by evolution, but by something that can't be measured. Love."

Oh, God. I lost it. The tears rolled down my cheeks and I

closed the gap between us and kissed him. "I love you. I want the exact same things you do. I want us. A home. A future."

He kissed me back, soft, delightful brushes of his lips over mine. "This is right. This is meant to be."

"So it was written in the stars?" I whispered.

He laughed. "In a manner of speaking. Though never, ever repeat I admitted that." Then he was pulling me onto his lap. "I love you so much. The last two months have been hell. I missed you so much."

"I missed you, too." I wrapped my arms around his neck and breathed in his scent. "I'm glad you want to be with me."

He laughed. "Kylie Ann. You put me through hell, but I get it. I hope the time was useful to you."

"It was. I learned to respect myself more. Does that make sense? I learned that I could dig myself out of an academic hole. And I learned that there is nothing wrong with wanting a domestic life some day."

"Well, you'll get to put some of that into practice if you move to Evanston with me. I'll be really busy with the program, and I know you'll have school, too, but you won't have to work. We can live off the grant money. If you're saying yes, that is, that you'll go with me."

"Duh. Of course I'm going with you." Nothing could make me stay behind, not when I knew that he wanted to be with me.

He laughed. "That's my girl."

"I doubt I can get into Northwestern, though. Most schools don't let you transfer for your final year, and certainly not when your grades suck like mine do."

"There are a million colleges around there. We'll find one that is right for you."

I laid my head down on his chest. "I trust you."

His arms wrapped around me. "I know that's hard for you. But yes, trust me. Trust me to take care of you without dominating you. Trust me to respect you. Trust me to love you."

Tilting my head so I could stare up at him, I said, "I do."

CHAPTER NINETEEN

One Year Later

"ARE YOU READY?" I ASKED JESSICA, ADJUSTING THE RIBBON on my fuchsia empire-waist maid of honor dress. "You look stunning."

She did. She was a beautiful bride, her hair in an updo, her makeup perfect, her body shown to advantage in a strapless princess gown. She had wanted a mermaid style, but out of respect for her father, had gone with something less revealing, in an ivory. She was also walking herself up the aisle, since her dad was officiating her marriage to Riley, and was waiting at the altar.

She gave me a solid nod, with virtually no sign of nerves. "I'm ready."

I gave the signal to Robin, who started down the aisle, followed by Rory, and Jessica's cousin. When I went down, I looked for Jonathon, and smiled at him when I spotted him midway. He smiled warmly back. My boyfriend was so cute. Then I looked up at the groomsmen and saw Tyler, standing solid next to his brother as his best man, and Phoenix, whose hair had grown even longer, looking comfortable and confident. Jayden was shifting restlessly next to Tyler, clearly nervous, and Easton, who had grown two inches in the last year, was fiddling with the cuffs of his suit jacket. Riley looked stiff, but very handsome, all the guys in matching black tuxes with black Converse on their feet.

Jessica's father, who I had known since seventh grade, gave me a wink when I got to the front. He seemed surprisingly okay with the whole marriage thing. Maybe because Riley and Jess had been living together for two years. He had to know it was going to stick at this point, but also he probably preferred them to be legally married instead of just shacking up.

I knew by looking at Riley the second Jessica appeared at the back of the church that this was the real deal. He looked stunned and in the best way possible. He swiped at his eye quickly and my heart melted. I glanced at Jonathon, who was watching me, his expression warm and intense. Then I saw Jessica come down the aisle, beaming, regal.

"She looks beautiful," Rory murmured to me under her breath.

She did. And her vows were strong, her voice clear as she repeated after her father. Riley's were, too, his shoulders back, his normally teasing voice solemn. Then without warning he went rogue.

"And I know this isn't part of the ceremony, but I have to add something. I need you to know that I understand that I'm committing to you, but that you have taken a vow, and a commitment, not just to me, but to my brothers and I want you to know how much that means to me, how much I love and appreciate you for that. I can't ever . . ." His voice cracked a little. "Repay you for that, but I can promise you that you've got me and these guys backing you up for the rest of your life."

Jessica was swiping at her eyes, trying not to screw up her makeup, and she leaned forward and gave him a kiss. "Thank you."

Riley gave her father a sheepish look. "Sorry."

"Emotions are never something to be ashamed of, son. Every woman needs to know she is appreciated. Marriage is a partnership."

I could feel Jonathon's eyes on me and as I adjusted my bouquet in front of my baby bump, I met his gaze. *I love you*, he mouthed.

Grateful there was no recording of the ceremony being done, I mouthed it right back, wanting him to know that I couldn't wait for the day when it was my turn to stand up there and commit to him.

Not that I hadn't already.

I had moved to Illinois with him and knew that I would go anywhere on the planet as long as we were together. We were having a baby, despite me going on the pill to ease his anxiety. Because it was meant to be.

It was written in the stars and I would never doubt him or myself again.

KYLIE LOOKED TIRED AS I PULLED HER DOWN ONTO MY LAP at the reception, her cheeks flushed from dancing. Resting my hand on her bump, I kissed the back of her head. "How are you doing? Do your feet hurt?" I had wanted her to wear flat shoes, but she had insisted on matching the other bridesmaids.

"They are totally killing me," she said cheerfully, kicking them off. "Of course, I'll never be able to get those back on, but whatever."

"I'll rub your feet tonight, and anything else you would like rubbed, for that matter."

"Ooh, yummy." She shifted and kissed me. "How inappropriate is it that I totally want to do you even though we're staying at my parents' house?"

"Not at all," I assured her. Now that she was in her second trimester, Kylie was eager for sex, and I was eager to take advantage of that fact. "I think your parents know we have sex."

She laughed. "True. What do you think gave it away?" She pointed with her two index fingers to her belly.

I ran my thumb over her bump, loving the changes to her body, loving that it was our baby growing in there. In defiance of two forms of birth control. Now that was science, though Kylie preferred to call it a miracle. She also didn't find the onesie I'd bought that said "Made with Love and Science" nearly as entertaining as I did. I'd give her the miracle thing publicly but I wasn't returning the onesie.

"Your family is being really awesome," I told her. I had met them during the holidays over the past year and they had been to Evanston once to visit, but we were in Troy for a whole week to celebrate Kylie's graduation and to be there for all the wedding prep and events for Jessica, and my girlfriend's family had been great. My mother had come up for the graduation party and she and Kylie's mom were definitely enjoying bonding over their future grandchild.

Who was a boy. According to the science of ultrasound.

"They're just glad to have us around."

We were going to be in Evanston at least two more years so I knew that was hard for them, but Kylie and I both liked it there.

Robin collapsed into a chair at the table with us. "I'm sweating bullets. I can't dance with Jayden anymore. He's like Patrick Swayze in *Dirty Dancing*. He's relentless."

I had to admit Riley's brothers were entertaining to watch. Easton had already stuck his face in the chocolate fountain, earning him a cussing out from Tyler, and Jayden was chatting up all the ladies.

Kylie laughed. "Totally. Where is Phoenix?"

I was proud of her for being able to forgive Robin and move past all of that. I knew it helped that Robin had been so clearly contrite, and that she had completely changed her life. She and her boyfriend lived an organic lifestyle, even growing their own food, and belonged to an artists' collaborative down in New Orleans.

"He is running the leftover reception food to the local food bank. It's something Riley worked out ahead of time. He'll be back in ten minutes." She pulled her dark hair off her neck and fanned herself. "By the way, you are like the cutest pregnant person ever."

"You should have seen me two months ago."

I nodded. "There was projectile vomiting. It wasn't pretty." It seemed Kylie was just going to be one of those women who were prone to aggressive morning sickness. It hadn't helped that I been on edge, worried about another miscarriage. Kylie had been serene, though, sure that everything was fine. Sometimes I watched her and I was amazed at how instinctively maternal she was, and how much she had blossomed into a mature woman. Or how mature she'd always been. I felt downright neurotic compared to her.

"Thanks, honey." She made a face at me.

"*You're* pretty. Just projectile vomiting isn't pretty."

"Quit while you're ahead."

"I'm not sure I'm actually ahead at this point."

She laughed.

Then she reached out and grabbed Jessica's hand as she came over and sank down into a chair next to us.

"Holy shit, I am having so much fun! And shit, did I just say holy shit?" Jessica asked.

"I didn't hear it," I told her as she glanced around guiltily.

"I mean, my father is being pretty awesome. I don't want to be disrespectful. I mean he didn't even say anything about you being knocked up, Kylie bug."

Kylie snorted. "No, he totally didn't."

"Hey," I protested. "It's not like she's just knocked up by some random guy."

Jessica yanked up the bodice of her dress and gave me a look. "This time."

Ouch. "Point taken."

"My eggs just want to be fertilized by his sperm," Kylie told her. "We can't help it."

I visualized her eggs with free will and was amused.

"Oh my God," Jessica said. "I can't wait for you guys to see our new house. It's the tits."

I had to laugh. It seemed the champagne had given her only arbitrary control over her tongue.

"That didn't sound right, did it? Anyhoo, it was awesome of Dad to give us the down payment to move to Pleasant Ridge. The only reason Riley would accept it was because he said it was a wedding gift, but you know it's totally because my father hated me living in that area. I'm kind of going to miss the old dump, but at the same time the new house is the cutest little Tudor, and it's a way better neighborhood for the boys."

The girls chattered away, offering each other decorating tips as I mostly tuned them out, content to feel Kylie on my lap, her neck enticingly in front of my mouth. I kissed her there, feeling an erection growing. She was sexy pregnant. Her body had swelled in all the right places and she was super responsive to my touch. It was just a perfect package and I had a hard time keeping my hands off her. But I figured it was a wedding and romance was in the air so I could go for it.

She didn't seem to mind.

"Where is Rory?" Robin asked. "I haven't seen her in awhile."

"There she is," Kylie said. "Coming out of the bridal room. With Tyler."

"Shut the door," Jessica said, sounding gleeful. "Did they just bow chicka bow wow at my wedding reception? They totally did! Her hair is a hot mess."

"Wow, I didn't know she had it in her," Kylie said. "You introduce her to a pierced penis and lookie what happens."

"What?" I asked. "Pierced penis?" Maybe I didn't actually want to know.

"Never mind, sweetie. You don't want to know."

Fine with me.

Riley appeared behind Jessica and put his hands on her shoulders. "What's that?"

She jumped. "Oh, nothing. We were just commenting on the fact that Tyler and Rory just came out of the bridal room together."

"Well, they've been at Rory's dad's with the boys. He's probably feeling blue balls as much as I am. This has been a long week of celibacy."

"I am not having sex with you in the bridal room," Jessica said. "My mother is still not happy with me; I am not going to risk that. We have a hotel tonight. You can wait another two hours."

"I never even thought about it, though thanks for putting the idea in my head, then nixing it."

"Who is having sex in the bridal room?" Phoenix asked, sitting down beside Robin and tossing his hair out of his eyes.

"Rory and Tyler," Kylie said, immediately.

"Don't sound so happy about it," I told her, shifting her weight slightly. My leg was falling asleep.

Rory came up and looked around at everyone, her smile for Tyler falling off her face. "What? What are you all talking about?"

"So what have you been up to?" Jessica asked. "Wink, wink."

"Tyler was giving me a gift for graduation and for getting accepted into med school."

"You got her to accept sex as a gift?" Riley asked his brother. "I am so jealous."

"We were not having sex!" Rory shot him a dirty look. "Tyler gave me this necklace." She leaned forward so her friends could see the diamond pendant dangling down from her neck.

"Ooh, pretty," Kylie said.

"Love it," Jessica said. "Though I'm surprised it's not an engagement ring."

Riley squeezed her shoulders. "Jess! None of your business, sweetheart."

"We're waiting until Rory graduates," Tyler said. "Then we'll get married when I go back to school and finish the degree I started nine million years ago. It's all good."

"It's totally working for us," Rory said.

"You've been together the longest," Robin pointed out. "It's been two and a half years even if you factor in your breakup. I think you've made it past the hump."

"True," Jessica said.

"Hey, how do we figure out how long we've been together?" Kylie asked me, glancing at me over her shoulder. "Because there's when we met, then when I told you I was pregnant, then when we started sleeping together again, then when we didn't talk, then when we were together, and—"

I cut her off. "We've been together since the day we met." I lifted my arm to show her my exposed skin where I had rolled up my dress shirt. "See?"

She traced the numbers of our anniversary tattoo with her finger.

"Maybe not technically." I touched her chest right above her breast. "But we've been together in our hearts since that night." Then I kissed her.

She sighed. "I love you."

"Smooth," was Riley's opinion.

"And this would be how she's pregnant," Tyler commented.

I threw a balled-up napkin in their general direction and I kissed my girlfriend.

Kylie was right. I was a romantic. It happened when you found the *one*.

Even to me.